www.ingramcontent.com/pod-product-compliance
Lightning Source LLC
Chambersburg PA
CBHW040524170726
48295CB00012B/322

The Sword of Ali Diab

The SWORD of Ali Diab

by Albert Payson Terhune

SCP Tête-Bêche
Book VI

Silver
Creek
Press

2024

CHAPTER I.
The Prisoner.

THE prisoner sat cross-legged on the beaded camel-saddle, staring reflectively at his very neatly bound wrists.

The Bedouins evidently had a way of their own in this matter of trussing up a captive like a roasting turkey. The rawhide cord was so thin, so seemingly weak. The knots looked so simple. Yet a score of furtive efforts had proved to the prisoner's own pained satisfaction that an Arab wrist-thong is as unbreakable as are a pair of police headquarters handcuffs.

The bound man gave over his futile inspection of his bonds and fell to wondering morosely why an all-wise Providence had constructed camels.

The brute on which he was strapped was mangy, hairy, and dust-colored—a weight-bearing creature, such as carry six-hundred-pound date-packs; as different from the sleek, shapely grayish saddle-camels of his escort as is a Percheron from a race-horse.

These others were of the unbelievably swift Bishareen breed that can carry the mails across the Syrian desert from Damascus to Bagdad in ten brief days—a full twenty-five days faster than the caravan camels can plod gruntingly over the same road.

Over a red sand-dune moved the cortege—six camel-riders, a dozen horsemen, and, in the center, two pack-camels; the prisoner on one, his belongings on the other. Over the dune's crest and down into the cup of ground beyond, where line upon line of long, low, black goat-hair tents were arrayed in slovenly order.

Before the largest and nearest tent a spear stood, thrust upright in the earth. And from the ridge-pole fluttered a dirty patch of green. By the spear the prisoner knew the tent was a sheik's; from the green banner that the sheik was a *hadji*, descendant of the Prophet, or a noteworthy veteran of Mecca pilgrimage, or both.

A horseman had galloped ahead of the procession some ten minutes earlier; and now it was evident that he had been a forerunner, for from every tent men and boys were debouching. Women in dusky blue robes and with duskier blue tattoo-marks on their dark faces were grouped shyly in tent doorways.

There was no swarm of hustling, squabbling curiosity-seekers pouring forward as when a stranger *howadji* nears an ordinary Syrian settlement. Curiosity there assuredly was—but of a stony sort and tempered with a courteous reserve worthy the folk of an American Indian village.

For these people were not peasants, but Bedouins. And, from the time of Abraham, the true Bedouin has been the unquestioned aristocrat of the East.

The riders halted before the spear-tent—the only tent from which no one had emerged at the sight of the newcomers. At a word of command the pack-camel sank gruntingly and heavily to its knees. A dozen hands unstrapped the captive's legs and lifted him to his feet.

Numb from the waist down, from cramped sitting, he stumbled and was saved from falling by the rough tug of a guiding brown hand. Half propelled, half led, he was conducted within the tent.

From the glare of the afternoon sun on the multihued desert sand to the cool gloom of the black tent was so keen a contrast that for an instant he blinked unseeingly.

Then he was twisted to one side, to face the far end of the tent. And his eyes, accustoming themselves to the change, he made out a figure seated on an embossed camel-saddle that in turn rested upon a heap of rugs.

The man thus seated was, as a single glance told the prisoner, a Bedouin of the highest type—tall, slender, with absurdly small hands and feet, a thin, high-bred face with aquiline nose, straight-bearded mouth, and dark, unfathomable eyes. Those eyes were now roaming unconcernedly over the prisoner as though over a none too comely horse or other new possession.

While the brief scrutiny endured no word was spoken by any one. Then, idly, the seated man let his eyes stray to the nearest of his captors. As at a signal the Bedouin thus singled out broke into flowery speech:

"Oh, Ali Diab," he intoned, *"Naharak saïd!"* ("May your day be happy!")

"Naharak assad," ("May yours be happier,") perfunctorily returned the seated figure a little impatiently, as though wishing to get through the cumulative series of compliments which, by rigid etiquette, must open every Syrian conversation.

"Sa-ar issar assad," ("It is happier for seeing you,") the other duly made answer. And, apparently feeling he had appeased the deity of politeness, he plunged into a vivid and rhetorical recital, gesturing much and pointing alternately to those around him and to the prisoner.

The latter scarce heard the first words of the tale. For he was gazing open-eyed at this man on the camel-saddle. The other had addressed him as "Ali Diab."

And no one, in that day, who had pierced the remotest fraction of an inch beneath the East's inscrutable outer skin, could be ignorant of the identity of Ali Diab; the desert sheik who, during his forty wild years, had performed deeds of daring that filled the mouths of a hundred camp-fire poets, and had won for him a repute that was a blend between that of *Bayard* and *d'Artagnan.*

His first curiosity as to the man of ballads satisfied, the prisoner gave heed to the recital of his captor. And, in the midst thereof he was so rude as to interrupt that eloquent story by a very genuine and spontaneous laugh.

The orator halted, chagrined. Ali Diab turned on the interloper with a slight frown of surprise.

"I crave your pardon," apologized the prisoner in reasonably pure Arabic; "I heard him describe me as a Feringee (European) prince—without any special amusement. But when he claimed to have overcome me, in single-handed battle, it struck me as a bit of a joke. You see, I was asleep when these worthy clansmen of yours came upon me. And when I woke up I was already bound. My servant had cut and run at sight of them, I suppose—without bothering to wait long enough to wake me. The story of my being overcome—"

"You speak Arabic, though it is the Arabic of cities," commented Ali Diab, a little contemptuously. "What are you?"

"Your man here says I am a prince."

"He is mistaken," corrected Ali Diab. "Princes do not laugh—only hyenas and women do that. What are you?"

"From your own statement I am presumably a hyena or a woman—whichever it most amuses you to have me be."

A little murmur of amazed reproof at the captive who could thus dare brave the lofty Ali Diab, ran through the tent. But the sheik showed no emotion.

"What are you?" he repeated quietly.

"A man who is suffering grave discomfort from bonds that cut into his wrists," retorted the prisoner. "Look here, sheik! If we are to talk man to man, order these things cut off my hands. If we are to be lordly master and cringing captive, you can go ahead and do what you choose—but you'll get no word out of me."

Again the murmur through the tent. Ali Diab leaned forward a little, surveying his prisoner with some faint interest. Then he nodded to a servant. In a moment the bonds were cut loose.

"Thanks," said the prisoner, chafing his half-numb wrists and drawing out a much-smashed pack of cigarettes; "and now, if I may borrow a light from somebody I'll be ready to answer your questions."

Catching sight of a brazier on the ground near by he sauntered across, bent, lighted his cigarette at the coals, and returned to his place before Ali Diab.

"Now, then," he said cheerfully—with purposeful flippancy—"you want to know what I am? I am an American. And I am not a prince, as you surmised. We don't keep them in stock. I am a civil engineer, if you understand what that means. And if you don't, I don't believe I can explain to you. My name is Ruyter—Paul Ruyter. Is that enough information—or do you want to know my favorite flower and what I think of the East?"

For an instant the sheik made no reply.

Then he whistled a peculiar note. From a dusky corner of the tent sprang a Bedouin, whipping out his curved sword as he came. Full at Paul Ruyter he leaped, blade in air.

Ruyter jumped nimbly backward as the sword awkwardly descended. Then, in practically the same move, he ran in; and, before the blade could be raised again, grappled its wielder about the body.

A twist and a heave and the Bedouin was hurtling, spread-eagle, through the air—his sword gone. He landed on all fours amid a heap of luggage—Ruyter's pillaged belongings—that had just been carried into the tent.

Ruyter, his back to the flimsy tent wall, glanced about him.

His knees were bent, his shoulders were forward, his arms out-stretched—he was ridiculously like a football back who braces himself to stop a flying attack.

But no such attack was made. No one moved save the fallen man who crawled awkwardly to his feet, a look of amazement in his face.

"It is well," gently approved Ali Diab; "your words were not wind. I wished to know."

CHAPTER II.
In the Black Tent.

"You wished to know?" echoed Ruyter, in open bewilderment. "You chose a pleasant way to find out. If your assassin—"

"He is not an assassin," gravely corrected Ali Diab.

"Oh, a humorist, eh? Just his idea of welcoming a guest?"

"You are not a guest," denied Ali Diab quickly—"you are a pris-oner."

Ruyter understood the reason for the dignified sheik's unwonted haste in contradicting him. The guest law of the desert is as old as the Book of Job, and no Bedouin may violate it. But it does not in any way apply to captives nor to others who do not voluntarily enter the encampment. Only to those who throw themselves upon the hos-pitality of a sheik.

"A prisoner, if you like," assented Ruyter. "But if you really wished me murdered—"

"If I had really wished that," explained the sheik, "any of the four men who stood just behind you would have stabbed you to death at my signal. Even now, if I so signal, one of those who stand without will wield the knife."

"But," demanded Ruyter involuntarily and very hastily shifting his position from against the tent wall, "if you did not wish me killed, why—"

"Why did I whistle to Massoud? To learn if you were a boaster. To learn if your mouth were brave and your heart a coward. He understood. No man of mine would otherwise attack so awkwardly. Is it explained?"

"I thought my hazing days were over when I finished freshman year," grumbled Ruyter. "But now that you have decided to your own satisfaction that I won't run screeching up a tree when a man comes at me with a bit of hardware in his hand, what comes next?"

"The words you speak are Arabic," observed Ali Diab coldly, "but their sense is as the bleating of goats. I do not understand it."

"I mean," translated Ruyter, "now that you find I have stood the silly test, what do you intend to do?"

"The test was for mine own desire to learn your heart. As to what I shall do—I shall do as ever is our custom when Feringee travelers are captured. I shall hold you for ransom."

"So I supposed. But if no one bothers to ransom me?"

The sheik shrugged his shoulders deprecatingly, his innate courtesy barring him from naming the alternative.

"I understand," rejoined Ruyter. "Custom of the country. What ransom shall you demand?"

"It shall be according to your rank. I—"

"And do I rank as a hyena or as a woman? And which of the two calls for the higher ransom?"

"What is your rank?" demanded Ali Diab, unheeding.

"I rank as a C. E. That's all."

"As what?"

"Civil engineer. As I told you."

"An engineer? I have heard the word. Is it hereditary or—"

"No. People are elected to it. By their hoodoo. Let me see if I can make it all clear. When were you last in Bagdad?"

"I do not enter cities."

"Too close to the pashalic garrisons, eh? And the price on your head is too high? Well—"

"Wait! Massoud was at Bagdad forty days ago. What did you wish to ask concerning the city?"

"Massoud," said Ruyter, turning to his recent opponent, "did you see the viaduct they are building on the north road from Babylon? Viaduct—high stone bridge—arch—like this. Water under it. *Viaduct*—see?"

"I saw the bridge, howadji," replied Massoud.

"So. Well, I built it."

"Howadji, there were ninety men building it. My cousin's son was one, and—"

"Oh, Lord! How can I explain? I drew the plans—made the— Oh, what's the use? You wouldn't understand. Let me try another way by telling you what my next job will be. (Always supposing the ransom comes in time.) There's a man named Greene—Joshua Greene— a fellow countryman of mine, who cabled me to meet him and—and his daughter and some mechanics—artisans, you know—skilled *fellaheen*—at Jerusalem a week from now."

"I fear they will wait," interposed Ali Diab courteously.

"I hope they will. There's good money in it for me. By the way, that's how your followers came to catch me, sheik. The Mecca pilgrimage was starting from Bagdad, and for the next month I knew I couldn't get a regular conveyance for love or money. So I hired two pack-camels and started with my servant across the desert on a short cut. But that isn't the point. I am to do some engineer work for Mr. Greene in the Land of Moab. Sinking wells and that sort of thing, I gather from his cable. Now, do you see? I'm the man who directs work like that and shows the workers the way to—"

"An overseer?" asked Ali Diab scornfully. "A driver of slaves?"

"Nothing of the sort. You're thinking of *Simon Legree.* I'm—"

"Of whom?"

"Never mind. I can't make you understand. And, after all, it hasn't much to do with the ransom. Unless Mr. Greene will ransom me and with plenty of other engineers within easy reach, I don't see why he should, for he isn't noted for philanthropy—why, I don't know any one else that will. For I haven't a living relative on earth, I always regarded that as a bit of undeserved good luck. But now, from mere family pride, they might come in handy. By the way, did you mention the size of the ransom?"

"Two thousand pounds, Turkish."

"You flatter me, sheik. And, I may add, you can order the execution as soon as you choose."

"You mean your friends will not pay the sum?"

"None of my friends but Joshua Greene could raise that much. And he assuredly *won't*. Why, he could buy a Legislature for less."

Ali Diab looked searchingly at the American.

But the latter's face still wore the same unconcerned half smile. When the sheik spoke again it was of another matter.

"Your friend seeks to dig wells in the Land of Moab? To what end?"

"A crazy idea, so far as I can see. But he hasn't lived out here, and I have. He seems to have studied a map and noted that the track of the caravans from Arabia and Persia is round-about instead of straight, because of the scarcity of water. He thinks if he can establish one or two wells—and perhaps provision stations, too—he can make money by charging stiff tolls to caravans that will then take the shorter cut to save time. My own experience in the East is that time is the one thing no native cares to save. But that's Greene's business, not mine. He's hiring me."

"Many fools have digged in the Land of Moab," commented Ali Diab. "And some few I and mine have captured."

"Oh, then the well-digging idea isn't new?"

"They did not dig for wells, but for gold."

"Gold? I never heard of any gold-mines in the Syrian mountains."

"Nor did another. It is for the treasure of Suleiman Pasha they dig."

"Who was he?"

"Pasha of Syria in the days of our fathers' forebears, as all men know. And when the hand of the Sultan was raised to crush him he fled to the Land of Moab, so runs the tale, and there buried the wealth of his pashalic. But his breath was in his nostrils. And he perished. And to this day none knows where lies his treasure, if indeed treasure there be. Though many have sought it, we of the El Kanah tribe do not soil our hands with digging."

"Cheaper and easier to pick up tourists and fat merchants and civil engineers and hold them for ransom, I suppose. Every man to his trade."

"Feringee," said Ali Diab, slowly, "for a man on whom death already smiles, you are wondrous light of heart and of speech."

"Would I gain anything by whining? If so, say the word, and I'll whine."

"You are a brave man," vouchsafed Ali Diab. "Is it the truth you tell me that none will ransom you?"

"Lying is not one of my pretty tricks," said Ruyter stiffly. "I see no prospect of being ransomed."

"Then you must die?"

"So it seems."

"You do not value life?"

"As I told you, lying is not my specialty. Of course I do."

"You swear you have no hope of ransom? You swear it by your father's beard?"

"The old gentleman died when I was a boy, and as I remember he wore only side whiskers. But I'll swear it by them if you like."

"It is well," assented Ali Diab, albeit evidently puzzled by the distinction. "Then listen to what I say. And on your answer hangs the life you say you cherish."

CHAPTER III.
One Chance—and Another.

THE sheik rose to his feet. At a motion of his hand the others quietly slipped out of the tent, leaving him standing alone in front of Ruyter.

And thus for a moment they stood; the tall, graceful Bedouin in his loose, white robes and scarlet headgear; the tall, heavier American in his soiled khaki outfit; fair, conflicting types of the ever-conflicting East and West.

It was Ali Diab who first spoke.

"Feringee," he said, "you are a brave man. And you can scoff at death. Not as the boaster scoffs, but from the heart. Such men are rare outside the El Kanah. And such men I love."

"Thanks," stammered Ruyter, embarrassed at the simple praise. "You're something of a man yourself from all accounts."

"You are strong, too," went on Ali Diab, impersonally, as though sizing up the points of a horse. "Strong beyond the strength of most men. You hurled Massoud through the air as you might have tossed a child. Such men are rare. I offer you your life."

"Thanks, ever so much!" exclaimed Ruyter. "That's awfully decent of you, sheik. I appreciate it. And—"

"I offer you your life," continued Ali Diab in the same measured tones, "on a condition."

"Oh!"

"On a condition I would offer to few men. For mine is a picked tribe."

"Well," asked Ruyter, somewhat ungraciously, "go ahead. What's the condition?"

"I offer you your life and I admit you to my following. I offer you a spear, a gun, a horse, a tent, a wife. All that a brave man can ask. I make you one of us. Is it understood?"

He paused in his grave, slow-spoken speech, with the air of one who confers an immeasurable favor. And Ruyter stared at him blankly.

"You offer me a position in your tribe?" asked Ruyter, wondering.

"You will be the first Feringee on whom such an honor has fallen."

"And that is the condition of my being allowed to live?"

"The condition?" echoed Ali Diab in cold displeasure. "No. The gift."

"Excuse me. I didn't understand. But what—"

"The condition," pursued Ali Diab, "is that you swear to serve us in all fidelity, giving up thought and memory of your earlier life and companions. To become a subject of the Sultan. The condition is light. It is accepted?"

An hour earlier Paul Ruyter would have given such an absurd proposition no second thought. Now, to his own astonishment, something about the idea thrilled him.

To turn his back on a civilization that had kept him poor and over-worked, to forget an existence that had been one long struggle against poverty and ill luck, to forget the vain, useless struggle in many lands, the loneliness, the friendlessness of it all. There was a lure in the thought.

To live the wild outdoor life his primitive spirit craved, to ride to battle and to foray, like his ancestors of old when the world was young, to live in the open, to serve this Oriental paladin, to feel the desert wind in his face, the muscles of a desert horse beneath his knee!

"A spear, a gun, a horse, a tent, a wife!"

And this in exchange for dreary mathematical calculations, of poring over blue prints, of acting as an unknown cog in progress's wheel. The temptation swayed, obsessed him.

Through the mist of conflict glowed softly for a moment a woman's eyes. The eyes of a woman he had seen a scant dozen times in all. He had dreamed of her, out there in Persia and in the Syrian wastes.

He had dreamed wondrous dreams. And when her father had sent for him to come to Jerusalem to embark on the foolish Land of Moab well-digging venture, he had dreamed afresh.

Yes, and he had cursed himself for a fool, as now once more he did, for having dared fancy a girl like Madge Greene could ever be anything more to him than the altogether glorious daughter of an overrich father who occasionally employed him. The dream was futile. And once and for all he put it behind him.

"A spear, a gun, a horse, a tent, a wife!"

To the tired, heart-hungry man there was a spell in the words.

"Well," Ali Diab was saying courteously, "I am waiting."

"I—I must become a subject of the Sultan, too, you say?" queried Ruyter.

"Assuredly."

"H-m! After all, I don't suppose it makes much difference. What do I do to become one?"

"The intent is all I ask. Forms mean little to us here in the desert."

"All right. I'm content."

"Good. This, then, that I may tell it to my people to prove your intent."

The sheik picked up a tiny silken American flag that lay amid the other plunder captured from Ruyter. He laid it on the ground in front of the captive.

"The one form I demand of you, as a sign to your new brethren, to prove your loyalty to the Sultan and to no other Padishah, is that you grind this emblem into the dirt with your heel."

"No!" thundered Ruyter, a half-maniac rage seizing and shaking him as with physical hands. *"No!* And ten thousand times no, you mis-

erable heathen! That emblem is Old Glory! I'll see you and all your worthless race, from the false Prophet down, in the red flames before I'll defile it!"

"What?" gasped the amazed sheik, for once roused out of his perfect calm.

"Yes!" roared the American, his big voice breaking grotesquely. "I refuse! Do you hear me? *I refuse!* I never realized before what it all meant to me—and to every American. But I'm awake to it now. Go ahead and have me butchered if you like. You'll come out of the world along with me, though, for asking me to do such a hideous thing!"

Still beside himself with the rage that mastered him, Ruyter flung himself bodily at the coldly sneering Bedouin.

And, before his outflung fingers could touch his prey, before Ali Diab's hand could close on the pistol at his own belt, a shriek from no mortal throat filled the whole world.

A shriek that made the sudden babel of cries from the Bedouins outside seem like mere whispers. The tent vanished from around them.

Ruyter had one fleeting glimpse of a sky the color of half-dried blood. Then the universal shriek from above rose to a deafening howl. And dead-black night crashed down upon everything.

For the most infinitesimal fraction of a second Ruyter thought the world had come to an end. Then a blow as of a billion tiny tongues of flame smote him in the face, strangling, burning, torturing him. And he was lifted bodily from his feet.

The sandstorm, rising unobserved, and with none of the warnings that sometimes prepare the weatherwise desert tribes for it, had whirled down into the cuplike hollow in the dunes, where the Bedouins' temporary camp was pitched, and had scooped up its contents as a broom sweeps out a corner.

Paul Ruyter was pitched headlong. Gasping, his hands over his face, he was rolled along, tossed along, twisted along, like a chip in a river's rapids.

Suddenly he came to a stop with a thump that knocked the little remaining breath out of him. He had struck against an obstacle soft, bulky, hairy—an obstacle that bubbled and grunted and moaned.

It was a kneeling camel. The beast had flung itself down with its back to the storm, its head buried in a clump of thorn. And at the contact Ruyter's numbed senses leaped to life. His face pressed against the camel's hump for protection, he ran his hands along its body.

From the short coat and the general shape, he knew it was one of the fleet racing camels. It had not yet been unsaddled. Also, a burnoose lay wedged against the pommel of its saddle.

Ruyter disengaged the burnoose, wrapped its folds about his face, crawled to the saddle and, seizing the bearing rein, jerked the reluctant beast to its feet. Then with fist and rein he goaded it into motion.

Before the storm the fast traveling beast staggered, moaning with pain and fear. Blind in that awful darkness, ignorant of direction, save that he was traveling with the storm, confident that the sand would wipe out every footprint, Ruyter urged on his mount.

The storm slackened, though the darkness still hung heavy. And the camel, goaded to frantic speed by its strange rider, settled into its long, tireless run—a run whose goal Ruyter could not guess. Nor did he care.

For at least his back was to Ali Diab's camp.

CHAPTER IV.
THE SUNSET HOUR.

IT was three days since Paul Ruyter, blistered and aching and at the verge of collapse, had entered Jerusalem by the Jaffa Gate, atop an exhausted and foot-sore racing camel of the famed Bishareen breed.

He had rolled off the dead-beat animal at the door of Gelat's Hotel and had spent his last shred of vitality in registering and in reeling to a room. Tumbling over on the bed, without so much as removing his red tarboosh or his boots, he had slept the clock around.

After which, a shave, a bath, and a breakfast that was liberally irrigated by black coffee, had put him wholly on his feet again. Beyond a slight stiffness and a face still smartingly sore from its sand-thrashing, his iron-and-wholesome system was none the worse for his wild ride.

He was not a little ashamed of the rage-fit that had roused him from his wonted coolness into so melodramatic a scene as had preceded his sudden parting from Ali Diab. Being a severely normal man, he hated heroics, and he wondered shamefacedly at his own in-explicable outburst. For this reason, if for none other, he resolved to say nothing of his desert adventure.

Out of his advance pay from Joshua Greene he replenished his pilfered wardrobe and outfit as best he could at the bazars.

He carefully overhauled the digging apparatus Greene brought along—an equipment Ruyter found hopelessly unsatisfactory. And he spent his spare time in showing Madge Greene the wonders of the Holy City.

It was at sunset on the third day. On he morrow, at dawn, the start for the east-of-Jordan country was to be made. Ruyter and Madge were standing on the hotel's flat roof, overlooking the world-old, yet ever-new panorama of Jerusalem and its environs.

To the north rose the grim hillock of Golgotha, starred with Moslem graves.

To the east, beyond Kedron's valley, swelled the gray-green slopes of the Mount of Olives; while far to eastward, dazzling clear by sunset, yet invisible at earlier hours of the day, the high purple-brown mountains of Moab rose rank on rank.

From minarets scattered through the city muezzins were intoning the evening prayer-chant. On other flat roofs where white-robed folk reclined or gossiped, a few of the faithful rose lazily from their desultory occupations and, facing Mecca, went through the prayer-form.

"And we are to start before sunrise, father says," observed Madge.

"We aren't to start at all," corrected Ruyter; "if we were, the prospects of escaping boredom would be decidedly brighter for me. Shall you wait here or run down to Cairo? It's more amusing there.

"Why, didn't you know?" he asked, surprised. "I explained to your father that you'd have to give up the idea of coming with us. The Land of Moab is not a safe place for any foreign woman. It is full of lawless wanderers, fugitives from Syrian justice, and all that sort of thing. Besides, more than one of the Bedouin tribes is usually camped among the Moab mountains."

"I know, I know," she made light answer. "He told me all about it. Your report quite startled him. For a while he was even tempted to stay here himself and not to risk the journey. But he had a talk with his bankers and with M. Gelat and some other people. And they all told him the Land of Moab is as safe as a church, now that the Sultan has it so well patrolled."

"I see," sighed Ruyter. "A lot of smug 'cits' who were never nearer it than the Jordan have settled it all nicely for him. Well, that's his own risk. But he has no right to let you take such a risk."

"So he told me. But I told him he was mistaken and that I was going, anyhow. He said I mustn't. But—"

"But you and he compromised at last by letting you go? I see. But it's dangerous. And I shall tell him so again."

"It wouldn't be any use. In all important things father and I have only one mind, and—"

"And that mind is yours and it is made up. Besides, he is like most other financiers: 'He weighs men's opinions by their ratings in Brad-streets.' These bankers, who tell him it is safe, are solid men. I am not. So they are right and I—"

"Isn't that just a little bit unworthy of a grown man?"

"I'm sorry. I suppose it was your possible danger that riled me."

"What a pity," she murmured solemnly, "that father engaged you as engineer for the work and not as nurse for me!"

"I wish he had. Then I could make you stand in a corner until you were good and promised to stay in safety instead of adding to our worries."

"Mr. Ruyter!"

"It is true. There will be worries. And your presence will make them ten-fold greater. Your father's 'concession' from the Sultan to permit us to dig wells in Moab will probably safeguard us to a great extent. Most natives will be afraid to bother us. And it will put the Sultan's troops at our service in case of need, always supposing we have a chance to get word to any of them. But—"

"But what?"

"There is danger," he finished rather lamely. "And I'd rather you weren't to be in it."

"If my presence is a bore—"

"I wish it were," he said grimly.

"Now," she commented, "I suppose that rude speech means some-thing or other. But—"

"It means," he said in cryptic brevity, "that women who are poor would be wiser to stay home and cook than to flatten their noses against jewelers' windows. Shall we let it go at that?"

"I think," she answered, "that I like you better when you don't try to talk like Bernard Shaw or Ibsen or a subway guard and then refuse to translate your meaning. Why do you never 'translate' at such times?"

"Because I have no right to. And the translation would interest no one but myself. Also, because it's pleasanter to flatten one's nose against the jeweler's window than to be banished to some place where there is no jewelry."

A violent and high-pitched quarrel in the street just below them broke in on their talk. Ruyter, glad of a chance to move away from the conversational quicksand in which he was floundering so helplessly, leaned over the parapet and looked down.

An old man and a younger, standing beside a coffee stall, were howling at each other in guttural Arabic, with much shaking of fists and waving of brown arms.

"Oh!" laughed Madge, it's that old coffee vendor and his son. They quarrel regularly three times a day. I've gotten so I set my watch by them. I wish I knew Arabic. I'd love to hear what they can find to quarrel about so often. Surely that's something you can translate?"

With a parting yell at each other, the father and son were stamping away in opposite directions.

"I caught only their farewell insults," said Ruyter. "The son said, *'I'n-al-Deenak!'* It's a black affront here in the East. It means 'Curses on your religion!' The father's religion, by the way, is the same as the son's, of course. But no Oriental has enough sense of humor to notice the joke in that. And the old man had even less sense of humor than the son. For he answered his son with the most dire insult known to the Oriental, by saying *'I'n-al-Abuk!'* That means 'Curses on your father!' He—"

A stoutish man, past middle age, bustled through the scuttle onto the roof.

"Madge," he called, coming toward the two at the parapet, "I've been looking for you. You can't carry all that luggage of yours to the Land of Moab. You're not going to Newport but to the wilderness. Two suit-cases is all the weight we can spare for your things. Better go down now and do the sorting and packing. Imbarak wants to have the luggage to-night."

Madge departed unwillingly on her heartbreaking mission of condensing the contents of three trunks into two suit-cases. Joshua Greene was about to follow her when Ruyter stayed him.

"Mr. Greene," he said, "I'd like a few minutes' talk with you if you're not too busy. There are several things that need clearing up."

Greene glanced up with quick suspicion. Then he settled himself to listen.

"In the first place," began Ruyter, "Miss Greene tells me you are going to take her along with us."

"Yes, yes," fidgeted Greene. "Now, my boy, don't start that calamity croak about danger again. I appreciate your thoughtfulness, and all that sort of thing, of course. But there's a line between caution and fussiness. And you've overstepped it. I'm told by people who have lived here all their lives that the Land of Moab nowadays is as safe as Pompton, New Jersey."

"And people who have lived around Pompton, New Jersey, all their lives," retorted Ruyter, "will tell you there's no danger in drinking from barnyard wells. But—"

"Drop it, Paul. My daughter's safety is more to me than it can be to an outsider like yourself. And I've taken pains to make certain there's no risk. Besides, she wants to go. And I want her to go. So that settles it. And now, if there's nothing else—"

"There is. I've spoken to you before about the equipment you've brought. It is hopelessly old-fashioned and incomplete.

"If we were going to excavate ruins or dig house foundations it might do well enough. But for well-digging it's it joke. I find I can hire a fairly good hydraulic drill apparatus from—"

"I don't need it."

"But—"

"I brought what we shall require. When I want advice as to what equipment I need for my own enterprise I'll ask it."

"I am not interfering. But as your engineer, it is only loyal to tell you you can do the work in half the time, and at half the expense, with a drill. Hogan, your foreman, agrees with me."

"I am paying for this. And I don't like to be dictated to. You forget your place. I'm hiring you to work for me. Not to order me around."

"You are not hiring me at all. I resign. You may be able to talk like that to Hogan and the rest. But not to me. I'll trouble you to look for another engineer."

"What? A good job and high pay—and you?"

"I didn't like the job from the start. It is a foolish idea and it will be a failure. I do not wish to be mixed up in a failure. It injures me professionally. And when you take to speaking to me as if I were a section hand, it is time to quit."

"My boy!" almost whispered Greene, "I wouldn't have hurt your feelings for worlds. I apologize. Don't desert me now. I need you. We all need you. Just think! If, as you say, there is danger to Madge out there, how can you turn your back on us and leave us in the lurch?"

Into Ruyter's brain flashed a picture of Ali Diab; a memory of the sheik's boast that he had reaped rich tribute by capturing Land of Moab tourists. With a sigh of self-contempt he gave up the fight.

"Mr. Greene," he said, "if you weren't my employer I'd take a lot of pleasure in telling you what I think of you. But for reasons that I'm afraid you understand I'll go through this thing with you."

CHAPTER V.
THE MAN IN THE DARK.

FOR days the expedition had moved eastward. The plains of Jericho and the Jordan were passed. So was the valley to the east of Jordan. And now for two days they had been amid the passes of the mountains of Moab. Nebo lay behind them. So did many a lesser peak. Yet onward they went.

After the second day's journey from the Jordan, Greene had ordered the exact direction of each day's march. The confident authority with which he set the day's course, named beforehand the location of the night's camp and directed every minor detail of the march, seemed to Ruyter little short of wonderful.

Greene, to Ruyter's knowledge, had never before crossed the Moab mountains.

His explanation that he followed a route suggested to him by his Jerusalem bankers rang false to Ruyter; the more especially since theirs was not the regular caravan course, but one Ruyter himself had never before taken.

The engineer, after some speculation, added the mystery to the several other unexplained features of the expedition and dismissed it from a mind already overfull of one girl's image.

There were eighteen travelers in all: the Greenes, Ruyter, Hogan, the foreman, who was also engineer of Greene's yacht lying off Jaffa; a native cook, a steward, two grooms, four muleteers and camp men, and six swarthy Syrian laborers whom Greene had engaged through his bankers.

The laborers and muleteers were to do the manual work of digging, bossed by Hogan, who, during a checkered life, had once served for three years as engine-driver for the quarry trains at Beirut and had picked up a handful of Arabic with a grief-inspiring accent.

The journey was pleasant enough—almost dangerously pleasant to Ruyter. Riding at Madge's side for hours through the sharp cold of morning and afternoon and the fierce mid-day heats, he lived in a fool's paradise—a paradise whose folly he never let himself forget.

At the evening camp-fires, before early drowsiness seized the party that had ridden all day in the open, he and Madge would sing together the old college songs of the land Ruyter so long ago left; while the little jackals beyond the radius of firelight yapped a restive accompaniment, and the native servants, used only to songs in minor monotone, listened in disgust to such outlandish music.

Then, in the dark of the tent that he shared with Greene, Ruyter would lie awake long enough to build wondrous air castles and alternately curse himself for a pitiful fool.

The hyenas and wolves, quarreling over some carcass in the hills above, would add their amen to his self-condemnation; and the stamp and snort of the line-tied horses would at last lull the man to sleep.

One night as he lay thus, listening to the recurrent "laugh" (a wail, with a hysterical catch of the breath in the middle of it) of a hyena that had ventured unwontedly close to the tents, the pad of unshod horse-hoofs caught his ear.

Some one was riding very quietly in a circle about the camp.

Ruyter got to his feet and made his way out of his tent. The camp-fire had sunk down to a bed of smoldering ash.

Beside it nodded the men who were on guard that night—drowsing half upright after the manner of all Eastern camp-guards.

And, just beyond, dimly silhouetted against the sky-line, Ruyter could see the shadowy shape of a mounted man. The rider had drawn in his horse momentarily and was surveying the camp, as best he could in the faint light.

Before Ruyter could move, a brand that had burned in two fell with a thump into the mound of camp-fire ashes. Up rose a protesting shower of sparks. And a flare of released gas blazed merrily for a single instant; then went out.

But not before it had bathed Paul Ruyter's face and body in momentary brilliancy, making every lineament stand out in startling distinctness against the gloom behind him.

So far did the tongue of fire throw its radiance that it even half illumined the more distant man on horseback. Ruyter had a fleeting impression of a bearded face whose deep-set eyes were peering at him in amaze.

Then the dark settled down, doubly black after the moment of light. And through the darkness thudded the fast receding hoofs of an unshod desert horse.

Ruyter stood staring into the blackness, forcing back to his mental vision the face he had so dimly seen. Then all at once he remembered.

"Massoud!" he muttered, half aloud. "The chap that came at me with the saber when Ali Diab whistled. And he was reconnoitering our camp. Yes, and he must have seen me more clearly than I saw him. I fancy—I fancy a few members of the Trouble family are coming to board with us."

He had gone back to his tent and was groping silently among the luggage piled there. Presently he emerged, carrying a repeating rifle. The weapon across his knees, he sat in the shadow of the tent door and began vigil that did not end till daybreak.

But the Bedouin did not come back.

Nor did dawn reveal from the hilltop any sign of his tribesmen.

Laughing at his own overcaution, Ruyter laid by the rifle, stretched his cold-stiffened body, and went back to his cot for an hour's sleep before the day's march should begin.

At sunrise the camp was astir.

By eight o'clock the march began. All morning it wound up and down through the maze of the little-traveled mountain trail, a trail on which any horse from Europe and America would have fallen a dozen times and would have ended by breaking a leg or a neck.

At noon, they came out on a hill shoulder, sloping down to a patch of valley a half mile below. A turn in the hilly road brought them abruptly to a deserted and half-ruined khan.

The inn, from its appearance, had been for years deserted—doubtless ever since the northern pass had been generally abandoned for the southern and had carried all profitable custom with it.

The khan stood in a fairly large enclosure surrounded by a stone and cement wall perhaps nine feet in height and still in fairly good condition. Within the enclosure, some twenty yards away from the inn and as far from the open gate, was a building of such odd aspect as to call forth an exclamation of surprise from Madge.

It was a mound of yellow stone, about ten feet high at its summit and with its narrow entrance sealed by a huge flat stone, laid upright and held in place by crumbling cement. Above and around and on every projection of the mound were draped hundreds of rags.

Some were large. Some were mere shreds. A few were fairly new and were of violently gaudy coloring. Most were faded by years of sun and rain into utter tonelessness.

"What on earth is that thing?" demanded Madge of Ruyter, who was as usual riding at her side along the narrow way.

They reined in their horses as she spoke.

"You never saw one before?" said Ruyter. "The rural districts of Syria are full of them. That's a saint's tomb."

"A what?"

"Hereabouts when some Moslem priest has lived for a century or so without washing and has achieved a few neat hand-made miracles, he is canonized. A tomb something like that one over there is built to hold his remains. And when the faithful pass by it they pause to pray. After which they tear off a shred of their garments and string it on the tomb. I don't know just why. But they do. Shall we ride on? If we're to reach the valley down there in time for lunch—"

"Hold on!" called Greene from behind them as they started their horses. "We stop here."

CHAPTER VI.
The Tomb of the "Saint."

"GOOD!" assented Madge. "We can lunch under cover, then. And I can get a chance to sketch the saint's tomb."

"You can get a chance to sketch it a hundred times, if it amuses you to," answered her father, "for we are going to stop here perhaps for weeks."

"Here?"

"Yes. Here is where our first well is to be dug."

Ruyter stared at him in wonderment.

"You're joking!" he laughed.

"No," denied Greene; "I'm in earnest. It's—why, it's an ideal place for a well. We can have better cover, close at hand, than the tents in case the rains begin before we're through. It's a high, healthful location—"

"But—"

"—and," finished Greene in triumph, "the fact that a khan is here proves it is a traveled road."

"The fact that the khan has evidently been deserted for at least twenty years," retorted Ruyter, "shows the road is hardly ever traveled. Why, we haven't met a traveler all day."

But Greene's enthusiasm would not be checked. Here, he declared, was the one perfect spot for the digging of the well. He enumerated a hundred advantages. Nor was he in the least downcast when Ruyter and even Madge pointed out the folly of each.

"If you insist on starting your well in this vicinity," urged Ruyter at last, "let us dig it in the valley down below there. Some caravans might pass that way if it were known there was a well. It is on the main track. But no sane traveler will choose a route where he has to climb a mountainside with all his camels and horses in order to get a drink of water."

"My friend," said Greene, stiffly, "let me point out to you once more that I am in charge of this enterprise. And my decisions must be regarded as final. I have been in a number of business ventures in the past twenty years. And I have yet to record my first failure. I doubt if you can say as much. And I owe my success to following my own ideas instead of taking other people's advice."

"Just as you like!" laughed Ruyter. "If it amuses you to dig wells on inaccessible mountain-tops; why, all right. We'll try Mount Everest's summit, next, if you say so. It would be a joy to Hindu pilgrims to take a twenty-nine-thousand foot climb just for a nice drink of water. Shall I go over the ground here before lunch and pick out the spot for sinking the well or shall we eat first?"

"I'll pick out the spot, thank you," replied Greene coldly.

"Look here, Mr. Greene," said Ruyter, with half-annoyed good-nature, "you've hired me for your engineer. Thus far my job has been a sinecure. Now that the first time arrives when my knowledge of engineering may come in handy, you take the task away from me and plan to do it yourself. I'm not likely to earn my board and lodging at this rate."

"If I don't complain about that, I don't see why you should," snapped Greene.

"Neither do I," cheerfully assented Ruyter. "I only wanted to save you trouble. For my experience in such things would tell me the best and easiest way to dig. While you—"

"While I have already decided," interposed Greene. "We will sink our well just to the left of that Moslem tomb. In fact, one side of our shaft will be the left wall of the tomb, as far down as its foundations go. That will save us something in shoring and—"

This time Ruyter's laugh was hearty and uncontrollable.

"Mr. Greene," said he, "may I beg you to change that location?"

"I shall not," returned Greene. "It is the best imaginable."

"Who is to do the digging?"

"Those brown fellows, of course. You know that."

"No, I don't. And I'll prove it to you. Hogan!"

The foreman slouched over to where Ruyter was helping Madge to dismount.

"Hogan," went on Ruyter, "go over and tell those *fellaheen* that the well is to be dug alongside the tomb,with one side of the tomb as a side wall of the well. That's the idea, isn't it, Mr. Greene?"

"Yes," growled Joshua Greene.

"Good. Go and tell them, Hogan. Now, then, Mr. Greene, watch the result."

Hogan crossed over to where the group of natives were unloading the mules. Ruyter and Greene watched him address to them a score of words in halting Arabic, accompanied by gestures toward the tomb.

Before the foreman had finished his brief address, a gasp of incredulous horror burst from the knot of *fellaheen.*

Then came a volume of cries and howls of negation in many keys; accompanied by waving of arms, impromptu step dances and frantic head shakes, and followed by a wild chorus of chattering, guttural Arabic.

"What is the matter with them?" asked Madge in wonder, while her father scowled heavily at the noisy scene. "Have they all gone crazy?"

"They have," answered Ruyter, gravely. "Just about as crazy as an American would go if he were ordered to tear down his own church and then dig up the bones of his ancestors. You can see, Mr. Greene, why I said your plan for sinking the well there was impossible. Most of those fellows are Moslems. There isn't money enough coined to tempt them to desecrate the tomb of one of their saints. You'll have to pick out another spot. Shall I stop that babel by telling them you'll change the location of the well?"

"No!" thundered Greene. "That is where the well is to be dug or not at all."

"Then," sighed Ruyter, "I'm afraid it'll be not at all."

"No," declared Greene. "It shall be dug. If not by those chaps, then I'll find men who will do it. What in blazes are they doing now?" he broke off.

"Nothing much. Only, out of the ten laborers and muleteers, seven are gathering up their goods and chattels preparatory to starting back from Jerusalem. They are Moslems. The other three are apparently Christians. For they are staying. But seventy per cent. of your working force is 'walking out.' The Land of Moab is being treated to its first strike. Better let me call them back."

"No!" reiterated Joshua Greene. "There the well is to be dug. There and nowhere else. And if seven desert us, we'll work with the other three and with Hogan. That's settled once and for all."

Ruyter felt his temper slowly rising at such pig-headed idiocy. And, to keep from showing it, he turned on his heel and walked away toward the khan gate. As he went he heard Madge say:

"Father, he is right. Why won't you listen to reason?"

To which Joshua Greene replied, with the gentleness that none but his daughter ever heard from him:

"Little girl, a great many people in my time have called me an obstinate fool. But can you now recall a single time I didn't win out? Well, this isn't going to be the exception. You can take your old dad's solemn word for that."

CHAPTER VII.
THE "LAW OF THE WILDERNESS."

IT was morning of the second day. Shorthanded, from the defection and departure of their shocked Moslem laborers, the remainder of the party had worked hard. As a result, the khan's dismantled lower rooms began to present a fairly habitable aspect.

They were furnished with the camp beds, tables, and chairs. The kitchen was equipped, and the provisions and tight-filled water-skins were piled up under shelter in corners of the enclosure wall.

Everything was shipshape for a prolonged stay. Joshua Greene was delighted over the comfort of his surroundings. Madge was pleased with the novelty of keeping house in a tumble-down khan. The remaining natives were pursuing their vocations contentedly enough.

Hogan, alternately wielding the pick and directing his curtailed section-gang, had already broken ground; and the excavation alongside the yellow tomb was well under way.

Paul Ruyter alone was decidedly miserable. There was little for him to do and there was much time left him for worrying. And he had—or fancied he had—enough to worry over.

The brief vision of Massoud, two nights before, betokened the probable presence of Ali Diab's band somewhere in the Moab mountains. That the Bedouins would happen upon them at the khan was problematical of course.

Still, it was a chance. And to guard a little against that chance he had commandeered the services of the entire party (to the contemptuous amusement of Greene) in the task of hunting out, rehanging and repairing the massive discarded gates of the khan yard.

Also, unknown to Greene, he had, on the previous evening, given two of the men, a half medjidie apiece to stand sentry-go around the walls until daylight. He had not told Greene or anyone else about his glimpse of Massoud. He had not wanted to frighten Madge, and he had not cared to submit his already frayed temper to a second dose of Greene's skepticism as to possible peril in Moab.

He was worried, too, over the defection of the seven *fellaheen.*

Not only did their desertion leave the work short of men, but it cruelly cut down the size of the garrison in the event of attack. Incidentally, the mutineers were quite certain to announce at every hillside village through which they might pass on their way to Jerusalem, that impious foreigners were desecrating a holy shrine.

And this rumor might well bring on the party an outraged mob of Moslems whose attack would be far more fanatical and merciless than that of any mere ransom-seeking Bedouins.

Altogether Ruyter was in a highly unenviable frame of mind. And, except in Madge Greene's presence, he took no especial pains to hide the fact.

Breakfast was over.

The phenomenally fat cook and the phenomenally lean steward were in the kitchen, clattering merrily amid the metal dishes. Madge had gathered a lapful of rock cyclamen and was busy arranging the flowers in the living-rooms.

Hogan and the three *fellaheen* were toiling pick in hand in a hole of twelve foot area that already was more than ankle deep.

Joshua Greene, after-breakfast cigar in mouth and pugreed sun-helmet on the back of his head, was seated on a corner of the tomb, watching the work with an air ludicrously like that of a terrier which views the unearthing of a rat.

Ruyter was taking measurements of the excavation and its relation to the tomb's side wall. No sound disturbed him. Yet, all at once, he alone of the six was impelled to rise to his feet and turn around.

Directly behind the workers stood two desert horses, whose unshod feet had been unheard amid the noise of pick and spade, as they had approached from the open gateway. On the horses sat two Bedouins.

Ali Diab and Massoud.

The sheik was surveying the scene of labor with not one trace of expression on his thin, high-bred face. But Massoud's fuller countenance was distorted with horrified rage as he beheld Hogan's pick rise and fall against the very edge of the holy man's tomb.

Only Ali Diab's presence, apparently, restrained him from flying to the punishment of such gross sacrilege.

Attracted by Ruyter's movement, the others turned, and beheld the intruders. The *fellaheen* looked upon the Bedouins with the mingled fear and respect the peasant class of Syria ever bestow upon the better born sons of the desert. But, to Joshua Greene's unprejudiced eye, the newcomers represented only two possible additions to his short-handed force.

"Hello!" he hailed them. "Savvy Inglese? Want job? Dig ground. Five piasters a day and grub. You want?"

As neither of the visitors so much as glanced at him, he gave over his industrious pidgin-English attempt to make them understand and turned to Ruyter.

"Translate, will you?" he asked.

"These men are Bedouins," explained Paul. "The tall one is Ali Diab, the famous sheik. He—"

"Pshaw!" scoffed Greene, "Ali Diab is a myth. Gelat and the others told me so. Every time a lie of wild adventure is made up, he is made to father it. There's no such person."

"Perhaps not—in Jerusalem," grimly retorted Paul, "but out here you will find he is about the most real thing in the place. And he isn't here to pay a friendly morning call, either. Shall I talk to him?"

Glancing uncertainly from the Bedouin to Ruyter and reluctantly impressed by the latter's words, Greene nodded. Ruyter faced the motionless and expressionless Ali Diab, and extended his right hand forward and upward, palm front, in the world's universal peace sign.

The sheik did not return the sign.

Instead, he merely touched his forehead and his breast with the finger tips of his right hand—the most formal of Eastern greetings and quite devoid of any hint of the servility which so often accompanies the same gesture.

Ruyter augured ill from the salutation. Yet he strove to keep up the great traditions of the East.

"May you be happy," he began pleasantly. "Will you alight and eat?"

"May you die in peace," was the ominous yet emotionless answer. "I will not alight nor be your guest."

"May you be where rose-leaves shall fall upon your tomb," continued Ruyter in the cumulative flattery wherewith every Oriental conversation must begin. "And if you will not be our guest, why have you come here?"

"To order you and your infidel friends away," was the cold retort, this time stripped of all verbal ornament. "To give you one hour to depart."

"What's he jabbering about?" demanded Greene. "And what does he want? Will he take the job?"

"He is ordering us away," explained Ruyter in English.

"The deuce he is! I like his nerve. Tell him to clear out, or—"

"Hold on!" put in Ruyter. "Let me handle this, please. Ali Diab," he went on in Arabic, "we are here by concession of the Sultan—the most sacred padishah—on whom be peace! He graciously grants us leave to dig a well here, for the future welfare of his people. If you wish to see his majesty's *firman*—"

"*Firman!*" scoffed Ali Diab; yet with no raising of his deep voice nor indulgence in the wealth of gesture beloved by the East. "What is the Sultan's 'concession' to me? Here in the wilderness, *I* am the Sultan. My saber is the law. I am Ali Diab, sheik of the El Kanah."

"By all means," assented Ruyter, "be as many things and as many people as you choose, including a connection by marriage to the latest comet. But here we are. And here we stay. That isn't quite original. But it's true. What are you going to do about it?"

Ali Diab's dark, brooding eyes rested on the *fellaheen.*

"I am Ali Diab," he said, raising his deep voice just enough to reach them, "and I order you to leave here." One of the natives dropped his spade with a clatter. The two others looked irresolute.

"And *I*," interpolated Ruyter, "hold the Sultan's order for us to work here. If you disobey that order, the padishah's arm is long."

"I do not chaff with fellaheen," haughtily returned the sheik, "and I have given my command. I go now to enforce it. If all leave within the hour I promise safe passage. Thus far do I yield to the Sultan's *firman*. Even in the case of you, Feringee," to Ruyter, "with whom I have hoped to have a reckoning. Yet if within the hour all are not gone, the Sultan and all his armies must look for you and your fellow infidels in the tents of Ali Diab. And to find the tents of Ali Diab is like tracking the mists of dawn to their home. I have spoken. *Taman*."

"Yes," agreed Ruyter, "you have spoken. And at some length. And rather melodramatically, it seems to me. However, that is beside the point. What business is it of yours that we are here? What harm are we doing you? We're not interfering with your gentle sport of tourist-catching. In fact, when our well is dug, there'll be three travelers along here where now there is one."

"The well will not be digged," replied Ali Diab. "This morning we met the faithful whom you sought to drive into impiety. They told us their tale and we come here. But only by my own word would my people believe that any Feringee dared to defile the tomb of the holy Sidi Hussein. Wherefore I have come in person to see. And I have seen."

"What concern is old Sidi What's-his-name to you?" grumbled Ruyter.

"He was a holy man of the Bedouins. His tomb shall not be desecrated. You have my commands. One hour is yours to obey."

He wheeled his horse, turning his back on them and rode slowly toward the gate. Massoud, who had not been able to take his horrified eyes from the exposed foundation wall of the tomb, started reluctantly to follow.

As he did so, Hogan, starting guiltily from his absorption in the interview, suddenly remembered the example of industry he owed his men. Swinging his pick in air he brought it down heavily upon the hollowed earth. The blow went an inch wild and struck the side wall of the tomb with a clang.

Massoud, at this seeming intentional insult to the sacred spot, lost all control of himself. Fired with the sudden religious zeal that lies so near the surface of all Moslems, he whipped out his curved saber and rode headlong at the foreman.

But Hogan did not need Greene's warning shout, nor Ruyter's forward leap to put him on his guard.

He had lived long enough in the East to read death in the Bedouin's frenzied glare. His back was to the tomb wall and there was no time to scramble out of the shallow trench before Massoud was upon him.

Not in vain were the years when Malachi Hogan had bossed rebellious and treacherous section gangs. As the Bedouin charged, the foreman fell swiftly to both knees, and the saber cut whistled harmless above his head.

Massoud wheeled.

But the soft, new dug earth impeded his horse's movement. And before he could launch a second blow, Hogan, striking as he leaped up from his knees, had driven his pick point through the Bedouin's skull.

Massoud's saber, in mid air, fell from his nerveless hand. Massoud's body collapsed like a shot squirrel's across his broad saddle. One hand, in a death grip, became entangled in his horse's mane.

His feet, in the death convulsion, wedged themselves far into the shovel-shaped stirrups.

The horse, affrighted, whirled about and thundered after Ali Diab's mount, which had just passed out through the gate. The already lifeless Massoud swayed to and fro with the maddened brute's long stride, ridiculously like a stuffed mannikin tied to the saddle. And down the hill fled the living mount and its dead rider.

Ali Diab halted in the gateway, and sat for a moment, motionless, expressionless, surveying the group of invaders. Then, disdaining to hasten (although Greene had drawn a revolver, and the steward was emerging from the khan brandishing a rifle, whose use he did not in the least understand), Ali Diab rode in measured pace down the hillside in the wake of his slain henchman.

"Well!" grunted Hogan, striking his pick into the soft earth, and speaking lightly to cover a shake of excitement in his voice, "I hit just in time, didn't I? A second slower, and goodby to Malachi Hogan! Git to work there, ye haythen tarriers!" he blustered, his basso suddenly scaling tremulously to falsetto.

"Thank Heaven that's over!" shuddered Greene, his florid face pasty.

"Over?" echoed Ruyter. "Over? It hasn't begun. Man, after what's just happened, do you suppose Ali Diab's going to let one of us get out of here alive, if he can help it? Well, he isn't."

CHAPTER VIII.
In the Day of Battle.

"D'YOU mean," quavered Joshua Greene—"that he will come back?"

"With a hundred Bedouins at his heels. Do you know what it means to kill a Bedouin? It means that his clansmen must take the blood-vow, whether they want to or not. And they do want to. It means they must avenge his death at the earliest possible moment."

"He hit me first!" growled Hogan from the trench; "or he tried to. Would ye have had me get me head sliced off and never say 'Boo' at him?"

"You did the only thing you could," answered Ruyter—"but the result's the same. We're in for a spree. Lord, but I'm glad Miss Greene didn't see the row! She—"

"Quick!" roared Greene, shaking himself into forcible action—"order the horses saddled. Never mind the luggage or the mules. There isn't a minute to waste. We must get out of here and back to Jerusalem at full speed."

"We must do nothing of the sort," contradicted Ruyter. "Stay where you are, Hogan, and try to stop those chattering fellaheen from making enough racket to disturb Miss Greene. We must—"

"We must get out, I tell you!" declared Greene—"and on the jump. Come!"

"And I tell you," reiterated Paul, "that's the one thing we mustn't do. I—"

"I'm the master here," vociferated Greene, "and I order—"

"You aren't even a two-spot here, just now," contradicted Ruyter. "You've made this toad-pie for us. And now, unless we're to eat it, some one with brains has got to take charge. Don't make me use force."

"Hogan!" appealed Greene.

"He's right, boss," replied Hogan. "He's dead right. Can't ye see? What chance would we be having to reach Jerusalem—yes, or half of a quarter of the way to the Jordan—before the whole blooming tribe would be down on us? These conthract-built horses of ours can't travel a mile to those Bedouins' four. They'd cut us to pieces in some mountain-pass. And the hyenas would have something foreign to laugh over. No, Mr. Ruyter has the idea—whatever his idea may happen to be. I'm trailing me bet with him. And where is he, at all?" Hogan broke off, staring around.

Ruyter had not waited to hear the foreman, but had run at top speed to the stone stables at the back of the khan. Scarce had Hogan reminded Greene of the engineer's absence when a thud of hoofs was heard.

Imbarak, the preternaturally lean steward, emerged from the stable, riding the fastest of the party's string of horses. Over his saddle-bow were slung a small goat-skin of water and a sack of biscuits. Ruyter, afoot, followed him, giving final directions.

The steward swung out through the gateway and galloped away to the westward, disregarding Joshua Greene's shouts of inquiry.

"What does this mean?" demanded Greene petulantly as Ruyter hurried across the enclosure toward the group.

"It means," said Paul, "that I've sent the servant that seemed most trustworthy and was the lightest rider to Jerusalem to tell the pasha about our plight and have a regiment of light cavalry rushed here. If we have the most phenomenal luck on record he may get here and we may hold out till he does. In the mean time—"

He shouted an order in rapid guttural Arabic to the three native diggers and set off at a run toward the gateway—the others at his heels.

Greene, staring after in panic-perplexity, saw them swing-shut the double gates, bar them and reenforce them with stones and shoring. Then, Ruyter still in the lead, they made the rounds of the enclosure, examining the wall for breaches and testing its more crumbling portions.

After which they bolted for the house and presently reappeared, bringing out the scanty stock of firearms and ammunition. While

Ruyter was investigating and apportioning these, Hogan and the cook began to drag indoors several of the provision boxes.

Madge Greene, returning from the other end of the khan with such few flowers as were left from her effort at decoration, found Ruyter feverishly counting cartridges while a muleteer swabbed out a rifle.

"What is the matter?" she asked in wonder. "Are you going hunting?"

"No, Miss Greene," he answered with forced lightness, "we are going to be hunted. Listen: A party of Bedouins have taken umbrage at our presence here, and it is possible they may attack us. It is best you should know. We've sent Imbarak for reenforcements. He'll probably be back with them before long. In the mean time we want to guard against surprise or danger. *Please* don't be frightened."

"I'm not frightened," she denied. "It's—the reenforcements will come in time, of course?"

"Of course," loudly declared Ruyter. At his tone she glanced keenly at his averted face.

"Mr. Ruyter," she said with quick intuition, "there *is* danger—grave danger! Why do you try to keep me from knowing it? I am not a child!"

"To you," he evaded, "there is no danger whatever, so long as one man of us is left to look out for you."

"Please don't think of me that way, as an impediment, as something to be guarded. If there is danger for you men, I want to share it. And if there is work, I want to share that, too."

"You'll *have* to share the work, I'm afraid," he laughed, "now that I've sent away our steward. By the way, if you really want to help, won't you go and superintend the storing of the provision cases in the room behind the kitchen? It isn't a heroic role to play, I know. But food is the most useful thing in a siege—except water."

"And speaking of water," he added to Hogan, who came from an inspection of the inner quarters as Madge moved away on her errand, "get one of the men to help you lug those waterskins out of the corner over there and into the house. If we're rushed, we can't hope to hold the enclosure with the pitiful handful of men we've got. All we can do is to defend the khan itself—as long as possible. You looked to the shutter-fastenings, as I told you to?"

"Yes," replied Hogan, "and I went up on the roof, too, to see if any of the parapet stones was good and loose. Likewise they are, praise be! They may come in handy. I learned that wrinkle about the gentle uses of stones dropped from a roof on Orangeman's Day, once. Say, Mr. Ruyter, down in the valley by the foot of the hill there's a swarm of Bedouins—hundred of 'em—pitching their black tents and making camp. I came down to tell you."

"So! They haven't wasted much time. I wonder when we may expect a call from them. Meanwhile, go and hustle those water-bags; then put a lookout on the roof, to let us know when—"

He got no further.

From the hillside came the unrhythmic beat of many galloping hoofs. In an instant Hogan was hustling the trembling Greene into the house. The natives followed, leaving orders for the doors to be fastened and the solid wooden window-shutters closed and barred.

Ruyter and Hogan, rifles in hand, raced up to the roof. About fifty Bedouins, with Ali Diab in the lead—resplendent in scarlet burnoose and snowy headgear—swarmed up the last rise of the hill and charged the gate.

"Hold your fire!" ordered Ruyter as Hogan covered the sheik with his rifle—"they can't break in that way, and I don't think they'll try. The less killing we do the less needful they'll think it to collect revenge."

The Bedouins, finding the gate barred against them, made no effort to force it. Indeed, they circled the wall of the enclosure at slow gallop, as thought seeking out the more vulnerable spots.

After which they ranged up silently behind Ali Diab in a maneuver ridiculously suggestive of the opening "mass formation" of a Buffalo Bill show.

The sheik had not joined in the gallop around the walls. He had halted directly in front of the gate, and there sat his pawing horse— an enormous old fashioned blunderbuss athwart his saddle-bow.

One panel of the gate's upper portion formed an iron grill, its fretted bars perhaps eight inches apart. Through these apertures Ali Diab was quietly gazing.

When the tribesmen drew in behind him, he spoke for the first time.

"Ali Diab, Sheik of the El Kanah, to parley!" he called aloud.

"Keep him covered, Hogan," said Ruyter. "But for Heaven's sake don't fire unless you have to. I'm going down to talk with him."

"But—"

"There is no danger. He sees us. He'll see your rifle is pointing at him all the time. Besides, treachery isn't in his line. I rather wonder, in fact, that he didn't carry the enclosure wall by storm. He could have done it without losing four men."

"D'ye notice that silly old blunderbuss he's carrying?" queried Hogan, as Ruyter prepared to descend. "Sure, 'tis more like a young cannon than a gun. I've seen those blunderbusses up at Beirut. They carry about a quart of old nails and scrap iron and they scatter their charge all over creation."

Ruyter was already on his way down-stairs.

He, too, had wondered at the blunderbuss. He knew most Bedouins carry long flint-locks. But the blunderbuss is to the flint-lock what the latter is to the repeating rifle.

And that a sheik should be armed with so antiquated a weapon was by itself worthy of note. The more so as Paul remembered having seen an excellent modern rifle—probably the spoil of a tourist—hanging in Ali Diab's tent.

Though Ruyter went to the door of the khan and unbarred it, he was far too conversant by hearsay with the etiquette of Eastern desert warfare, to sally forth in response to a single summons. And, as he waited, his hand on the latch, he heard the second deep-mouthed, resonant call:

"Ali Diab, Sheik of the El Kanah, to parley!"

Madge was at Paul's side as he stood there.

"You are going out alone?" she whispered.

"It is perfectly safe." He went on, "This is all my fault. I mean that I am here."

"And to think that we trusted those foolish bankers' word about the danger, instead of yours!" Madge exclaimed.

"Please!" Ruyter laughed. "We're here now. And no good ever comes of holding a post mortem over dead actions. So let's just make the best of it. And as for your being here, well, your presence is the one thing in the world that makes the battle worth fighting. Remember that. I—"

"Ali Diab, Sheik of the El Kanah, to parley!" came the customary third summons.

And, etiquette being fulfilled, Ruyter sallied forth to greet his foe.

CHAPTER IX.
WHAT THE BLUNDERBUSS WAS FOR.

OUT into the glare of sunshine from the cool gloom of the house, walked Paul Ruyter. He leaned his rifle against the door post and advanced unarmed toward the barred gate.

Madge Greene, watching him from behind the chink of a closed wooden shutter, felt a strange little thrill at the man's quiet fearlessness in going forth bare-handed to parley with a Bedouin chieftain. Erect, leisurely, almost carelessly, Ruyter made his way to the gate.

In front of the grill, whose lower edge was at the height of his shoulders, he halted. Discarding the formal salute and series of compliments which would ordinarily have opened such a talk, and feeling he had sacrificed enough to etiquette by awaiting the third summons, he nodded curtly and demanded:

"Well, sheik, what do you want this time?"

"I bear you the decree of my council," gravely answered the sheik. "You have desecrated the tomb of our saint. You have slain one of our warriors. For this there must be payment."

"Well?"

"My tribesmen would have put you all to the sword or to the torture," went on the sheik. "But I, Ali Diab, forbade."

"Very decent of you, old chap. Thanks."

"First," slowly resumed Ali Diab, "because in your party is a woman."

Ruyter's pupils contracted involuntarily. He had hoped against hope that the Bedouins might not know of Madge's presence.

"And," continued the sheik, "we wish no ill to a woman. Second, you yourself are among this party. And once in the face of death I saw you bear yourself like a man. Also you outwitted me once. And for that I would make mine own payment. Not by the sword of my people. For these reasons and because of the Sultan's *firman,* I forbade the massacre."

"I get the idea," laughed Ruyter. "As long as you prey only on obscure travelers, the Sultan is content to send out against you a stray troop of horse now and then, which is easy enough to dodge or defeat. But when a man of prominence like Mr. Greene comes here with the Sultan's concession, it's another matter. And it is likely to call for wholesale punishment."

"It is true," replied Ali Diab, with no shadow of hesitation or attempt at denial. "And yet," he added quickly, "do not presume on that. For it cannot stand in your behalf unless our terms are obeyed."

"You've said much about 'terms,'" answered Ruyter a little impatiently. "What are they?"

"These. For the family of the man who is slain, ten thousand medjidie blood money, for he was a man of rank and of prowess. He was mine own cousin's son."

"We'll hear the rest of his obituary later," interposed Ruyter. "Ten thousand medjidie, that's about $8,500 in American money by my reckoning. And if we refuse to accept your gilt-edge appraisal of his worth?"

"Hear first the whole of my terms," commanded Ali Diab. "I am not wont to be interrupted like some Cairene camel boy."

"Excuse me, sheik, go ahead. I won't butt in again."

"For the man whom your Feringee laborer slew," went on Ali Diab, "Ten thousand medjidie. One of your number may ride to Jerusalem for the sum. The rest will stay in my camp as hostage for his return. That is the first clause. The second is that the Feringee who slew Massoud shall be delivered into our hands for punishment. Those are my terms."

"All of them? You're sure that's quite all?"

"All."

"Good. $8,500 and Hogan turned over to you for punishment. What kind of punishment?"

"That which shall suffice the dead man's dear ones," answered the sheik. They demand the punishment of the sun."

"The *which?*"

"The punishment of the sun," repeated Ali Diab, as though teaching a lesson to some overstupid pupil.

"That's a new one on me, sheik. Explain it, won't you?"

"It is as old as the tribes," replied Diab. "The Feringee shall be taken, according to custom, to a spot on the desert. There he shall be tied in the sun. And there, while all look on, shall he die."

"Die?"

"By thirst and by heat. Probably within the third day. It is the custom."

"And that's the punishment of the sun, is it? A nice, quaint, gentle little game, to be sure. And it's the program you've framed up for Hogan, a white man?"

"So shall Massoud be avenged," evenly continued the sheik. "And when the ten thousand medjidie are paid, you and yours may depart in safety. On the honor and oath of Ali Diab, Sheik of the El Kanah."

"Sheik," asked Ruyter, with ominous gentleness, "if the situations were reversed, if it were our people here who demanded one of *your* men for such torture, what would be your reply?"

"A Feringee cannot be judged by the standards of Ali Diab," loftily returned the sheik.

"But what would you do?" persisted Ruyter.

Long and closely the sheik looked into Ruyter's flushed face. Then slowly he said:

"Feringee, I should do as you are going to do. I should refuse. And I would protect my clansman to the last breath."

"That's the answer, sheik," nodded Ruyter. "We'll see you in Gehenna before we give up Hogan to you. And you can make the most of it. I wonder you wasted breath in making such a fool offer."

"It was needful to give you the chance, if but for form. Our laws require it."

"And now, sheik?"

"And now, Feringee, we shall fulfil our sentence upon the slayer of Massoud. We shall put him to death by the punishment of the sun."

"I think," said Ruyter with labored patience, "that I've already said we should not give him up."

"It is not requisite."

"You talk in riddles."

"Perchance. But I do not act in them."

"But how?"

"You shall see. I regret that all must suffer alike for the fault of one. But perhaps when the heat bites deep you may repent and yield him to us."

"Bites deep? Say! There's nothing gained by chattering in conundrums. Attack, if you're going to! The parley is over."

"The parley is over," gravely assented Ali Diab. "And—the punishment of the sun begins."

He still made no move to go, and the dense ranks of desert horsemen behind him sat their mounts like gaudy bronze statues.

Ali Diab looked up into the eye of the blazing hot noonday sun. It seemed to Ruyter almost as though the sheik were silently invoking the sun god.

Then, with a gesture so indescribably quick that Ruyter could not follow it, the sheik snatched up his huge blunderbuss from across the saddle pommel, leveled and fired it.

There was a roar that deafened Ruyter and that reverberated fully for miles among the brown naked mountain gorges. The hot air was filled with blinding acrid smoke.

Like a tardy echo came the answering spit of Hogan's repeating rifle from the roof. And a bullet flattened itself with a vicious splash upon an iron grill-bar in direct line with Ali Diab's head.

"Don't shoot again!" yelled Ruyter to the foreman.

The sheik saluted punctiliously, turned his steed's head and descended the hill at a walk; his followers falling into place behind him as he rode away.

Ruyter, recovering from the noise of the shot, realized all at once that Ali Diab had not fired at him nor at the house. That blunderbuss had been leveled at a point far to the right of Paul's body and still farther from the house.

Ruyter, turning to see what had been the target for the inexplicable shot, stood suddenly inert, wide-mouthed, sick with horror.

Then, half-dazed, he babbled:

"The punishment of the sun! The punishment of the sun! The brown devil!"

CHAPTER X.
"THE PUNISHMENT OF THE SUN."

JOSHUA GREENE, first making very certain that the unwelcome guests had departed, ran out of the house to learn the nature and result of the interview with Ali Diab.

"Well," he called, "I see you got rid of them. Good boy! Now we'll— Why, what ails you? You look as if you were seeing a ghost."

He followed the direction of Paul Ruyter's stupefied gaze, then broke out in pettish annoyance:

"So! *That's* what he fired at, is it? How babyish!"

"Yes," acquiesced Ruyter, finding his voice. "Almost as babyish as a cyclone or a prairie fire."

And as he spoke, he was running toward the spot on which his horrified gaze had been riveted. Hogan, too, descending from the roof, just then caught a glimpse of the scene and cried aloud at what he saw.

The water supply that was to have lasted until the first well could be dug, had been bottled, after the Eastern method, in goatskins. These skins had been piled temporarily in one corner of the yard in a fairly regular heap.

Ali Diab's trained eyes had, apparently, on his first visit, taken in every detail of the defenders' surroundings. And, on departing just now from Ruyter, he had fired point-blank into the pile of swollen skins.

The nails, pebbles, scraps of iron and bitten slugs wherewith the ancient blunderbuss had been crammed almost to its flaring bell-muzzle had ripped and torn their way through the heap of water–bags. Not in concentrated "pattern," but wide scattered.

Some skins were only punctured. Some were burst. Water, precious life-saving water of the arid mountain wilderness, was gushing and avalanching down into the thirsty sands of the kahn yard.

If Greene did not see the tragedy of the thing, Hogan and Ruyter undoubtedly did. Both had dwelt long enough in the East's desert places to know the surpassing value of every drop of stored water.

And, on seeing them hurl themselves upon the wreck, frantically seeking to stanch the rents that were not hopelessly large, a slow realization came to the onlooker.

"The beast!" he yelled. "He tried to cut off our water supply."

"He not only tried it," growled Hogan, holding together the torn gap in one goatskin while Ruyter wound a pack thread tightly around the ragged opening, "but he came plenty close to doing it. For a single shot it did more damage than a ten-inch shell bursting in the Sub-Treasury. Grab the other side of this bag, will you, and help me plug this second leak?"

The others came out.

For the time all fears of attack were merged in this greater horror of thirst. Madly they toiled to scoop up and save such pools of gritty water as had collected in hollows and had not yet sunk into the ground.

Madge sewed rents as ardently as a poor woman making over her one ball gown. Even Greene was pressed into service. The water-saving was carried on as feverishly as any treasure hunt.

At last when the task was finished Ruyter took account of stock and made known his report.

"We've got enough to keep us on half rations of water for the best part of a week—with luck," said he. "Of course none of it can be used for cooking or washing or any luxuries like that. It goes under lock and key in a separate room. I'll keep the key and portion out each day's supply. I may add," he said, speaking in English and then repeating his words in Arabic, "that I shall shoot dead any man caught trying to take more than his right share or tampering in any way with the lock of the room it is to be stored in."

"Look here, Ruyter!" blustered Greene, making one more effort to gain the leadership which Paul had so naturally assumed. "You're pretty free with your orders and threats. I appreciate your zeal. But don't forget for one moment that you are my employee. And as employer here I give all orders. Of course I shall be glad to receive good suggestions. But just because I have allowed you to take control to-day in a few matters—"

"Just because there's no one else fit to," put in Hogan, "he'll keep on doing it. And every mother's son of us is going to mind him."

"You will take your orders from me, Hogan, and no one else," loftily declared Greene.

"I'll take orders from the only man in the crowd that's got the wit and the experience to keep us all from being killed," doggedly returned the foreman.

"You are discharged!" flared Greene.

"By all means," agreed the imperturbable Hogan. "Will ye kindly give me my pay and my fare to the coast, and safe passage thereto? That's what my contract calls for, you'll remember. Listen to me, Mr. Greene. Come off yer high horse. We're up against it, one and all. And in a pinch like this, the man who's fit to be leader is leader, be he water-boy or emperor. And if we don't hang together and obey that leader, it's slaughtered we'll all be. So let's hear no more silliness. When we're out of this you'll be our boss again. And then you can fire us all till you're black in the face, if that's yer diversion. In the mean time, you and me and the rest of the push will do just what Mr. Ruyter tells us to do. What next, Mr. Ruyter?"

The mutiny was over.

Under Ruyter's direction the precious water was carried to a storeroom. A padlock from a camp chest was affixed to the door of the room. And Ruyter pocketed the key.

A lookout was stationed on the roof, and the hours of sentry-go were apportioned. Madge insisted on doing her share of duty, and Paul accordingly sent her to the roof for the first turn as lookout. Then Ruyter addressed his male garrison.

"Imbarak will probably get safely to Jerusalem," said he. "If he does, we ought to expect help inside of a week. Our water should hold out that long, our food much longer. I don't think the Bedouins will rush us. They are playing another sort of game."

"What do you mean?" asked Greene.

"They have a pleasant form of torture known as the punishment of the sun. They stake out a victim on the sand and let the sun and thirst do the rest. They're trying that on us. Figuratively, they have us staked out. For we can't escape. They'd catch us in the passes before we had traveled a half day. So they are sitting quietly, waiting for us to die of thirst and heat. It is a merry sport and worthy the sons of the desert."

"Won't they take ransom?" said Greene, "or didn't you ask?"

Ruyter did not hesitate in his reply. Already he had resolved not to tell the price Ali Diab had demanded for letting them go. His own judgment of character told him that Hogan would probably insist on giving himself up to save the rest, were the Irishman to learn that his life was part of the price.

So Paul answered:

"No. They won't take ransom alone. It is life they demand. And it is up to us to see they don't get it. After all, I'm glad they've decided to kill us by thirst instead of attacking us. It gives us time. And Imbarak ought to get the cavalry here by the sixth day."

"The well," suggested Greene with furtive eagerness, "sha'n't we keep on digging it? It—it may supply us with water in case the cavalry are delayed a day or so in getting here. Sha'n't we go on with it?"

There was a concentrated appeal in the man's almost fawning manner in which he spoke, which Ruyter, even in that moment of stress, wondered. But he answered:

"By all means. It will keep us busy and take our minds off our worries, even if we don't strike water. It's a good idea. Nothing like work to dull a man's troubles."

"If we're looking for water," observed Hogan, "suppose we go over the enclosure again and see if maybe we can't hit on some more likely spot for it than alongside that old tomb."

"*No!*" almost shrieked Greene.

"No," said Ruyter more quietly. "I've been over the whole ground pretty carefully. There's no other likely spot. And often those old Moslem tombs were built alongside a spring. The spring—if there is one—has receded long ago. But perhaps if we dig deep enough we can tap it."

"Oh, thank you!" cried Greene.

"For what?"

Madge's voice, from above, calling in quick excitement, broke in on the colloquy. The girl was leaning over the parapet, her field-glasses to her eyes, staring down toward the Bedouin camp in the valley.

"Look!" she called. "They have captured a prisoner and they are dragging him into one of their tents. It's—it's—oh, it's *Imbarak!*"

CHAPTER XI.
THE SIEGE AND THE CHALLENGE.

THE siege was a week old. For six days and nights Ali Diab's men had been encamped in the valley below the enclosure. For six days their vedettes had ridden back and forth over the mountain trail that led to the Jordan.

For six days, each morning, the sheik himself had ridden, fearless and alone, from his camp up the hillside to the gate-grille of the khan yard, and, glancing carelessly in, had ridden back again. There was a quiet contempt in his action—contempt not only for danger, but for his present opponents—that was daily more and more maddening to the besieged as their nerves waxed more and more taut and racked.

It was as the sheik might have made daily inspection of a cageful of rats captured by him and on whose daily change of demeanor hung the results of some scientific test.

It was a waiting game, this "punishment of the sun." And if there is one art wherein the true Oriental not only excels but revels it is in waiting.

This same waiting was beginning to play havoc with the defenders' nerves. Even as to the first of two opponents to enter a prize-ring, the wait for his foe's advent is the most trying phase of the whole contest.

For an attack they could have braced themselves, and excitement would have served as tonic. But to know they were playing a hideously slow game with death, and that their fast-dwindling store of water served as the score of that game, was enough to send Greene well-nigh into nervous prostration, and had latterly begun to affect Hogan's stolid good humor.

By day the men worked doggedly with pick and spade at their task of well-digging.

Even Greene took a hand at it as a relief from tension, until he found that pick-wielding under a glaring sun was horribly thirsty work for a fat man, and that he could neither cajole nor bully Ruyter into giving him a drop more than his allotted daily ration.

The half quantity originally ordered by Ruyter had been cut down still further from the moment it had been discovered that a group of Ali Diab's vedettes on the mountain had intercepted and seized the reenforcement-seeking Imbarak.

Now that all hope of relief from Jerusalem was cut off, the finding of water was the one chance of prolonging life. And, cursing the inadequacy of their equipment, the men slaved manfully in double shifts at the work.

Far down the shaft had sunk. And now Ruyter's engineering skill was called into play to arrange the angle of digging, the shoring, and other details of which the rest were ignorant.

The foundation of the tomb still formed one side of the shaft. And, deep as they had dug, they had not yet reached the base of that foundation.

On the morning of the seventh day Ruyter came from the water store-room, his face haggard, his eyes dead. Hogan, waiting to dispense the supply of water for the day, stared at him in amaze.

"What's up, chief?" he demanded. "Touch of sun?"

"No," said Paul dully.

"Where's the water?"

"There isn't any."

"But you said—"

"Come and look."

He stood aside and Hogan came to the room's threshold. A deflated goat-skin lay on the middle of the stone floor. Around it the damp stones were already drying.

"In the night, I suppose," said Ruyter jerkily. "A rat! See the teeth-marks. The goatskin must have been greasy. He gnawed clean through. The water has had hours and hours to ooze out. All gone!"

Hogan's wide mouth flew open to make a clear path for a flood of useless execration. But the words died unsaid. He and Ruyter looked at each other in sullen silence. Then:

"At the rate you were doling it out it would have lasted us the best part of another week," said Hogan. "By that time we might have dug down to a spring in our well-shaft. No use crying over spilled water any more than milk. I s'pose."

"No," said Ruyter.

"'What's to be done?'"

"If I knew I'd do it. But I *shall* know. Come!"

Paul led the way out to where Greene and the natives were eagerly awaiting their morning drink. The tense, craving, expectant look in their eager eyes was more than Ruyter could bear just then.

Turning abruptly, and leaving Hogan to explain matters, Paul went up the stone stairway to the roof.

It was Madge's turn as lookout. She glanced from the scant shade of the parapet and smiled as she caught sight of him. But at the expression in his face the light in her own died out.

"What is it?" she asked, hurrying toward him.

As briefly as possible he told her.

"That means?" she asked as he finished.

"A few minutes ago," he answered, "I thought it meant distraction. I know now it means I'll be able to find some other way of getting water for you."

"Don't think of me," she begged. "I've shared with the rest, and I've tried to work with the rest. We will all take together what comes. You mustn't think of me—"

"It's a habit I can't break," he laughed ruefully. "And I'm going to get water for you. How, I don't know. But I'm going to. I wonder if you half realize what a brick you've been this past week? Any other girl brought up as you have been would have gone to pieces under the strain, the privation, the fear. You have worked splendidly. And, better, you've kept heart in all the rest of us."

"*I?* It was *you.* But for you, Mr. Ruyter, we should all have been lost long ago. You have been the brain and backbone of every move."

"And at the last," he murmured bitterly, "I've brought us to a point where there's no next move. But—"

"Look!" she interrupted; "Ali Diab is riding up the hill for that horrible morning inspection of his. How I hate him!"

"Wait!" Paul exclaimed: "I am going to speak to him."

He ran down the stairs and was at the grille by the time Ali Diab drew near enough to hear him.

"Sheik," said Ruyter formally, sinking his voice so that it was audible only to the Bedouin, "I call a parley."

"If it is to beg mercy—" began the sheik.

"I am not of the begging breed," returned Ruyter; "I'm no Oriental. And when I turn to begging it will not be to ask mercy from the merciless."

"Speak on," answered the sheik, as if not wholly displeased at the retort. "But first, why not eat and drink? I will await you here. From your sunken eyes I fear you have neglected to break your morning fast."

"You are mistaken," snapped Ruyter; "I did not forget my breakfast. I wanted none. I have been made sick by guzzling too much water at a time from our new well."

"My friend," observed the sheik in genuine admiration, "Allah has forked your tongue."

"In other words, I'm a liar?"

"The look of thirst on a face is as plain to be recognized by us desert born as are the blotches of the plague," evaded Ali Diab. "Too many thirst sufferers have reeled into my tent from time to time during my life in dire anguish and claiming the guest right—for me not to read the first signs. But you called a parley. Speak on. I will hear you."

"So good of you!" growled Ruyter with a heavy sarcasm that was quite lost on the Oriental. "Here's my suggestion: You claimed last week ten thousand medjidie and the life of one of us. Are those still your terms?"

"The sheik of the El Kanah is not a Damascene seller of rugs," coolly replied Ali Diab. "My word once is my word ever."

"Then the terms are still the same?"

"Of a certainty."

"Then," replied Ruyter, "I accept."

The handsome mask of Ali Diab's face broke up into a look of crass unbelieving amazement.

"I accept," went on Ruyter. "The money shall be paid, and the man shall be given over to you."

"It is well," agreed Ali Diab, albeit with disappointment in his voice. "And it is also well that you once refused my offer to join my people, for we have scant use for weaklings. For the first time in Ali Diab's days he has misjudged a man."

"Quite so," assented Ruyter. "Put it any way you like, so long as you let the rest of us go."

"And the man shall be delivered to us—when?"

"Here and now," said Paul, beginning to undo the gate.

"He consents? Or shall my men bear him forth?"

"Oh, I consent, all right," retorted Paul. "That's what I'm here for, and I am trusting in your sworn word that the rest be allowed to return to Jerusalem in perfect safety. It is so understood? Then I'm ready."

"You?" queried the puzzled Bedouin, as Ruyter opened one-half of the gate and stepped out unarmed into the road.

"Yes, I. Say, old chap," added Ruyter, embarrassed, "I'm not given to being melodramatic, and I sure do hate a scene. Let's say nothing more about it, but go along quietly."

"You would trick me!" declared the sheik. "It is not you whom we demand for the torture of the heat and the thirst. It is the Feringee who slew Massoud."

"But," urged Ruyter, "I'll prove a dandy substitute. I'm better born and of more importance than he. And those details count in the East. Why, Hogan's little above the *fellaheen* class. There's no honor in torturing him. Now, with me it is a different proposition. You're making a good bargain all around by taking me instead. Come along."

Something very close to a smile wreathed the thin lips of Ali Diab.

"I am glad," he said simply. "I am glad. It seems I can still point out a *man* and that my judgment does not err."

"Never mind the hot air. Come along. They'll be strolling down here to the gate presently, asking awkward questions and interfering. I want to be out of their reach before then."

"My friend," said the Bedouin, "you are brave. But what you have proposed is folly. Your death would not atone for the slaying of Massoud. Nor would it satisfy his kindred's demand for blood vengeance. I cannot take you in his stead, O brother of eagles!"

"You can't, hey? Well, then, are you sport enough to light me here and now—with any weapons you choose—and if I win, let us go scot-free?"

"Why should I take half when the whole is mine?" said Ali Diab. "You are all in my power—in the hollow of my hand. Why should I fight for stakes that are even now mine own? For that reason, partly, I have not stormed the khan. For when the Sultan's people find you all dead of thirst—not slain by my men's weapons—they cannot lay the blame at Ali Diab's door."

"That's corking good logic," admitted Paul ruefully; "but it isn't the line of talk I'd expected from the heroic Ali Diab. Why," he went on, deliberately seeking to force upon the Bedouin a contest that might give himself and his the loophole he sought, "I've been forever hearing about the romantic fights waged by Ali Diab. And here's the most romantic one of the lot—a fight for the lives and liberty of besieged white men. It must be you are only a heroic warrior when your opponents are donkey-boys and porters. You seem to have a positive genius for skulking out of a fight with any one who might lick you. Myself, for example. Oh, your reputation is well earned! It rests on the breath of a tribe of liars."

For the briefest instant the sheik's face was transfigured into a mask of murder. Then; by mighty effort, he controlled himself; though when he spoke his deep voice still shook from his battle at self-mastery.

"You are familiar with saber and pistol?" he asked.

"I've shot a pistol perhaps ten times," answered Ruyter. "And once I broiled an antelope steak on a saber. That's the tale of my experience with both. But that needn't bother you. I've the pluck and you haven't."

"You are brave," mused the sheik—"brave beyond measure. You would fling away your life on the bare chance to save those with you—and knowing my prowess, too. Your insults are but part of it all. And I grant you credit. I grieve that such a man must die by the punishment of the sun. But better than by my hand. You would be as a child in battle with me. Even now thirst has made you so weak you can scarce stand. *Ma-Salami,* O brother of heroes!"

Ere Ruyter could check him the sheik had galloped down the hillside out of ear-shot.

CHAPTER XII.
Upon One Cast.

Ruyter moved slowly back inside the enclosure, barred the gate behind him, and walked up to the khan door. He had failed. And for the moment there seemed to him no other possible move.

Yet, as he walked along, rehearsing in memory his odd colloquy with Ali Diab, one chance phrase of the sheik's leaped forward in his mind, sharply, incisively; and with that fugitive recollection came inspiration.

For an instant, as the amazing idea struck him, he stopped short in his path, well-nigh overwhelmed by the simplicity and the abounding peril of it.

"What was the talk about?" asked Hogan, coming across to him from the well.

"Oh, I offered to fight him for our freedom. He's just the chivalric, impractical sort of chap that I hoped would be caught by such a sporting proposal. But he was too chivalric. He saw what rotten condition I'm in. He could have beaten me in no time, at any weapon, as I am now. He knew it, and he wouldn't do it. He's a good deal of a man, in his own way, is Ali Diab."

"Then," commented Hogan, who was not especially impressed by the recital of the sheik's virtues, and who had his own very positive notions on the subject—"then there's no chance left?"

"Oh, yes, there is!" denied Ruyter. "A brand-new idea."

In a few words Ruyter outlined it to him. At the conclusion of the brief speech the dumfounded Hogan broke out in a torrent of angry protest.

Ruyter silenced each argument with the same retort:

"It's our one chance. And I'm the one man here who can put it across."

"But if you don't?" said Hogan at last, when every line of appeal was exhausted.

"If I don't, the rest will be no worse off than now."

"The deuce we won't! Without you? Let *me* do it."

"And make a certain bungle of it? Not much! It's my job. Keep mum about it. If I don't come out of it, take charge. But I'm going to come out of it. It's a way I have."

"We've come to the bottom of the tomb's foundation wall!" hailed Greene from the edge of the shaft.

"And no sign of water?"

"No."

"From your tone I thought we had."

"Are you going to take a turn at the work?" went on Greene.

"Not to-day. And I don't advise any one else to. It's thirsty exercise and may lead to heat prostration. There's not a chance in a million of our striking water to-day. Wait till to-morrow."

"Why to–morrow more than to-day?"

"There may be water to-morrow," answered Ruyter cryptically; and he would give no further explanation, but went up to the roof to Madge.

The rest followed his counsel about ceasing work. But Greene, who had always had a morbid dread of thirst and of the chances of sunstroke, surprised everybody by climbing down into the shaft, pick in hand, and starting briskly at the task his employees had just abandoned. For hours he toiled unremittingly.

Dusk had fallen. Ruyter left the roof. He had spent the bulk of the day there, field-glasses in rest, studying minutely each detail of the valley camp of Ali Diab.

Before twilight he had learned every approach: the lay of every tent; the space where the horses were tethered; the pasturage where grazed the tribe's lean cows, its long-haired goats, its dirty Syrian sheep, with their beaver-like, twenty-pound tails. And at last his lesson was learned.

Through the dusk Ruyter made his way to the gate, Hogan at his side. They shook hands in silence, and Ruyter softly let himself out of the enclosure.

He was unarmed. For their weapons were few; and, in event of a rush, the defenders would have ample use for every firearm they could muster.

Once outside the gate, Ruyter called into play all the old scout training of his youth. From rock to rock of the hillside he dodged. His soiled khaki blended with the dun earth. His step was noiseless, his direction sure.

Beyond setting vedettes at either end of the pass, the Bedouins kept no special watch on prey which they knew could not possibly escape. And, as is almost invariably the custom with the desert tribes in peace times, there was practically no organized sentry guard of the camps.

Hence, Ruyter found his work, as he had anticipated, ridiculously easy. The very last thing any Bedouin expected was that one or more of the besieged should make for their camp.

Early night had settled when Paul Ruyter paused at the curtain of the center portion of Ali Diab's own spear-marked tent. Thrusting the curtain aside, he strode boldly in.

A pace within the threshold, Ruyter halted and sharply clapped his hands together, the universal form of summons in the East.

"Coffee!" he called in Arabic. "Coffee, food, and tobacco!"

From the service section of the tent, at the summons, four or five persons hurriedly came into the central space. From the other curtained compartment entered Ali Diab himself, staring questioningly in the half light cast by a charcoal brazier at this imperious visitor.

Ruyter wheeled and faced him, his right arm raised in the peace sign.

"I claim the rights of the desert guest law!" announced Paul. "In the tent of Ali Diab, which I entered of my free will, I demand his hospitality."

The others, save the sheik alone, broke into exclamations of angry amaze as they recognized the intruder. Ali Diab's high-bred face gave no sign of emotion. Saluting Paul with a proud humility, he came forward, a lithe majesty in his mien.

"You are welcome, my guest," said he. "I and my possessions and the swords of my people are yours."

Never before had Ruyter so admired the sheik's wondrous self-control. By no word or look did the Bedouin show the stark surprise and chagrin that must have been his. And Paul could now well believe a tale that had been told him in Persia of Ali Diab's hospitality.

The sheik's direst foe, so ran the story, had once strode into the camp of the El Kanah, crying: "What treatment does Ali Diab grant to such a guest as I?" And by way of reply the sheik had, with his own hand, slaughtered two hundred of his choicest horses and cattle as a sacrifice to the hated visitor.

At a sharp word now from Ali Diab servants brought rugs and cushions and bore a coal-lighted narghile to Ruyter, and coffee upon a tray garnished with pungent sweetmeats. From the kitchens came the bustle of preparation as for a feast.

The sheik motioned Ruyter to a seat upon a pile of rugs propped by cushions, and with his own hand set the narghile before him. Then courteously and first begging permission, the sheik seated himself cross-legged at the feet of his guest.

"Honor my tent by making known your wishes, I pray you," he said.

"Well," replied Paul ruminatively, "just for the moment I think about a gallon of cold water would taste better than anything else on earth. And after that maybe another gallon or two, just to sip as we talk."

A huge *ghoola* of water was fetched by the nearest bearded servant. And Ruyter plunged his parched, thirst-cracked lips into its cool contents.

After an interminable time he drew back from his draft, sighing in utter relief. Then, reaching forward, he lifted one of the loaves of unleavened bread from a platter near him, broke it in two, and ate the smaller portion.

"Sheik," he said formally, "I break bread with you."

"You bring bliss thereby upon my poor abode," was the ceremonious rejoinder.

Taking a pull at the narghile, the American went on, more colloquially:

"If I'm rightly informed, sheik," said he, "the immemorial guest law of the desert may not be broken."

"Yourself have but now proven it."

"And," pursued Ruyter, "by that law a Bedouin host is not only obliged to feed and care for his guest for so long a time as the latter may choose to remain, but must also speed him on his way, granting him such food and drink as he may require for the journey and affording him the full protection of the tribe against all enemies for a certain space of time."

"It is so."

"You're a good loser, sheik. I'll say that for you. As I understand it, the guest who breaks bread with a Bedouin sheik is inviolate and is protected by the tribe for forty-eight hours after his departure?"

"Yes."

"And—if I still quote the guest law correctly—the guest who not only eats but also sleeps beneath a sheik's tent-roof is inviolate and protected—and, if need be, provisioned—not for a mere forty-eight hours, but for fourteen days. Is it so?"

"It is the law."

"A good law. Sheik, I'm drowsy. If you'll excuse my rudeness, I believe I'll take a nap."

Incontinently, Ruyter leaned back among his pillows, stretched himself out, and shut his eyes, Ali Diab all the while watching him inscrutably, the tribesmen huddled at the far end of the tent glaring in impotent wrath through the half light.

Fatigue, the deep drafts of water he had taken into his parched body, the sharp reaction from the week of stress, all did their work. Paul knew he was safe. Since the birth of time no Bedouin has ever broken, in letter or spirit, the guest law.

It was no false snore that presently echoed through the tent. Even Ali Diab realized that.

For a full hour Paul Ruyter slept heavily under the roof of his enemy, Ali Diab never once relaxing that fathomless, inscrutable gaze into the slumberer's face.

At last Ruyter yawned, stretched, and sat up.

"I feel like another man," he announced cheerily. "And now, sheik, if you please, we'll have a little business chat. First, though, how about another quart or so of water?"

CHAPTER XIII.
The Guest Law of the Desert.

"ALI DIAB," observed Ruyter, with studied formality, as he set down the dripping earthen *ghoola,* "I have broken bread with you. I have slept beneath your roof. I have claimed and received the hospitality of the sheik of the El Kanah. Accept my thanks."

"Thanks are *your* due, *howadji,* for honoring my wretched home," said All Diab mechanically, using the formula custom decreed.

"And now," went on Ruyter more naturally, "we pass lightly to the next cage—or, rather, the next point. I so far take advantage of the guest law's privileges as to ask of you two double goatskins of water to bear away with me. I could carry no more. I demand no food, for with that I am well supplied. But, where I am going, we are wofully shy of water."

If the Arab felt new chagrin he showed none. He clapped his hands. A servant appeared. The sheik transmitted Ruyter's command. A minute later two hundred-pound goatskins of water lay in the tent door.

"Should I or mine thirst again within the allotted fourteen days of time wherein you and your tribe are bound to protect and succor me," said Paul cheerfully, "I'll come back for more."

"*Howadji,*" remarked Ali Diab after a short pause (and using for the second time the term of honor instead of the contemptuous "Feringee"), "you have conquered. Mine own laws and those of my people—from the days of that Sheik Ibrahim whom Allah loved and whose deeds are told in your Bible—you have turned against me. You have made a mock of the sacred guest law. And, as upholder of that law, I have no recourse but to obey—to see you set at naught my careful plans and to abet you in doing it. But after the fourteen days are passed I shall capture you, if half my tribe die in the attack, and make you give payment for this victory. Not in piasters and medjidies, but in such tortures as shall make death seem a boon. This I swear by the awful triple oath—by the beard of my father, by the sword of the Prophet, by the—"

"In fourteen days," interposed Paul lightly, "I and mine shall be safely out of Syria. To-morrow, under your safeguard, I ride to Jerusalem. I shall return post-haste with a regiment of the pasha's cavalry, who will escort my friends out of this land of desolation. You must search far for us."

"Your friends?" echoed the sheik in cold mockery. "Their breath is in their nostrils. The protection of the El Kanah does not extend to them. They are not my guests. Nor shall any of them ever be. For from this hour a double guard shall be set on my camp to seize all Feringee who seek to approach it."

"Yes? But—"

"Ride to Jerusalem, if you will, for the pasha's troops. Yes, and return with them at what speed you will. But before you go bid farewell to those in the khan up yonder. For before your return the jackals shall fight over them. This I swear."

"I don't quite get you. That is—What do you mean?"

"You are inviolate. But those with you are not. At dawn we attack the khan."

"That's hardly playing the game, is it?" commented Ruyter, with an assumption of carelessness.

"The punishment of the sun is averted by your trader trick," said Ali Diab, with a gesture toward the wet goatskin bags. "We can no longer sit patient and watch the thirst do our work. But we still can capture. And on the oath of Ali Diab those who fall in the attack will die happiest."

"Several things will happen before that capture," hazarded Ruyter. "The khan is strong and we are well armed. We can give a fair account of ourselves, I fancy."

"You have made my guest law a mock. And if the tale goes abroad Ali Diab shall be the laughter of fools. To wipe out that laugh is worth the lives of fifty of my men. And I am prepared to waste such lives in the attack. *Howadji,* ye be four Feringee men, four Syrians, and a woman. In my camp here alone are one hundred and forty warriors. How long will you withstand our attack when we come ready to die if only first we may slay?"

"There are moments," remarked Paul, with profound conviction after a thoughtful pause—"there are moments when I am half inclined to revise my list of the world's great men and give myself a rather lower place in it. When I turned that water trick just now I was tempted to fancy myself as one of our shrewdest little diplomats and four-time winners. But from where I sit I can't see that I've accomplished anything except to secure my friends a good drink of water and to end a little sooner the suspense of waiting for the attack."

"You have gained immunity and protection for yourself," the sheik gently reminded him. "Think what joy it will be—and what safe hunting—for so brave a man to fire upon assailants who are bound by oath to do him no harm."

"Drop that!" growled Ruyter, wincing. "D'you suppose I hadn't thought of it?"

"Also," pursued Ali Diab, "if you ride to Jerusalem for reenforcements, the work will be easier for us. Without you, your friends are as sheep whose head is stricken off."

"You are going to attack at dawn?"

"At the sun's rise."

"We shall await you, sheik," said Paul, rising, "and we shall make your visit as interesting as possible."

"*Bismillah,*" gravely indorsed the sheik.

"By the way," added Ruyter as he stooped to shoulder the heavy water-bags; "you aren't overfond of bargains, sheik. But I've one more to propose. There is, as you have said, a woman with us. If from the moment I enter the khan I will waive the rights of the guest law, will you spare her?"

"The guest law cannot be waived," returned the sheik. "As for the woman who is at the khan, I am Ali Diab, not an Armenian nor a Kurd. She is safe from me and mine, as is every woman."

"Sheik," remarked Ruyter as he slung the second bag over his shoulder and bent under the weight, "by all rights I ought to hate you. But, somehow, I can't. You're a good deal of a man. So-long!"

"*Ma-Salami!*" returned the Bedouin, with a courteous salute of farewell.

Half an hour later Paul Ruyter, panting from his slow and difficult climb, reached the outer gate of the khan. At his whistle Hogan ran forward to admit him.

Into the enclosure and so on to the main hall of the khan staggered Ruyter under his burden, answering in panted monosyllables Hogan's whirlwind of questions.

There, laying down the water-bags, he stood, recovering his breath while Madge and Hogan and the four natives proceeded to quench their thirst.

"Not too much at first!" he warned them. "Go easy. There's plenty of it. But too much is bad for you after you've gone without it so long."

Madge had not taken her great eyes from him since the moment he had appeared. She had said no word. But her face was deathly white. And in her dark eyes' depth lurked a strange light that Ruyter dared not translate.

Scarce touching the water Hogan offered her, she took advantage of the general absorption of the rest in their new-found treasure to cross to where Paul stood.

"Why did you do it?" she demanded; and there was a tense quality in her low-pitched tone.

"Do what?" he asked, perplexed at the strange note in her voice.

"Risk your life so foolhardily and leave us to suffer such awful suspense for fear you wouldn't come back?"

"If I'd known you were bothering yourself to worry over me," he said, "I'd have taken a shorter nap."

"Nap!"

"Yes. I was dead tired. Besides, it was a part of the guest game."

"You could sleep in such danger?" she asked incredulously. "Oh, you are of iron, not flesh! You have no human weaknesses."

"I have nothing else, thank goodness," he laughed. "As for danger, that stopped the minute I entered Ali Diab's tent. If I'd been caught before I got there I'd have been a goner. Once there, the guest law made me as safe as if I were in a church."

"How could you be sure of that? They might—"

"No, they mightn't. That's a law no desert tribe can break; it's stronger than their religion, and it's necessary, too. You see, in the desert there are no restaurants and no police stations. Thousands of years ago the Bedouins made up for those two deficiencies by instituting the guest law. Why, there are instances of it in the Book of Genesis. For example, where Abraham—By the way," he broke off, "where's your father?"

"Why," she answered in surprise. "I don't know. I haven't seen him since dusk. I suppose he's asleep in his room. I'll go and wake him. He'll be so glad the water has come. He's suffered horribly to-day from thirst."

As she left the room Ruyter beckoned Hogan to him.

"This is just a respite," said Paul. "We're goners. They attack us at sunrise. We can't hold the outer enclosure for a minute against them. Get the men busy barricading the house. We must fight to the death—for I imagine death will be the pleasantest fate in store. It may comfort you, though, to know they'll not harm Miss Greene."

"Praise be!" exclaimed Hogan.

"I'll go out to the shaft and gather up the picks," decided Paul. "They'd come in too handy for breaking shutters and doors."

Ruyter left the house and strolled through the starlit night across to the well-shaft. As he fumbled for a match to locate the scattered picks, a sound directly under his feet made him stop in bewilderment. He waited an instant. Then, from below, the sound was repeated. And again a third time.

CHAPTER XIV.
THE SECRET OF SULEIMAN PASHA.

THEN Ruyter understood. Some one was in the bottom of the well-shaft and at work there with pick and spade. He recalled the absence of Greene and the khan, and the brief mystery of the night-time toiler was at once solved: though why Greene, already sick with thirst, should have chosen to come out here and labor alone in the shaft so late at night was still inexplicable to Paul.

In fact, so odd did it seem to him that he restrained his first impulse to halloo down the shaft the glorious news about the water. Instead, he stepped over the edge and, finding the short rope ladder, let himself down hand over hand into the shallow depths below.

Ruyter made no effort to move softly. But the clang of the pick on stone reechoed now through the narrow shaft and quite drowned the slight noise of his approach.

Reaching the bottom and finding the earth under his feet, Ruyter let go of the ladder and turned around. Within a yard of him was Joshua Greene, his back to the newcomer. And now Paul saw why the pick had been striking hard mineral instead of soft loam.

Greene was not deepening the shaft. Instead, he was hammering upon the lower foundation wall of the tomb.

The shaft had at last reached the bottom of his preternaturally deep foundation of yellowed brick. And Greene was smashing in the old brick wall. Already he had made a breach almost large enough to admit the passage of a man's body. On the ground beside him burned a gauze-protected lamp.

The engineering sense that was his second nature made Paul wonder instinctively at the thinness of this brick partition. Surely no sane architect or builder would have sunk so deep a foundation wall so thin that a pick-blow could pierce it.

Another sweep of the pick and a dozen broken bricks caved outward, clattering around Greene's feet and widening considerably the breach.

Within gaped black darkness. The space within the partition wall, then, was evidently hollow—not even filled in with loose stones.

"Raw work," mentally commented Ruyter. "Some one must have made a tidy bit of money if the contract called for solid foundation."

Greene dropped the pick. His face was purple and apoplectic. His breath came in dreadful gasps. His stout body shook as from desert fever. He stooped to pick up the lamp. And as he did so, half turning, he caught sight of Ruyter.

A scream like that of a wounded horse—raucous, unhuman, hideous—burst from Greene's lips. His face was horribly distorted. He reeled back against the wall, writhing as though in a fit. His nerve and his nerves had snapped at the same instant.

Ruyter stepped forward to catch him as the stricken man toppled as though to fall. At Paul's movement Greene, with a twist, straightened himself, groped hastily at his belt, tugged out a revolver, and leveled it point-blank at the intruder upon his nocturnal labors.

Paul, with a lightning-quick move of his open hand, slapped the weapon from the other's grasp. It fell to the ground. Greene made no move to recover it; but, all the action suddenly going out of him, collapsed weak and gasping against the flimsy foundation wall.

"A touch of heat and too much thirst," announced Ruyter. "Didn't you know me, or did I frighten you? Let me help you up the ladder. I've some water at the khan. Plenty of it. Come and—"

But Greene drew shuddering back from the reassuring grasp Paul would have laid on his shoulder.

"Hands off!" he croaked weakly. "Don't kill me. There's enough for both. I—I—"

"Of course there's enough for both and for all," said Ruyter soothingly, as to a panic-stricken child. "I brought two big goat-skin bags of it from Ali Diab's camp. Come along. We'll—"

"You tracked me here!" cried Greene, emboldened as he noted the other's pacific intentions; "you want to get me out of the way. You've stolen my secret. You'd kill me for it. As Suleiman—"

"There, there! No one is going to kill you or even hurt you!" soothed Ruyter. "You're all worked up over nothing. The heat and the thirst have gone to your head. Your nerve's all in. By the way," he added, by way of turning the hysterical man's mind to indifferent topics as he strove to draw him gently toward the ladder, "that's a good big hole you've made in the wall—big enough to go through."

"No, no!" vociferated Greene, struggling to escape.

"Funny that a little ten-foot mound should have had any deep foundation at all," continued Ruyter. "Funnier still that it should have been so deep. And funniest of all that at the bottom of it should turn out to be just a hollow shell of brick wider than the tomb above it. I don't understand it. Do you?"

As he spoke his foot touched the fallen revolver. Reflecting that in the coming Bedouin attack every available weapon would be needed, Paul stooped and picked it up.

The stricken Greene, at sight of the other's movements, dropped heavily to his knees.

"Don't murder me!" he babbled. "There's enough for both. Come, we'll go in there together," pointing toward the aperture. "There's enough for ten men, let alone two. Don't shoot, I say!"

Ruyter looked down in open-eyed wonder at the gibbering creature that clung to his knees. And as he looked he realized that though Greene was in the throes of hysteria brought on by privation and shock, yet he was not in the least delirious.

And Paul, noting his furtive glances at the ragged hole in the partition wall, and recalling his maunderings about there being enough of something "for both" and "for ten men," began to wonder, piecing together scraps of half-forgotten happenings.

Through the engineer's mind flashed a chain of events he had never been able to explain. The fact of so shrewd and successful a man as Greene having embarked on such a wildcat venture as the digging of caravan wells in an almost caravanless district.

His directing so unerringly the march from the Jordan to this out-of-the-way mountain khan. His choice of that particular and unprom- ising spot at the tomb's edge for his first well; his seemingly pigheaded adherence to that site, and his feverish toil there, alone, late at night.

It all needed explaining; doubly so in view of his present agony of uncalled-for fear. Ruyter resisted his first impulse to pick up the frightened man and take him by force to the khan for water and for rest. Instead, he merely lifted Greene to his feet and supported him against the wall.

"Now," he remarked, facing the still trembling man, "let's talk this thing over. Or, rather, let's hear your end of the story. I can tell you mine later. Go ahead."

Greene set his thick lips obstinately. Then he chanced to notice the revolver which Ruyter still held unconsciously in his right hand. And the sight of it opened the clenched lips.

Disjointedly he spoke. Ruyter interrupted by many questions. At last, through skilled cross-examination, he gleaned a tale that for the instant left him well-nigh as unmanned by excitement as was Greene himself.

Joshua Greene's story, stripped of its countless repetitions, evasions, and incoherences, was the complement, in a way, to certain chance words of Ali Diab at the sheik's first meeting with Ruyter.

Early in the eighteenth century—so Ruyter pieced together his employer's rambling narrative—Suleiman Pasha had been Turkish governor of Syria. Years of oppression, of inspired graft, and of methods whose details read like Inquisition romances had enabled the pasha to amass a fortune whose fame at last reached the ears of the Sultan and whose magnitude aroused that potentate's ever-eager cupidity.

Suleiman's fall was ordained, with the wonted bow-string accessories. A friend near to the Sultan sent advance warning from Constantinople to the pasha. And Suleiman wasted no time, but made his preparations accordingly.

The year's pay for all the troops and government officials in Syria had just arrived. The taxes, too, were but newly collected and not yet forwarded to Constantinople.

Apart from such fortune as he had amassed—and rumor had perhaps invented, certainly magnified, the hoard—Suleiman promptly seized the pay chest and the tax money and fled. The ports were watched. Therefore the pasha, with a handful of trusted adherents, had borne the treasure to the fastnesses of Moab's mountains.

A holy man of the Bedouins had just died, so ran the tale. To secure the safety of the treasure from molestation, Suleiman had erected a tomb for the "saint," and under it had dug a sort of sub-cellar, wherein he had packed his wealth.

His plan was to seek refuge among the desert tribes for a year or so, until the hue and cry should have subsided; then to unearth the hoard, smuggle it aboard a ship somewhere along the coast, and make good his escape to Christian Europe.

The idea was excellent. But it failed through a not uncommon Eastern mishap. In short, the worthy Suleiman Pasha was assassinated by an industrious emissary of the Sultan who had sought to win imperial favor by following the disgraced pasha into the wilderness and putting him to death.

A desert band had fallen on the pasha's followers, mistaking them for Kurds (with whom that tribe was just then carrying on a flourishing blood feud), and had put them to the sword.

The only survivor was a renegade Englishman who had been Suleiman's secretary and right-hand man. The Englishman, Hodgson, had escaped to the coast and there had taken ship to England.

He alone now possessed the secret of the hoard. And he resolved to raise an expedition to recover it; since, single-handed and penniless, he could do nothing. With this in view, he wrote out during the voyage a full recital of the facts, with a chart of the region, addressing it to the daredevil Earl of Rochester, whom he hoped to interest in his scheme.

The ship had gone down with all on board during the passage of the English Channel. The wooden trunk containing Hodgson's effects had floated ashore on the French coast, where some fisherman had rescued it. The finders divided the box's contents among themselves. The lap writing-desk containing the letter to the Earl of Rochester had fallen to the share of one Duvard, who could read no English or any other language. And the desk, undisturbed as to contents, became an heirloom in his family.

As Greene had been motoring through western France a year earlier, he had stopped at a coast cottage while waiting for his chauffeur to buy some petrol. He had seen the desk and, admiring its lines and its antique look, had asked its history. Interested by the tale of the wreck, he had ended by buying the desk for eighty francs, including its yellowed, water–stained papers.

The story of the pasha's hoard had amused him as first he read it. Then the idea had begun to take hold of him. Cautious inquiry into Turkish archives verified the main facts of Hodgson's letters. And Greene had become convinced that the venture was worth while.

Knowing the crass insanity of setting forth openly upon a treasure hunt in the Sultan's dominions, Greene had evolved, as a mask, the well-digging scheme. By copious use of tips and political influence he had secured the imperial "concession."

The only white men he had chosen to accompany him were Ruyter and Hogan, both of whom he could trust. His yacht lay off Jaffa; and the port authorities were already bribed to let him carry aboard it, unchallenged, any quantity of "geological specimens" and worthless "antiques" he might chance to discover amid the mountains of Moab.

The plan had been very complete—as complete as had been that of Suleiman Pasha. And, despite the strike and the Bedouin siege, it had in the main worked out according to schedule.

The bottom of the tomb's foundation wall had that day been reached. And Greene had stolen out to the shaft after dark to explore the bricked treasure chamber and to arrange for the hiding of the hoard where the natives would not find it.

So much Ruyter gleaned from the rambling recital.

CHAPTER XV.
The Treasure of the Pasha.

AT the news he so fragmentarily dragged out of Joshua Greene the younger man felt his own pulses stir and throb with the treasure-lust.

Behind him, beyond that irregular gap in the wall, lay wealth—the key to all the world, the mastery of men, the bringer of happiness. It was there—lying, like Aladdin's lamp, waiting for human touch, to bring its possessor all that the earth can afford—of comfort, luxury, power.

The thought of it sanded Paul Ruyter's throat and misted his eyes. He could understand Greene's emotion now. But almost at once he steadied his nerve and came back to reality. There would be plenty of time for visions when the treasure was actually in hand. For golden visions and—for Madge!

"How did you guess?" he heard Greene asking.

"Guess what?" he asked abstractedly.

"That I was after treasure?"

"I didn't."

"Then how did you happen to come spying on me here, at dead of night, like this?"

"I didn't come spying on you. I came to tell you—"

"D'you expect me to believe that you—"

"It doesn't matter to me what you believe. Spying isn't in my line—neither is lying."

"And I, like a fool, blabbed it all!" croaked Greene in crass self-contempt. "But I only did it as a joke, Paul. There isn't—"

"Oh, yes, there is," grimly laughed Ruyter. "And we're going in to get it, you and I. But before we go, there's something to be arranged. You hit on this secret. You equipped and financed the expedition, so the bulk of whatever we find is rightfully yours. But Hogan and I are to get a look in, too. Don't forget that."

"It's preposterous. I paid you both—paid you handsomely to—"

"To act as foreman and as engineer for a well-digging job. Not to fight Bedouins, undergo thirst and starvation, and risk our lives, while you reaped all the benefit. We've done more than our share—a lot more, and you've deceived us. Three-fourths of this treasure goes to you. The other fourth Hogan and I divide. Is that understood?"

"But—"

"Is it?"

"Y-yes."

"Good. It's only fair to tell you there isn't one chance in a thousand that any of us will ever get away with a pennyworth of it. Ali Diab is going to attack us at sunrise."

But Greene, tugging at Ruyter's restraining arm in an effort to get to the treasure room, neither heard nor heeded. Paul loosed his hold and Greene bolted through the gap in the wall like a rabbit into its warren.

Paul, lamp in hand, followed little more slowly. The rays of the lamp eerily lighted the vaulted, earth-floored room, perhaps ten feet wide and nine feet high. In the room's center stood two huge, iron-bound chests. At sight of them Paul's heart beat like a trip-hammer, while Greene flung himself bodily upon the nearest of them.

The man clawed and tugged at the rust-eaten padlock that secured the chest, growling and whining like some hungry animal. Paul, watching him, felt a wave of disgust sweep through his own brain.

"The Circe touch used to turn men to swine," he mused contemptuously. 'Circe' must be allegorical name for 'treasure.'"

Meantime, he had returned to the gap. He reached through into the shaft and found the pick Greene had dropped there. Bringing it back with him, he set down the lamp in a corner and approached the nearest chest, the one at whose fastenings Greene was still tugging.

"Now, then," said Ruyter in the brisk, incisive tone that doctors employ to the semidelirious, "if you'll stop your dramatic rendition of 'Gaspard the Miser' for a moment, I'll smash this thing open."

Greene fell back, again fighting, and this time somewhat more successfully, for his customary self-mastery.

Poising the pickax, Ruyter aimed a blow at the hasp of the padlock. The rusty metal snapped like glass under the stroke. A second blow loosed the rust-cement of two centuries on springs and liddage.

Paul Ruyter dropped the pick, caught the heavy chest-lid with both hands, and by main force lifted it, the hinges squeaking and groaning most lamentably.

Back he threw the lid and raised the lamp so that it would shine into the chest. Greene was already bent eagerly over the opened receptacle.

The light's rays showed two close-jammed sacks of woven goat-hair. Each was bloated with its contents, and the two, side by side, wholly filled the big chest.

With his pocket-knife Ruyter slit the moldering rawhide thong that tied one of the sacks. Greene thrust open the sack's mouth and plunged both hands into it.

He drew them out full of greenish disks. So high had he heaped his joined palms with the sack's contents that two or three of the disks were shaken out of the pile and fell to the ground.

One of them rolled almost to Ruyter's foot. Setting down the lamp again, Paul picked up the fallen disk. It was about the size of a twenty-dollar gold-piece and was coated with verdigris.

Paul turned it over in his hand, his brow clouding. Then, first scraping it with his knife, he began to rub it briskly on his rough sleeve.

So dry and protected had the coin been kept during its long concealment underground that most of the surface greenness was easily rubbed off.

Paul surveyed it once more, holding it closer to the lamp. Then he crossed abruptly to Joshua Greene, who was still busy over the sacks.

Greene had just managed to break the thong that bound the neck of the second hag and revealed a similar mass of disks therein. Ruyter tapped him on the shoulder.

"Here," he said, "I've polished one of these a bit. Take a look at it."

Greene, his eye caught by the yellow sheen of the disk, snatched it almost fiercely from Paul and leaned over the lamp, inspecting it.

For a full half-minute the inspection lasted, Paul sardonically watching him the while. Then Joshua, with a cry, dropped the disk as though it burned him and reeled backward, staring wildly at Ruyter and gasping incredulously the monosyllable:

"BRASS!"

CHAPTER XVI.
Ruyter Makes a Discovery.

"QUITE so," solemnly assented Ruyter. "Perfectly good brass. A whole chestful of it here, and another over there. We've crossed the world and thrown away our lives for two chestfuls of brass disks. There must be pretty nearly five dollars' worth of old brass there in all."

As he spoke he smashed the lock of the second chest with the pickax and broke open the lid, revealing contents precisely similar to those of the first chest.

Greene scarce turned to notice this second experiment. He was staring, dull-eyed, jaw agape, at the disks that lay strewn around him.

"Well," suggested Ruyter, "shall we call it a day and quit?"

"I—I don't understand," moaned Greene dazedly. "I don't understand at all. Why should Suleiman Pasha have dug this underground room and taken such pains to hide its existence, and then put two chestfuls of worthless brass in it for safe keeping?"

"I think I get the idea," said Ruyter, picking up once more the disk he had half polished and pointing to half-effaced Arabic characters stamped thereon. "These disks are worthless now except as old brass. But in Suleiman's time they were worth their weight in gold."

"Nonsense!" snarled Greene. "Brass has never been a currency medium. Certainly not as recently as Suleiman Pasha's day."

"You're right," agreed Ruyter, "and you're wrong. These were never coins. They were tokens. I've read of the system. And so much as I can decipher of this inscription bears out the theory."

"Tokens?" repeated Greene blankly. "Tokens of what?"

"Here's the idea," explained Ruyter. "In the old times it wasn't safe or easy or convenient to transport big sums of actual money from the capital to the provinces or overseas. Pirate and robber bands were too plentiful. So the Turks and some other Eastern nations, I've read, hit on the plan of using these 'tokens.'

"Each token entitled its owner to a certain sum of gold, payable at the government treasury, like our own treasury notes or like bank checks. The government could safely send brass tokens when it couldn't send gold. And in the more distant provinces the tokens passed as currency for the full value of the amount named on them. They were always redeemable at par by the government. A sort of provincial 'credit system,' you see. The custom, with variations, runs back to Pharaoh's day."

"But how—"

"You say the year's pay for all the Syrian troops and the year's taxes had just been received when old Suleiman Pasha lit out? Well, beyond all question, this is the form it came in. In tokens, redeemable at Constantinople for cash. Suleiman probably counted on getting them across to Greece or some other of Turkey's European provinces, and cashing them in for his own benefit. They were quite negotiable, and—"

"And this is the treasure?"

"*Was*—not *is*," corrected Paul. "At present the disks would be no more redeemable at any bank than would a sight-draft with Cleopatra's signature. Which brings me back to the news that the attack will begin at dawn. We'd better get some rest. There's water at the khan, as I told you. I got it from the Bedouin camp."

For a long space Joshua Greene sat huddled on the corner of a treasure-box, his head on his breast. Then he rose, impatiently shaking his shoulders. The shock and the hopelessness had restored him to his former shrewd self and banished his hysteria and treasure lust.

"All right," he said wearily—"let them attack; I'll be ready to do my share—and *suffer* my share, too. In the mean time I'm going to get about a hogsheadful of that water you told me about. A drink just now is next best thing to a fortune. You're a plucky chap, Paul, to have ventured out for it, and it was white of you to hunt me up and to let me know about it. I'm sorry I behaved so babyishly just now."

He crawled back into the shaft and clumsily clambered up the rope ladder leading to the outer world. Ruyter took up the lamp and the pick and prepared to follow. Suddenly he paused.

By mere chance he had glanced upward, and his engineer eye at once had noted an oddity in the construction of the "treasure chamber's" ceiling. He sat down on a chest and leaned back to get a better light on it.

By rights, according to his ideas, the floor of the tomb above should have been of concrete or of cemented stone, supported by a series of the heaviest cross-beams, to prevent the weight of the floor and of the tomb above it from bearing down too heavily on the very flimsy under-foundation wall of brick.

He could see where the thicker foundations of concrete ended, nearly at the top of the room, jutting far out on each side beyond the narrow lower brick wall that extended thence to the floor.

But in the central space of the square ceiling he could see no trace of cross-beams, nor even of a supporting arch. The center of the ceiling was a mere rectangle of shriveled sticks, laid all in one direction, like a thatch; and not even interwoven. He fell to wondering whether or not this were good engineering, and conjecturing just at what points of the side masonry the strain of the weight must probably fall.

Then came another query: Where, in the tomb above, had the

body of the Moslem saint been laid? Surely not on that absurdly weak flooring of long willow wands.

Perhaps the body had been laid on the jutting stone and concrete foundation shelf at one side of this small stick-covered rectangle. There was ample room. But it seemed odd to him that the only occupant of such a tomb should be shunted off to one side instead of lying in state in the center of the structure.

And, as often happens to one whose mind is oppressed by far weightier things, this trivial mystery began to annoy Ruyter. He knew he would be trying to puzzle it out for hours and would always be bothered by it, unless he made some effort now to solve it.

A somewhat gruesome idea occurred to him. Besides the rope ladder that was fastened in place between the top and bottom of the well-shaft, there was a spare ladder coiled at the shaft's bottom. He had had it tossed there the evening before when the shaft had been closed for the night.

He scrambled through the opening, secured the spare ladder and came back. Uncoiling it, he stood on a chest and reached up to the square of twigs above him. These he pushed aside with no difficulty at all. And he fixed the grapples of the rope ladder's end to the side of the ledge that surrounded the opening.

Tugging on this, he tested its strength. The grip held. Stepping down, he secured the other end of the ladder to the bottom of one of the heavy chests. Then, lamp in hand, he ascended to the tomb above.

By this time a fresh and far saner idea had supplanted mere curiosity in Paul Ruyter's mind: Why would not this tomb above the treasure chamber serve a splendid purpose? Properly provisioned, the others might well stay there snug and safe while he rode to Jerusalem for reenforcements.

If there were room for them and they could live there with any degree of comfort, it was the ideal hiding-place. By blocking up with bricks and dirt the gap between the shaft and the treasure chambers they could conceal their whereabouts from the Bedouins, and no Moslem would commit the sacrilege of breaking into a saint's tomb in search of his prey, nor would he suspect them of intruding on so hallowed a spot.

The question of fresh air could be solved by knocking out stones here and there in the roof where they would not be noticeable. It would be an eery, unpleasant place wherein to dwell for days. But it would be safe from attack, and at best they could not hope to hold the khan against the besiegers for more than a few hours.

The idea seemed inspired, and Ruyter tingled with pleasure at his own ingenuity at devising so clever yet so simple a plan.

Meantime, to explore the place and see if really it were habitable.

His head and shoulders were already above the opened central rectangle, and in the dense darkness of the tomb itself. Insensibly he noted that the air, though musty, was breathable, arguing cracks in the outer masonry of the tomb. As he was about to raise the light to peer about him into the open space around his head a soft voice, apparently close to his ear, breathed his name.

Then something struck him lightly across his mouth.

CHAPTER XVII.
WITHIN THE TOMB.

THE surprise of it all well–nigh caused Paul Ruyter to lose his footing on the shaking ladder. At the moment he fancied his over-strained senses had played him false.

The tomb had been sealed for two centuries. That a voice could whisper his name there and that some tangible thing could brush across his parted lips was impossible.

Yet it had happened. And even as he crouched there, the cold sweat breaking out all over him, his head and shoulders still in the blackness of the abode of death, he was again struck across the face, though with no great force, by what seemed a small, clammy hand.

For the instant he actually had not strength left to raise the lamp to illumine the dark horror about him.

Then once more he heard his name called; still apparently from close beside him in the dark tomb. But at the sound the fear dropped from him like a garment, for the voice was the voice of Madge Greene.

"Where—where are you?" he managed to stammer.

"Down here," came the answer.

And, the dread having lifted from his mind, he knew his ears had played an odd trick on him, for the sound of Madge's voice now came unmistakably from the treasure-room beneath. A trick of acoustics had deceived him.

He backed down the ladder to join her, and as he emerged into the light below a bat darted out of the rectangular opening from the tomb over his head.

And now the cold touch on his face was explained. Also, he was assured there must be sufficient fresh air in the tomb to sustain life, for a crack in the mound's outer masonry large enough to admit a bat would assuredly let in a goodly volume of air.

Ruyter stepped to the ground from the ladder's last rung. A lantern in her hand, Madge Greene was standing beside the open chests. Brick-dust on knee and shoulder gave trace of her passage through the wall-gap from the shaft.

To Ruyter, in his overstrained state of wits and nerves, it all at once seemed the most natural thing in the world that this girl whom he loved should be by his side at such a moment. Forgotten were convention and formality. All he realized was that in his hour of loneliness and responsibility and reaction she had come to him.

And all his soul welcomed her. Impulsively he stretched out his hand in greeting, as though they had not met for days.

"Father has just told me about it," she said breathlessly. "I knew how terribly unhappy and disappointed you must be. So—I came to find you."

There was a moment's pause—tense, wordless. Then, to cover the embarrassment of his silence, she glanced down at the piled brazen disks and asked:

"This is the 'treasure'?"

"Yes," he answered briefly.

The theme was one on which he could not yet trust himself to speak.

"What were you doing up there?" she asked, pointing to the rectangular opening that gaped above them.

He told her, explaining the reason for his desire to explore the tomb.

"Then we are going to be attacked?" she asked quietly.

"At sunrise. Yes."

"Not earlier?"

"Ali Diab does not break his word. But oughtn't you to go and get some sleep?"

She shook her head with pretty obstinacy.

"I am glad," he smiled. "It is wonderful to have you share this hour with me. By the way, you are in no personal danger from the Bedouin's attack. I have Ali Diab's assurance for that."

"Do you think I would live," she asked scornfully, "if the rest of you were—"

She checked herself with a little shudder.

"There may be no question of any one's being killed," said he, "if that tomb up there will hold you all while I go for help. If you aren't afraid to wait down here a few moments alone I'll go up and investigate."

He took up the lantern she had brought and, holding its swinging handle between his teeth, remounted the ladder.

As he reached the top he stepped off onto the masonry platform that served as floor for all save that open central square of the tomb's floor, and looked around him.

The tomb's interior was perhaps nine feet in diameter, rising slopingly from the edges toward a low roof that was shaped like an inverted cup. The trap-door in the center, through which Paul had climbed up, was surrounded by an irregular circular flooring several feet wide.

Ruyter glanced about for a sight of the entombed "saint's" bones. But save for a receptacle, no larger than a cigar-box, which was resting in a rude niche in the side of the curving cement-and-brick wall, the tomb was empty.

No skeleton, no scattered bones, no trace of such clothing as must have wrapped the body. Nothing to indicate that ever the place had been used as a tomb. Except for that little box in the niche, there was absolutely nothing in the tomb.

As Ruyter stood peering about him in perplexity, Madge Greene stepped to his side. She had climbed the ladder unnoticed by him, and was beside the puzzled man before he was aware of her presence.

"Where—" she began, looking around.

"I don't know," said Paul. "It's a mystery. In two hundred years that saint might well have been crumpled to dust. But there would certainly be some trace of him, some shred of clothing, or bit of metal. You see—there's nothing. And no one can have broken in and taken the body away, for, see, over there to your left stands the flat stone of the entrance, and it is cemented from the inside."

"From the *inside?* How could that be?" she queried. "Whoever sealed the tomb would have had to get out afterward."

"Whoever did it," decided Ruyter, "did not go out that way, but probably went down through the opening by which we came up; and so through a hole in the treasure-room wall that was afterward filled."

"And then up through ten feet of solid earth?"

"What a fool I am!" he laughed. "Of course not. Then through a hole in the wall of this mound, and afterward the hole was bricked up."

"It seems to me it would have been simpler to use the doorway and fit the slab in place afterward."

"It would. But it wasn't done. You can see that by the cement at the edges of the entrance-stone. Do you know what I think? I think that doorway was sealed up before the tomb was finished. I don't think it ever was used."

"But—"

"I don't believe," he went on in growing excitement—"I don't believe this place was ever used for a tomb. I don't believe any one was ever buried here."

"Then, why—"

"I believe the whole thing was built by Suleiman Pasha as a blind to cover the treasure-room below. Those willow branches were just a screen—not a flooring. He built this semblance of a tomb to scare away people from digging hereabouts. If there was a saint buried at that time I believe he was buried secretly somewhere else by Suleiman and his followers. The subtleties of the simplest Oriental mind are beyond the understanding of the most astute Westerner."

She had been studying the tomb's interior as he talked, and now her gaze fell on the little box in the wall niche.

"Perhaps," she suggested eagerly, pointing to the box—

"perhaps he was cremated and his ashes entombed in that iron box?"

"People aren't cremated in Syria," he returned. "For the instant I'd forgotten the box in trying to work out the rest of the puzzle. Let's have a look at it. Shall we?"

CHAPTER XVIII.
PRISONERS!

THE niche was on the far side of the trap-door opening. Ruyter went around the edge and drew the box from its alcove.

It was an ordinary, old-fashioned iron despatch-box, eight inches long, five inches wide, and about three inches in depth. Two centuries had eaten it deep with rust.

The coping floor on this side of the tomb consisted not of concrete like the other, but of two enormous flat slabs of stone roughly mortised and cemented together.

As Madge stepped on these, following Ruyter, there was a distinct snapping and sagging. Bits of mortar fell to the room below. Her added weight had had a visible and audible effect on the two ancient and ill-laid masses of stone which formed that side of the flooring.

"Back!" ordered Ruyter sharply. "The whole thing is likely to give way. It's a rotten piece of jerry-work and age has weakened it."

As he spoke he thrust the box into the breast of his khaki tunic and stepped toward her to help her back over the sagging floor to the safety of the cement on the far side.

For the fraction of a second, as he stepped, their double weight chanced to rest on the jointure of the two monoliths. And that was a fraction of a second too long for the crumbling mortar to uphold the stones under their weight.

Ruyter saw the danger barely in time to thrust the girl backward with all his force. She reeled back before the impact of the thrust, collided rather heavily with the far wall, and fell—startled but safe—to the strong cement flooring alongside the opposite section of the trap-door.

Ruyter was far less fortunate. The impetus of his sudden movement had completed the strain put upon the tottering stones. They collapsed from under his feet.

Throwing out his arms, Paul was able to seize the far side of the floor opening, near where Madge had fallen. With a wrench and a heave he drew himself up and crouched on the cement platform beside her.

But before he had reached that perch the whole place reverberated with the crash of descending rock. Like an avalanche the two enormous floor stones had overbalanced and tumbled into the treasure-chamber below, carrying with them half a ton of cement, smaller stones and bricks from the flimsier foundations they struck against on their downward flight.

The rush of air generated by the fall of the monolith and of the lesser debris put out the lantern's feeble glare. The jar of the fall knocked it off the ledge into the pit beneath. The stuffy atmosphere of the tomb was all at once filled to suffocation by choking clouds of mortar dust.

In total darkness—strangling, deafened, horror-stricken—the two refugees clung together on their narrow shelf of cement, midway between the dome of the tomb and the floor of the treasure room below.

It was Ruyter who first recovered voice.

"Did I hurt you?" he asked anxiously. "I had to hurl you over here. I'm so sorry—I had to. There was no time to waste."

"No," she said shakily. "I don't think I'm hurt—but I'm horribly frightened. Don't apologize for what you did—it saved me from being killed. Oh, *what* happened? Was it just part of the flooring that gave way? It seemed as if all the universe was tumbling."

"A full half of our present universe did," he answered. "And we're lucky to be on the other half. Is the lantern anywhere near you? I can't find it."

"No," she answered, groping about her in the dark.

"It must have fallen—so did our ladder. I can't feel the grappling hooks anywhere."

"What are we to do?"

"Wait till they come out here after us from the khan. The noise of the falling rocks ought to bring them. It must have been heard from here to New York. Then they'll toss us the end of the ladder. We can make it fast to the cement here and climb down. For a minute or so don't try to talk."

They were silent for a few moments—straining their ears for the sound of their rescuers' voices. But no such sound came. Then the truth dawned upon Ruyter.

A noise in a tightly enclosed and partly underground space may seem incredibly loud to persons who chance to be in that place, but it sometimes may also be quite inaudible to persons who are shut up in a stone-walled house some distance away.

And it soon became quite evident that the people in the khan either had not heard the sound of the avalanche or else had not located it as coming from the direction of the tomb. Madge, as if reading her companion's thoughts, said suddenly:

"I don't believe they heard it at all. None of them but father would know you are here—or that there's any subterranean room. And by this time he is probably asleep from utter fatigue and heartbreak. When he is asleep it is almost impossible for him to be waked by the loudest noise. If the rest heard, it wouldn't mean anything to them."

Ruyter was groping in his pocket for matches. He found a few and drew one forth.

"I'm going to see the extent of the damage," said he. "Perhaps the rocks are piled so we can step down onto them and reach the gap leading into the shaft."

He struck one of the matches as he spoke and leaned perilously far out over the ledge, peering down. What he saw made him extinguish the match in haste—lest Madge also see. But he was too late. Her glance had followed his, and a gasp told him she understood.

The gap in the wall leading to the shaft and to life and safety was buried under tons of debris. The larger of the two fallen monoliths was jammed down over the rest of the rubbish that blocked the opening, forming an obstacle that no three men could have shifted.

For a minute neither of the two prisoners spoke or moved. Each was realizing just what the situation meant and its stark hopelessness.

CHAPTER XIX.
A Man and a Maid.

MADGE GREENE broke the pregnant silence.

"There is nothing to do, is there," she asked quietly—"nothing but to wait?"

"Don't be frightened!" he begged. "We—"

"I'm not," she denied. "It will be all right, somehow, won't it?"

"Yes," he answered, with a confidence he did not in the very least feel. "Wait a minute. Bats can crawl in here through the cracks in the mortar. Perhaps those same cracks will let my voice reach the khan."

He drew in a lungful of air, then expelled it in a shout that filled their whole prison-chamber. Again he shouted with all his power, and a third and fourth time, pausing after each cry to listen for an answering hail.

"No use," he surrendered, at last. "I see how it is. The hollow dome of the roof drives my voice back into the tomb again and downward to the room below. It's a simple matter of acoustics. We might fire a cannon in here and no one a hundred feet away would be likely to hear it. Besides, Hogan barricaded the khan long before this. I told him to. Every door and every window will be shut and barred."

"But they'll miss us and—"

"They won't miss you. For all they know, you're in your room and asleep. As for me, Hogan's used to my reconnoitering and my absences from the khan. He probably thinks I'm on another visit to Ali Diab or else out on a walk planning some new trick of defense. If any of them should pass close by the tomb we might possibly be heard. Otherwise it's out of the question."

"Then," she exclaimed, relieved, "at worst we'll have to stay here only till morning. As soon as they begin work in the shaft we can shout. And—"

"At sunrise," interrupted Ruyter in sudden dismay at the thought, "Ali Diab will attack."

"Oh!"

"And I'm out of it!" he groaned. "Pocketed here while better men fight for their lives against impossible odds. Out of it—not striking a blow, while two men of my own race battle against a horde of Bedouins! Oh, it's unbearable!"

"Don't!" she implored, shocked that the light-hearted, self-controlled man should so utterly give way. "I—I thank God you *are* out of it."

"Madge!"

"I mean it. I love my father dearly. And I would be willing to die at his side if I might. But—"

She hesitated.

Ruyter reached out in the dark and found her hands.

"Madge!" he began, all his soul in his voice.

Then abruptly he dropped her hands, drew out another match, and again held its blazing tip over the edge of their shelf. A moment he gazed down.

"Gone!" he announced.

"What?"

"Pickax and revolver, both. They are buried. I thought I might be able to hammer our way out through this wall with the pick or wake some one by firing."

"They were our last hope?"

"Yes. That is why I looked for them at that instant. Because if there were a shadow of hope I'd have no right to say what now I can. You know, don't you, dear?"

"Yes," she whispered.

"I love you," he went on. "I have always loved you, my glorious sweetheart. You knew it, didn't you?"

"Yes," she whispered again.

They drew closer together instinctively there in the darkness. Very simply, like two little children, they kissed each other.

"I love you," said the girl.

For a space neither broke the stillness. They sat, hand in hand. Then Ruyter sighed in complete happiness.

"This is worth it all," he said.

"Yes," she said dreamily—"worth it all; a thousand times worth it, my lover. Nothing can harm us now. For we shall face it together. It is *good* to know that."

"If there had been a shadow of hope," he said presently, "I should have had no right to speak, and I should have had the bravery to be silent. I *hope* I should. For I couldn't let you throw yourself away on a penniless chap like me—with no prospects and no steady job; you, a girl who has always had everything."

"Hush!" she reproved him, laying one little hand across his mouth. "Up to now I've had nothing that mattered. It is only now I have-everything."

As her hand fell away from his mouth, her finger-tips brushed against the box that he had thrust into the breast of his tunic.

"Isn't that uncomfortable?" she asked. "Why don't you lay it on the floor beside you?"

He drew out the box from its resting place. As he dropped it carelessly on the ledge its contents rattled noisily.

"Ashes wouldn't make that sound," he commented in idle curiosity. "Shall we open it? The lock must be almost worn away by rust. I think I could pry it open with my penknife."

He picked up the box once more. Feeling for the hasp, he slipped a blade of his penknife between box and lid. For a few moments he worked as best he could to break the rust-worn lock. As a result, he ended by snapping the knife-blade.

He opened the other and larger blade and fell to work again, this time more carefully. And presently the weak lock gave.

"Shall we have a look at it?" he suggested, taking out another match.

"Yes!" she exclaimed eagerly. "If it isn't too gruesome. If the box hasn't ashes in it, it probably holds some sacred relic or—"

The sentence was never completed. For just then, wrenching open the resisting lid, Ruyter struck a match.

And the flare of the wood splinter was answered by a hundred glittering points of fire. Madge cried out in amazement, and even

Ruyter almost let fall the match.

Together they stared, hypnotized, at the contents of the iron box until the dying match burned Paul's fingers so painfully that he dropped it. He groped feverishly for another.

Match after match was consumed while they stared, wordless. At last Ruyter muttered:

"Here is the treasure!"

Heaping pell-mell, with no semblance of order or care, to the very rim of the box was a tumbled collection of jewels. Some were in old-fashioned settings, some lay loose. Bracelets, brooches, necklaces, rings, clasps, unset gems—all were piled in a wonderful, disordered mass.

Diamonds ranging in size to a filbert or larger; rubies in whose great hearts glowed the eternal fires; emeralds, rough cut yet flawless, in their cold, green glory; sapphires; milky pearls of many a size and tint; opals and lesser stones—all gave back a rainbow of shimmering light from the match-gleams.

Long they sat there, the man and the maid, in hushed bewilderment, feasting their eyes on the marvels before them. Mechanically Paul lighted match after match as each died down. At last he lit no more.

"Another light, please!" begged the fascinated girl impatiently.

"There are no matches left," he answered with rueful apology.

Then, closing the iron box, he handed it to her.

"My engagement present to you," he said whimsically. "I never dreamed a poor, down-at-heel chap like myself could afford such a gift to the girl I want to marry. I'm a fair judge of precious stones, though I've had few enough of my own. There must be well over a million dollars' worth there. The spoil of harem and province and official bribers, I suppose, for many years."

"And you think the chests of 'tokens' down there were just a blind?" she asked.

"No. They represented a great fortune by themselves. But the pick of Suleiman's treasure was this box of jewels. And this he hid in the tomb itself for better safety. Yes: and for the sake of the box he must have built the tomb. For lawless folk might dig in the earth, even under the tomb, in search for his wealth. But no Moslem would lay hands on the tomb itself, nor permit any outsider to desecrate it. No one would even suspect that the tomb could be used by a Moslem pasha for such a purpose.

Suleiman had all the cleverness of his scriptural namesake."

Long they talked. Sometimes the sweet foolishness of new-told love. Sometimes of the gems and of their fabulous value. Sometimes of the past few weeks' experience. But, by tacit consent, never of the certain fate that lay before them.

Each knew the position was hopeless. At dawn the khan would be attacked. After a short fight it would be stormed and its pitifully small garrison be put to sword.

Then the victors would ride away with such plunder as they could lay their hands on. And again the mountain pass, whereon the khan enclosure fronted, would be given up to the wilderness and to solitude. Weeks might go by before a single traveler would ride along that road; months before a pilgrim might halt to pray at the saint's tomb.

Meanwhile, immured, without food or water, the two lovers must remain where they were. They must remain there—they who held in their grasp a treasure that would have bought half of Jerusalem.

At last, as they talked softly together, a pencil of blue-gold light struck downward from a crack in the summit of the dome and fell athwart their white faces.

"Dawn!" cried Madge.

And as though her words were a signal, the muffled fusillade of many guns broke upon their ears.

CHAPTER XX.
The Last Fight.

RUYTER leaped to his feet; and as he did so the firing broke out afresh, this time nearer. An answering volley sounded. Then came a melee of shots of faintly heard yells.

"They're at it!" gasped Paul. "At it hot and heavy. And by the noise they're making, the khan seems to be giving a good account of itself. Oh, to be there in the thick of it!"

Louder and more rapid grew the firing. No longer by volleys, but in an almost unending ripple of reports.

"The Bedouins are wasting a lot of powder blazing away like

that," declared Ruyter; "and if Hogan can keep the other men from exposing themselves foolishly, the shots won't do any great harm. The Arab is nearly always a bad shot. It's when they stop firing and rush the house that the real danger will come."

Madge had risen, too, and was clinging to his arm, listening to the detonations that swelled rather than sank in volume as the moments went on. The pencil of light dimly illumined their ledge prison.

Madge recalled the tomb scene from "Aïda" and the two lovers' death duet in it. Thus in the East had *Rhadaumes* and *Aïda* perished—glad to die in their narrow tomb, because they could die together; even as Madge for the same reason was now content to die.

"Ali Diab said he'd bring up a hundred and forty men to the attack," remarked the more practical Ruyter, breaking in on the girl's operatic vision. "But it sounds like double the number. *Listen!*" he broke off.

Through the spiteful bark of the firearms came a new note— the faintly heard ring of steel against steel.

"Our ammunition's gone!" groaned Ruyter. "And our men are trying to stand them off with some of those old junk sabers we found in the khan cellar. Why didn't Hogan make them reserve their fire, as I told him to? He knew we were pitiably short on cartridges. It will all be over now in a moment. God help them! At saber play they'll be children in the hands of the El Kanah—and six untrained men against more than a hundred veteran warriors!"

The tumult died into sudden silence. Then the earth shook as though with the thunder-tread of many hard-ridden horses.

"It is all over!" said Paul Ruyter, and his voice was dead. "They are riding away!"

He had drawn Madge into the circle of his arms. Now he released his hold and she slipped gently to the ground. Ruyter bent over her in dread. She had fainted.

"Her father's death!" he muttered. "And as the sun gets higher this place is like an oven. She can't breathe."

He worked over her in frantic awkwardness. And at last her great eyes opened. She sighed and looked dazedly about her. Then she met Paul's anguished gaze and smiled pitifully up at him.

"It's all right," she breathed weakly. "I'm sorry! I never fainted be-fore. I—"

He glared about their prison pen like a trapped beast. His eye fell on the upright slab of stone that served as an entrance to the tomb. It was just behind where Madge lay.

With hopeless desperation he drew out his penknife, and with its one remaining blade sought to loosen the stone by scratching away the crumbling mortar that held it in place.

Obsessed by a plan that his common sense told him was rank folly, he bent all his strength and furious energy to the task. Stubbornly, and scrap by scrap, the mortar yielded to his knife-blade.

But it was drearily show work. After a full half-hour of it he had cleared away a bare six inches of the crumbling yet tough material.

And as he worked a great, blind rage shook him. He was loved. He was now rich past all fear of future poverty. Even had Greene lived and had claimed the lion's share of the gems, there would still have been enough left to make Paul independently well-to-do.

And, with all this golden future before him, he must die cooped up here like a rat in a drain. He and this wonder-girl whom he adored and who had stooped to love him in return.

At the thought he drove his knife deeper into the obstinate mortar. And the blade—his last blade—snapped off at the handle.

As though the stone slab were a sentient enemy that stood mockingly between him and freedom, the frantic man smote it with all his rage-given force.

The blow numbed his right arm to the elbow. It ripped the skin from his knuckles, tearing them to the bone. And at that puny human blow the stone quietly toppled outward!

Sealed only from within, and slanted at the wrong angle, it had for two centuries been pulling its own weight outward against the grip of ever-weakening concrete. A child's push would have ripped it out from its moorings. And Paul Ruyter's blow was assuredly no "child's push."

Outward swung the upright slab and tumbled flat on the

ground outside, raising a little puff of dust as it fell, and letting into the tomb a gush of light and fresh air.

Paul, half stunned at his own unlooked-for victory, cried out incoherently. He half led, half carried Madge out into the enclosure, under the sky's clear radiance.

For an instant the change from gloom to glaring sunlight smote their eyes to dimness. Then they saw. Throughout the enclosure all was peaceful. Not a shutter of the khan was bullet-marked. The double gate stood wide open.

And the narrow ribbon of road beyond was choked with the bodies of men and horses.

CHAPTER XXI.
THE NEWEST ALI DIAB LEGEND.

AS the lovers stared, dumfounded, two men walked out from the khan. One was in the uniform of a colonel of Turkish cavalry. The other was Joshua Greene.

At sight of Madge, Greene set up a cry and ran forward to greet her.

"You escaped from them?" he bellowed joyously. "Colonel Stambouli was sure they had captured you both some time during the night. His men are scouring the rocks for you even now."

"We weren't captured," answered Madge. "We were in the tomb there."

"What? Oh, under the tomb! I might have guessed. Ruyter was there. I left him there last night with the 'tokens.' But how did *you* get there? When I woke up at daybreak and Hogan said Paul was missing—"

Colonel Stambouli joined them. He bowed to Madge, and then saluted Paul, whom he had met in Jerusalem. To the query in Ruyter's eyes he responded:

"Some of your *fellaheen,* who left you the first day you were here, brought me word at the barracks, in the Tower of David, that Ali Diab was here, and that there had been some sort of a quarrel between him and yourselves just before they came away. The governor ordered me here at once with my regiment. We arrived at daybreak this morning."

"Daybreak?"

"Just as the Bedouins were massing before the gate yonder. They had called in their vedettes to join the attack. So they had no word of our coming. But they fought as only the El Kanah can fight. We outnumbered them four to one, and yet it was as hard earned a victory as I care to win."

"Then it was your men who—"

"We go back crowned with golden laurels," went on the colonel jubilantly, "for we have Ali Diab."

"No?"

"The man we have hunted in vain for ten years. His horse was shot under him. Before he could rise one of my men stunned him with the butt of a carbine. He's bound hand and foot in a room of the khan. We start back for Jerusalem with all of you in an hour, and Ali Diab will come along—to justice."

Ruyter took advantage of the arrival of several Turkish officers to slip back unnoticed to the tomb. Overcoming with difficulty his horror of the place, he entered, secured the iron box, and hid it in his shirt. Then he strolled across to the khan.

Seemingly careless inquiries located for him the room where Ali Diab was confined. Two sentinels stood in front of its locked door, carbine on shoulder. Ruyter passed them by with a second glance and went to his own room.

Thence he emerged a few moments later, a bunch of keys in his hand and a knife in his pocket. Unlocking a door, he passed down the corridor, and thence through an anteroom whose inner door he stealthily unlocked.

He found himself in a storeroom, on whose floor, bound and trussed, lay Ali Diab, sheik of the El Kanah. Outside the room's second door still stood the two faithful sentries.

The sheik turned his emotionless, high-bred face toward the visitor. Paul motioned him not to speak.

Tiptoeing across the room, Ruyter bent over the Bedouin.

"Sheik," he whispered, "that door leads to a hallway. Turn to the left and you are at the rear of the inn. There are a number of cavalry horses tied there. The black one with the white blaze on his forehead seems to me the best, but use your own judgment."

As he talked he was busily engaged in cutting the thongs that held the prisoner.

"I suppose I'm breaking all sorts of international laws by doing this," he remarked. "But I'm told there's no capital punishment in Turkey and that you'll pass the rest of your days in a rather dark dungeon. I've just passed a few hours in one, and I wouldn't wish that job on my worst enemy. Besides, as I think I said once before, you're a good deal of a man. And, if the law of the desert protects a guest, it sure ought to do something or other to a host. So-long, old chap!"

Ali Diab rose to his feet as the last bond was cut.

"First I called you *Feringee*," he said slowly. "Next *Howadji*. To-day will you take at my hands the better title of *Ukh*—my blood brother? There is no thanks for what you have done. To me, your foe, it is beyond thanks—my brother."

Like a shadow he was gone from the room. Ruyter, following, carefully locked each door behind him.

"When they find those cut bonds on the floor and the prisoner gone through a line of locked doors," he mused, "there'll be another unbelievable Ali Diab legend for the campfires. I wonder now if I'm a fool or a good fellow. Maybe a bit of both. But it's a cruelty to animals to coop an eagle in a cage, and I always did admire the work of the S. P. C. A."

He strolled out into the veranda to find the courtyard in a fearful uproar. A black horse, so Hogan informed him—a black horse with a blaze on its forehead—had just dashed out from behind the khan through the gate and off to nowhere.

And on the horse—which Colonel Stambouli declared was his own—was a man whose face was hidden in a burnoose; a man that some imaginative soldier vowed was Ali Diab, which last statement, added Hogan, was a patent falsehood, as Ali Diab—bad cess to him!—had done forever with riding.

"Just the same, sweetheart," said Madge a moment later. "It *was* Ali Diab. I saw him myself. Thank Heaven, we're done with him and with danger!"

"Done with danger?" laughed Ruyter. "Not much we aren't. We've still got to face your father with the news that we're engaged."

THE END.

Appendix
Original source publication

This novel was serialized in two issues of *The Cavalier:* January 10 and January 17 of 1914.

January 10, 1914

Front text:
Author of "A Complete Tweed Suit," "Articles of War," etc.

End text
TO BE CONCLUDED NEXT WEEK. Don't forget this magazine is issued weekly, and that you will get the conclusion of this story without waiting a month.

January 17, 1914

Front text:
Author of "A Complete Tweed Suit," "Articles of War," etc.

SYNOPSIS OF PRECEDING CHAPTERS

WHILE crossing the Syrian desert, Paul Ruyter, an American civil engineer, is captured by tribesmen of Ali Diab, a famous sheik. Ruyter is bound for Jerusalem to join Joshua Greene, a wealthy man who has hired him to dig wells in the Land of Moab; and when he is brought into the presence of the Bedouin chieftain he demands the reason for his capture. Ali Diab replies that he is going to hold him for a ransom of two thousand pounds, Turkish. Ruyter protests that he can't pay that sum. The sheik, who has been watching the young American narrowly, and admiring his coolness in the face of death, offers to spare his life if he will join the tribe and renounce his flag and his country. Ruyter spurns the offer and escapes on a camel during a blinding sandstorm which descends on the camp at the conclusion of the interview. He meets Greene in Jerusalem. With the well-digging expedition

Cover, January 10, 1914 issue

is Greene's daughter, Madge, whom Ruyter loves. He protests against her presence in the party, fearing that Ali Diab will attack them. But he is overridden and Madge goes along. Beside the Greenes and the young engineer, ten laborers (seven Mohammedans and three Christians), their boss Hogan, a cook, and a steward comprise the small company that pushes out into the desert and takes up its abode in an abandoned khan, or inn, hard by the crumbling tomb of Sidi Hussein, a Moslem prophet. One night during the journey there, Ruyter sees a Bedouin skulking about the camp. It is Massoud, one of Ali Diab's men. Greene insists upon digging the first well by the side of Sidi Hussein's sepulcher and incenses the Moslem laborers, who leave and inform Ali Diab of the impiety. The sheik, accompanied by Massoud, comes to register his protest. Hogan gets into a quarrel with the latter and kills him. All Diab rides off, swearing vengeance. This frightens Joshua Greene and he wants to hurry back to Jerusalem; but Ruyter points out that they would be quickly overtaken by the swift Bedouin horses. He suggests that the inn be barricaded against a possible siege and despatches Imbarak, the steward, to the Pasha of Jerusalem for help. Ali Diab comes with his tribe, and upon being refused unconditional surrender, shoots the waterskins of the beleaguered party with a blunderbuss and prepares to give them the "Punishment of the Sun," death by thirst. After the Bedouins withdraw out of range and form their siege lines, Madge goes to the top of the khan, where she sees them dragging a prisoner across the sands. It is Imbarak!

* This story began in The Cavalier for January 10.

Did you like this book?
We have more APT available!
All with original illustrations

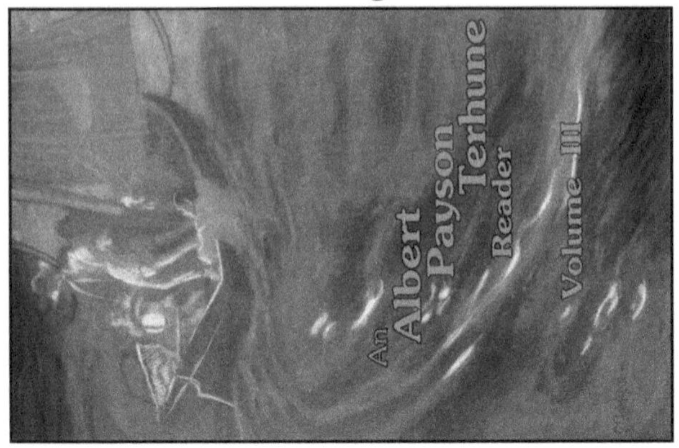

The Albert Payson Terhune Reader series

3 Volumes available

The White Way
Novel serialized from
The Green Book, about
financing Broadway shows

The Woman Tamers
Men who charmed the ladies:
Articles from The Green Book

The Flood Fighters
Two boys and a Collie!
Serialized from The Country Gentleman

In Treason's Track
Novel serialized from Argosy:
On the trail of Benedict Arnold!

The Tête-Bêche series

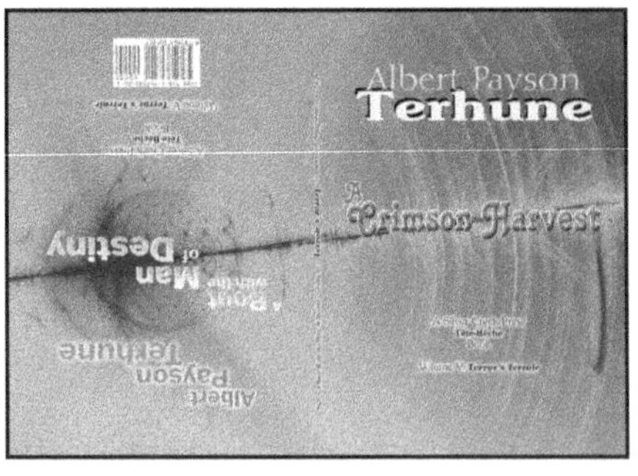

Volume I

The Fugitive

Forty Ali Babas and a Thief

Volume II

Their Last Hope

From Flag to Flag

Volume III: Dice Twice

As the Dice Fell

Fate Throws the Dice

Volume IV: Enlightenment's Ambiance

The Man Who Could Do Everything

When Liberty Was Born

Volume V: Terror's Terroir

A Crimson Harvest

A Bout with the Man of Destiny

In the Name of the King

APT

Swords and Scepters

A Silver Creek Press
Tête-Bêche Book
Volume VI

featuring:
In the Name of the King (from 1911)
The Sword of Ali Diab (from 1914)

The stories in this book are works of fiction. All names, characters, places and scenes described herein are the results of the author's imagination and genius. Any resemblance to actual persons, living or dead, is purely coincidental; and that includes actual persons depicted.

These stories were published at a time when political correctness had not yet caused serious cultural and moral damage. Certain ideas, terms and social conventions found herein are no longer considered acceptable (some for rational reasons, others not) and threaten to create crass incredulity among weak-minded readers. A mentally healthy reader (the kind for whom this book was lovingly compiled) will understand that, and not give the matter further thought.

Swords and Scepters
ISBN: 978-1-945307-41-6

Book compilation and design by Rodney Schroeter.

Cover design generated by Amberlight, www.escapemotions.com

The Silver Creek Press
PO Box 334
Random Lake WI 53075-0334

rschroeter@silentreels.com

In the Name of the King

By Albert Payson Terhune

SCP Tête-Bêche
Book VI

Silver
Creek
Press

2024

CHAPTER I.
I Am in Great Company.

I DREW myself up and made shift to look as cool as might be. Yet, Heaven alone knows what a tattoo my poor heart was banging against my ribs.

'Tis no light thing—when friendless, penniless, and alone in a foreign land—to feel, as it were, the noose tighten about one's neck.

Yes, and I doubt me if ever such another forlorn and coinless outcast, under sentence of death, had had the luck to stand in the king's own palace of Whitehall, as did I; in the very cabinet study of his majesty.

Let me paint, in a stroke or two, the odd scene.

A room hung in scarlet damask, blazoned with the royal arms of England, and lighted by a score of candles in wall sconces.

On a divan of satin sprawled a dark, stocky, swarthy man in black.

Behind him stood another man close to the other in aspect, yet— as it seemed to me—meaner, more shifty of gaze. In the doorway crowded a squad of the palace guard.

In the room's center—disheveled, torn of clothing, tousled of hair, and blood-streaked of visage—stood a young man of twenty-five. The guards had just thrust him forward from the door. He was a broad-shouldered, deep-chested giant of a fellow, yellow of hair, tanned of face.

I caught a reflection of him in a wall mirror. Seldom have I seen a youth less fitted to be in a royal apartment. And the glance at the mirrored form brought a dull flush of shame to my cheek. For the unkempt person was—my humble self!

The dark man sprawling on the divan nodded carelessly to the guards in the doorway. They withdrew and closed the door.

"Scrape me raw!" expostulated the other swarthy man, who

remained standing, "but this is a very desperate fellow! Do we well to have him here without a guard?"

"Tut, Jamie!" laughed the first, pointing at my pinioned arms and empty scabbard. "Is he not trussed up like any fowl? If you fear lest he may bite you, or butt at you with that yellow shock head of his, I will call one of the maids to protect you."

The standing man still glowered doubtfully at me from those shifty little black eyes of his. But his companion ended, more seriously:

"Is our business with him such as to warrant a dozen gossiping guardsmen to overhear and spread the tidings? Use your wits, Jamie. Also, take firmer hold on that too urgent prudence of yours.

"Now, sirrah," he went on, wheeling lazily on the divan to face me, "let me play magistrate for the nonce. Your name?"

"Dirck Dewitt," I made answer.

The shifty-eyed man broke in pompously:

"Knave, when you address—"

"Oh, be silent, Jamie!" ordered his companion petulantly; then, to me, he resumed:

"Dirck Dewitt? A Dutchman, eh?"

"No," said I; "an American. A native of his majesty's New England colonies."

"H-m! With a name that fairly reeks of Rotterdam and Amsterdam and all the other—"

"My Christian name," I explained briefly, "was given me in memory of a Holland friend of my father's. The name Dewitt—"

"Is as English as it is Dutch," he assented. "Let that pass. Your name is like to matter little enough to you in future. Your age?"

"Twenty-five."

"From the colonies, you say?"

"Plymouth born."

"How came you here?"

"A wander-love led me from one colony to another. And my journeyings gave me a certain idea, which I sought to lay before His Majesty Charles II. It was that idea which brought me overseas here."

"To the king?"

"To London," I corrected, "and, once here, I found no way of laying my plan before his majesty. Had I possessed the secret for some new gambling device, or known where a new breed of lap-dog could be procured, I fancy I might have gained access to the royal presence right easily. But as my idea concerned only the welfare of the kingdom, I was turned away from Whitehall on every—"

"Peace!" roared the shifty-eyed man, bustling forward angrily.

But the swarthy one waved him back and fairly rolled on the divan in a spasm of mirth.

"Oh, Jamie!" he panted, when he could get breath. "This alone makes the adventure worth while. It is thus that his most Christian majesty, Charles II of England, is talked of by his loyal, loving subjects."

"No, it is not," I broke in, nettled (as man ever is at a jest he cannot grasp). "It is far more lenient than the speeches that are made concerning him by most of his subjects."

Another fit of laughter, and the man on the divan once more continued his deliberate catechism:

"You came to England from the American colonies, you say? On a high-souled mission of patriotism? The king's gay life pained your worthy soul. Yet what manner of life have you yourself led since you came hither? Do I not recall some old-wife proverb anent the pot calling the kettle black?"

"My life is clean as any man's," I flashed back. "As for my present plight—"

"As for your present plight," he caught me up, "that same upright life of yours has very quickly led you into the shadow of the hangman's noose. The city watch tell monstrous tales of you."

"The true tale is told in a mere mouthful of words," I retorted. "I left my Cheapside lodgings to-night to make one more attempt at audience with the king. Here, in the very colonnades of Whitehall, was a licensed gambler at his booth—one of the gamblers from whom his majesty ekes out wealth by granting a license and taking a percentage of the pickings—"

"I know," interrupted my inquisitor dryly.

"An aged man," I continued, "was waiting, like myself, for audience. In passing, he brushed by accident against the booth. A pile of ivory counters was knocked to the ground. Some of them broke. The gambler, with an oath, struck the old man full in the mouth, knocking him senseless and bleeding."

The recital awoke no interest in either of my hearers' faces. I went on:

"I sprang at the gambler and beat him into helplessness with one of his own dice-boards. While I was engaged in this pleasant task, up runs a young gallant, shouting that he is the gambler's patron, and making at me with drawn blade. We fought. I wounded him—perhaps mortally.

"Friends of his then set upon me, and two of them fell before the watch rushed in and overpowered me by force of numbers. I fear me I may also have slain or badly harmed the watch captain during the struggle, for my blood was up and I was fighting for my life. They bore me to the nearest jail. Thence, a half hour ago, some of the palace guards brought me here. That is all."

"A most desperate fellow!" repeated the shifty-eyed man with a shudder. "Oh, lay me bleeding, but he is a murderous rogue! I trust his wrist-bonds are strong."

"Quite strong," I sneered, "else had I burst them long ago. I may add that my jailers stole what money I had about me—every penny I possessed. They be true imitators of their palace betters."

"He has pluck, Jamie!" approved the swarthy man. "Rare pluck, even if his wit be a trifle provincial.

"See you, fellow," he went on, again addressing me, "d'ye understand that your life is forfeit? You've wounded three nobles of the court; you've resisted the king's own city watch, and mayhap slain its captain; you've beaten a very worthy and licensed gambler so that he lies in hospital, 'twixt life and death. For one-half of these crimes any man must swing."

I made no answer. Nor, I flatter me, did I show aught of the cold terror that was beginning to grip at my brain. The dark man scanned me closely, then nodded approval.

"Where got ye your trick of fence?" he asked of a sudden. "Fitzroy and Rochester saw the whole affray. They protest you fought like a madman—yet, that you showed more than a bit of science, too. A man who attacks with strong fury and defense is a more perilous foe than many a cleverer fencer. Who was your master?"

"My master?" I repeated. "I picked up swordsmanship, as a lad, from a grizzled man who had once been a mighty warrior. He was Captain Miles Standish, of our Plymouth Colony. Since his day it has been my amusement to practise the use of the sword whenever I could find a worthy adversary. Yet, until to-night, I never drew weapon in actual conflict."

"The man for our purpose!" observed the swarthy one to his comrade. "The very man. Brave, strong, a born fighter, and—unknown. Friend, would you buy back your forfeited life?"

"If the price be not too high for my empty purse and full honor," I answered.

"Well turned!" he applauded. "A clever bit, worthy to be the tag for a stage play—'Empty Purse and Full Honor.' Well, to business! The price of your life is a slight service to us."

"What is the service?" I asked.

"A certain man—a nobleman—is a menace to the peace of the realm," replied he, "or rather, to the peace of my good brother here, and thus, indirectly, to *me*. By the stiff-necked notions of Parliament he may not be beheaded decently and in due order. Yet, he is of quarrelsome turn. A man who might meet him at the Cocoa Tree or the Cheshire Cheese, and by accident affront him, would have scant trouble in picking a very pretty quarrel. Then, out swords, and—"

"Wait!" I cried hoarsely. "Let me understand you. There is a man you wish killed. You have no legal means to compass his death. You are too cowardly to fight him, man to man. So you scour the city prisons for a condemned bravo who will put him out of the way for you? Am I right?"

"As right—and as unpalatable—as a dose of physic!" he laughed, again checking his companion's remonstrance. "Are you willing to buy life and liberty—and perchance a few pounds over—for rendering us this slight service?"

"To buy life by turning murderer?"

"No," he replied, rising and walking slowly toward me, "by serving your king."

"My *what?*" I echoed stupidly.

"Your king," he repeated, not without a certain jolly dignity. "I have the honor to be that same luckless monarch whom you so fiercely criticized a few moments back."

"The king!" I muttered, bewildered.

At first I fancied it a jest. But common sense came to my aid. A man not of royal blood would scarce be lounging in this inner cabinet of Whitehall.

Yes, and the swarthy personage resembled in looks and manner the descriptions I had so often heard of the "merry monarch," Charles II. It was he, past doubt.

He had referred to his shifty-eyed comrade as his "brother," and as "Jamie." King Charles had but one brother—James, Duke of York, heir apparent to the English throne.

I looked from one to the other in silence, then at my bound wrists.

"Well," observed the king, smiling at my awed confusion, "I have asked you to buy your life and serve your king—by doing this thing for me. Your answer is—"

"My answer," I snarled, "is that were my wrists free I should break every bone in your body for daring to propose so dastardly a crime to me. King or no king, that is my reply! Now, have me sent to the hangman! His is better company than yours."

CHAPTER II.
I Start on a Strange Mission.

THERE was a second of crass, stark silence following my furious outburst. Then the Duke of York, smiting a silver table-bell, howled:

"Guards! Guards, ho!"

On the instant a half-score of men burst into the room. York pointed at me, apoplectic, stammering, and incoherent in his rage.

"Take him away!" he sputtered. "To the—"

"Jamie," intervened the king, drawling the words with languid amusement, "cannot your patience await my poor life's end before you give state orders in my very presence?"

"But, sire," expostulated the duke, "this scoundrel—"

"This scoundrel," finished Charles, "is as entertaining a novelty in our truckling, time-serving court as a raging ice-storm in a tropic plague-center. Gentlemen of the guard, you may withdraw. And,

Jamie," he added as the door closed behind the puzzled officials, "if honest words chill your hothouse soul, you may follow them if you choose."

Behind his idle good nature, as he spoke, I seemed to note a flash of cold decision. The duke heeded it, too, for with a gesture of contemptuous resignation he returned to his place.

The king was eying me again with the admiring, half-amused curiosity that I have seen holiday crowds in Kew Gardens lavish upon that wondrous monster, the African elephant.

"I have seen men laugh in the face of death," said he musingly, after a little pause, "though, ods-fish, I always doubted as to their mirth's verity. I have seen men beard kings, too. But, faith, that outburst of yours, young man, savors of a far stranger thing—*of honesty!* Oft have I heard of it. Many a time have I seen its clever imitation. Little thought I that any king—least of all, myself—should live to behold the genuine thing."

I had caught his keen interest. I saw that. I knew, from all I had heard, that this paradox of a king—this royal blackguard—ever sought feverishly for some new sensation. It seemed that *I* had given him one.

Had I won him a victory over the Dutch, or discovered for England a new continent, I could not have won that quick flash of regard which my hot words of scorn had evoked. Yes, in the shadow of the rope, I, a humble provincial, had succeeded where a whole crafty, ever-scheming court had daily failed—I had interested an overbored king!

Does this seem odd to you? Read the tale of Charles's reckless, ill-spent reign if you disbelieve. There you will find scores of far more eccentric instances than that which I relate here.

"Is it your customary way, young sir," he queried now, "to run riot through courtiers and city watch, and then to voice yearnings to thrash your sovereign? Or is this but an exceptional case? I fain would know, so that I may be present at the next outburst."

I had been thinking rapidly. And through my head had run the old saw: "Smite while the iron is hot"! I had come to England to lay my idea before this very man. Here was my chance. Yet, to fit his humor, I must word my plea differently from my original intent, and, speak carefully so as to hold his attention.

"Sire," I made reply, "to-night was my first chance to call notice to myself as a swashbuckler and braggart. Yet, since my antics have amused your majesty, I am minded to repeat them on a larger and more glittering scale. Have I your leave to outline my project?"

"By all means!" he cried.

"To-night," I continued, "I overturned a few angry men and threatened violence to England's king. 'Twas a small beginning, but a hopeful one. Next, I mean to overthrow a province and do violence to a whole nation. Doth the program give promise, sire?"

"Excellent promise," he retorted. "None better since the Gunpowder Plot in my more or less sainted grandsire's day."

"Then will your majesty grant me patience while I lead up to my plan by speaking briefly of certain prosy matters? Believe me, the end will justify such doldrums as the hearing may cost you, and I hope for your approval when you have heard."

He nodded, still smiling, and lolled back on the divan. James, interested despite himself, stood eying me sourly.

"Sire," I went on, "across seas lies the greatest land on earth. From keys where endless summer burns, it reaches north to the dim, icy cape that yearns vainly for sight of sun. From the Atlantic shores, across thousands of rich miles, it stretches even to the Pacific. A wonder country that—"

"It seems to me," yawned Charles, "that I have heard much talk of this sort, and heard it to weariness. Pray get on with your tale."

"To the south of Canada," I continued stolidly, "lie your majesty's New England possessions. To the far south lie the Virginias, where also flies the English flag. Between—"

"I have read geography," he reminded me. "I looked to-night for an entertainer, not a schoolmaster."

"Between those two English possessions," I resumed, "is one of the richest, most wondrous tracts of land on all this earth. It is called the New Netherlands. Your foes, the Dutch, hold it. Were that territory England's, then your majesty would rule the whole Atlantic coast from Canada to the Floridas. That means, in effect, you would be master of the bulk of a continent larger than all Europe—a treasure-house of wealth—a future nation—"

"If—if!" he mocked. "History is ablaze with *ifs*. What does this lead to?"

"The Dutch hold the New Netherlands," I proceeded. "They hold it with a feeble, ever-failing grip, as a drunken man might grasp a bag of pearls. One strong wrench, at the right moment, would tear free their hold on those New World pearls and give your majesty dominion over a continent. Is is not worth while?"

But the king looked genuinely bored. I could see he was disappointed in the nature of my story. I felt baffled, hopeless.

Help came from an unexpected quarter. I chanced to glance at the Duke of York. His sallow face was alight, his shifty eyes agleam with cupidity.

"Sire," he cried, "the bumpkin is talking sense! Hear him out, I pray."

"As you will, Jamie," sighed the king, who had risen, but who now sank resignedly back on the divan. "You two are in treasonable conspiracy to make my evening stupid. Proceed. Mayhap history will have cause to call me—as well as my father—'Charles the Martyr'."

This poor jest at the expense of his own slain parent seemed to afford him vast amusement, and almost restored his good humor. I went on, more eagerly:

"The Dutch are England's foes. Ever they threaten Britain's coasts and shipping. Wise and thrifty as they are, they have no realization of the greatness of their American prize. Without progress, but with endless dissensions, they misgovern the New Netherlands. Petrus Stuyvesant, the governor at New Amsterdam, is at loggerheads with his people. His people are at odds with the Indians. And the states general at Holland is ever quarreling with *him*.

"The plum is ripe for the picking. Save for a weak Swedish colony or so on the Delaware, the conquest of this New Netherlands will give England all the Atlantic seaboard."

"What money have I for a costly war overseas?" fumed Charles. " 'Tis absurd."

"There is no need for warfare. A trusty agent at New Amsterdam can apprise you of the right moment to smite. A British fleet, appearing unheralded off the Battery in New Amsterdam harbor, would find city and colony too weak to strike a blow. I crossed seas to lay this simple plan before your majesty. It—"

"All would depend on the right agent," put in York. "A move too sudden or too slow would ruin all. We need a man who could stand close enough to Stuyvesant to learn all things, and whose ready wit could tell the exact minute to advise us on sending the fleet. Such men are not easy to find."

"On the contrary," answered Charles, "we need not look beyond this very room for such a one. Folk have said much to my disparagement, from time to time. But, none have yet doubted my judgment of human nature. We need, for the purpose, a man of daring, of ready brain, of fearless, accurate judgment. In short, Master Dirck Dewitt, if we carry out this precarious scheme, we need—*you.*"

"*Me?*" I cried, amazed. "No!"

"And why not, pray?"

"In the first place," I answered, "the responsibility is too great. My failure may mean the failure of my country's future—"

"England's future," he commented dryly, "is, I think, fairly well assured without your valuable aid, Master Dirck Dewitt."

"When I said 'my country,'" I retorted, "I referred to America, the land of my birth. The land which, one day—with or without England's aid—is going to rise to a height no nation of this age could understand."

"A prophet?" he sneered.

"No," I replied. "A man with enough common sense to look into the future. World-greatness has ever moved westward. And toward the far western land—the land of boundless possibilities—it is steadily moving. England, to-day, is America's best hope for progress. That is why I come to *you* with my plan. In another century the New World may be strong enough to stand on its own feet. Meanwhile—"

"Meanwhile," interrupted Charles, with another yawn, "you are avoiding the real question. I said you were the agent needed for so ticklish a scheme. You refuse, pleading your lack of ability. If *we* can take a gambler's chance on that same ability, surely *you* can. So let us consider it settled."

"There is another drawback," I insisted. "The work savors overmuch of spying to suit my taste."

"Spying?" he echoed coldly. "To do your sovereign's bidding?"

"No man—sovereign or other—can command my conscience," I answered, with a touch of pride.

"And your precious conscience tells you this will be spy's work?"

he scoffed.

"I am not quite sure," I said with all seriousness. "If I were, I could answer you the more readily. I do not like the thought of worming myself into Governor Stuyvesant's confidence in order to learn his secrets. On the other hand, if I am caught, I will pay the price with my life. And that makes it a fairer game. Moreover, I shall be serving America. Oh, I know not *what* to think!"

"Perchance I can decide you," suggested Charles. "I care little for this wild plan of yours. I enter upon it solely to please my good brother of York, who seems more overjoyed by the prospect than I have seen him since my physicians declared my illness hopeless, a year ago."

"Sire! Brother!" expostulated York.

Charles went on, unheeding.

"I shall let you, Master Dewitt, tip the balance. If you will accept the office of agent, then well and good. The scheme shall be carried through. If not—"

"I accept," I growled.

"Good! And your terms? "

"My terms?"

"Tush, man! Never look so stupid. Each man has his price. I take it you are not going to run your head into mortal peril for the sheer pleasure of it. What ask you, in case of success? A grant of wilderness? A hundred black slaves? A court office? A baronetcy? Or a cash—"

"Sire," I said, "this will seem to you the rarest jest of all. I ask, as reward, the privilege of serving my country. If I do so, with peril and without pay, my service is noble. If I go to the task with prospect of reward, I sink to the level of a hired informer—a spy. My price is— *nothing*. Nothing, at least, that any king can pay me."

"You talk well," he commented, "though your odd prate of patriotism hath more the ring of the playhouse than of the real world. For my brother's sake, I trust, your actions may worthily back your words. 'Tis said *mine* do not," he ended, with a quizzical smile that was half a sigh.

On the moment, I was reminded of the newest coffee-house gossip; how, pinned on the door of the king's own bedroom, a week earlier, this scurrilous verse had been found:

> "Here lies our sovereign lord, the king
>   Whose word no man relies on.
> He never said a foolish thing
>   And never did a wise one."

"By the way," continued Charles, "have you any plan of action mapped out? And—ass that I was, not to think of it!—do you chance to speak Dutch? Even stupid old Stuyvesant would scarce employ a man known to be English, in these days when Holland and England are ready to fly at each other's throats."

"My father," I replied, "spent his youth in Holland. His dearest friend and our most frequent guest at Plymouth—the man for whom I was named—was a Hollander. Dutch was spoken well-nigh as much as English in our home. I learned it when I learned to speak. I am told I have no accent."

"Good. Then get to Holland secretly. See my ambassador there. Arrange to send to him your reports, and for him to receive them under some feigned name and to forward them to me. I will see you get credentials to him and funds for the enterprise. Sail from Holland to New Amsterdam on the first possible ship. After that, your own wit must be your guide."

"There is one trifling detail," I ventured, "that your majesty has overlooked."

"Well, well!" he cried impatiently. "Out with it, O man of many objections!"

"I fear," I said quietly, "lest, on my quest, I may attract undue notice and, perchance, move somewhat awkwardly—with bound hands."

Charles broke into a merry laugh.

"The boy seems to have a true eye for detail!" he cried, cutting my bonds with a dagger he lifted from the table.

From me his jolly gaze roved to his brother (for whom he alone, of all England, seems to have had any genuine affection).

"Jamie," he said, throwing his arm over the duke's shoulders, "when next you blame me for crossing your wishes, remember this favor I have done for your sake against my better sense."

"It will pay rich interest," declared York.

"I doubt it," contradicted the king; "but—for your faith in the mad scheme, I am anxious to make you a gift. The more so since it costs me naught. Should we win those same New Netherlands—they are *yours!*"

"Brother!"

"Save your thanks," returned his majesty. "Save them until New Amsterdam is New—York!"

CHAPTER III.
I Fall in Love.

OUT from Zuydam Harbor rolled the good, if ungainly, ship Stadtholder. We were a mere handful of passengers; but the hold fairly bulged with casks of liquors and gunpowder. Heavy weighted, we sailed westward. My quest had begun.

On the ship's book Captain Stein had entered my name and identity thus:

"Dirck Dewitt, gentleman adventurer. Age—twenty-five. Trade—clerk. Home—the Cronstad, Haag. Destination—New Amsterdam."

The British ambassador had done his secret work well. I was at last bound for the New World in my accepted role. As the king had said, the rest depended on my own wit.

I read, the other day—long years after this tale I am chronicling—a maxim by a sage philosopher, who, 'tis said, is a man of fame in London now—one Dr. Samuel Johnson. This quip of his reminded me of my sensations as I began the fateful journey from Zuydam. He writes somewhat as follows:

"Being on shipboard is like being in jail. With the added danger of being drowned."

And truly, after the first few days out, I found time grow monstrous heavy on my hands. I had kept aloof from the other passengers, deeming such privacy less apt to draw me into notice than were I to be a boon companion.

But as the days went on in their dreary monotony, I fell wistfully to observing these same passengers as might a man on a desert island. For the most part, the little group was made up of plump merchants and commission folk, with here and there a staid *vrouw,* the wife of one of them.

None of my fellow sufferers interested me to any degree, save a young man and woman who, like myself, stayed apart from the others. The man was perhaps my own age; tall, lean, dark, with a certain dashing air about him.

The woman could not have been more than twenty. She, too, was tall, infinitely graceful—almost regal—in carriage and movement. Her hair was like spun gold, her complexion as snow-drifted roses, her eyes dark and inscrutable.

Never before in all my provincial life had I seen any one so lovely. My gaze followed her, wherever she appeared on deck, with a silent wonder that daily grew near and nearer to adoration.

Once or twice the tall man at her side—her husband, I gathered—intercepted these half-unconscious glances of mine, and scowled at me in return.

I did not like him. Not only because he was apparently the chosen of a glorious woman whom I admired, but because of a nameless antipathy that sprang up between us when first our eyes met.

The voyage was well advanced when, one day, as I leaned against the "house," smoking, the girl chanced to come up from the cabin alone.

Without a glance at me, she fell to pacing the narrow confines of the deck, steadying herself now and then against a stanchion as a gust of the ever-freshening wind slapped the sails and made the ship careen.

She was exercising briskly, an art most of our passengers did not seem to understand; and the quick movement sent a glow to the delicate oval of her cheek. Twice she passed and repassed me where I stood, pipe forgotten, in dumb admiration.

On the third turn of the short deck the filmy scarf that covered her hair was snatched away by a sharp puff of wind. Into the air whirled the gossamer thing, even as she gave a little cry of dismay at its loss.

Outboard it flew, carried on the wind's breath. But quickly as it went, my spring was quicker.

At a bound I had flung myself across deck and half over the rail. A wild sweep of my long arm—and I was so lucky as to seize an end of the fluttering lace between two of my outstretched fingers.

The impetus of my leap carried me beyond my balance. Over the rail I toppled, the lace still gripped in one hand.

With the fingers of the other I managed to grasp a bit of outrigging and, with a wrench, to bring myself back against the ship's side, my head on a level with the rail.

A tug, a scramble, and I vaulted over the rail on to the deck again. It had been well-nigh a case of "man overboard." But luck and an athletic frame had saved me a ducking.

Panting a little from my exertion, and annoyed at cutting so awkward a figure before her, I turned toward the girl and proffered the rescued scarf.

"Oh, sir," she cried, in Dutch, "you might have been drowned!"

"Could man die in sweeter cause?" I made answer.

Yes, it was a heavy reply, all lacking in grace. Yet, such as it was, it did not seem wholly to displease her.

Her great, dark eyes widened as she accepted the scarf from my shaking hand. Then, her gaze still on mine, she said in a pleasant tone:

"How strong you are! I gave you up for lost, and I was about to cry for aid, when over the rail you came, like—like a monkey!"

The simile did not please me in the very least. I am afraid I showed this by my face; for she added quickly:

"It must be splendid to be so strong—to be such a giant and to feel one could crush one's fellow men! My pretty rose-point scarf," she went on with a smile. "Louis would have been furious if I had lost it. It is from Venice, and—it cost him ninety guilders. I cannot thank you enough, Mynheer—Mynheer—"

"Dewitt," I supplied. "Dirck Dewitt."

"I have seen you so often on deck and at table, Mynheer Dewitt," she continued, "and you looked lonely. You *were* lonely. Is it not so?"

"Only since first I saw you," I answered with perfect honesty. "And then it seemed to me I was the very loneliest man in all this world."

She glanced at me in quick doubt. I suppose my face must have reassured her. For she answered:

"I do not care for compliments, *mynheer*."

"I do not pay them, *mevrouw*," I replied.

"You were lonely?" said she, after an instant's pause. "Then why did you not make our acquaintance?"

"I dared not."

"Yet you are brave. Otherwise, you could not have risked drowning for the sake of my paltry scarf."

"Paltry? At ninety guilders?"

I spoke somewhat lightly so as to mask my embarrassment.

"You think, then, of its mere cost?" she said, disappointed.

"No. But you forbade me to pay you compliments. How, then, could I tell the truth?"

I had unconsciously fallen into step with her. And, side by side, we were now pacing the deck together. When she spoke again, it was with a total change of the subject.

"You are merely to visit New Amsterdam, or to become a settler?" she queried.

"I am to stay. If not there, at least in America," I replied.

"So are we. A dreary prospect, is it not?"

"Dreary?" I echoed. "Why?"

"To turn one's back on home, on friends, on all the gay, pleasant life of civilization, and to plunge into the wilderness."

She shuddered as she spoke in mock despair.

"But," I urged, "New Amsterdam is not 'wilderness.' 'Tis a town of—"

"Oh, spare me the statistics!" she begged. "America is a wilderness. New Amsterdam is in America. Therefore, New Amsterdam is a wilderness. What schoolmaster could give wise logic? I am glad, *mynheer*," she went on more gently, "to have met you. Now, we shall not be wholly strangers in a strange world. I trust we may see much of you when we reach the—wilderness!"

A flash of audacity overcame my odd, new diffidence. Looking her full in the eyes, I quoted a couplet of the olden song:

> "The flow'ret blooms. But not for me, alas!
> I'll walk where I'll not see it when I pass."

She flushed, and I felt she understood. What further idiocy I might have perpetrated I know not. At this moment (luckily for my sanity and, unfortunately, for all my inclinations) the man who usually accompanied her appeared on deck.

Again our eyes met—his and mine—and once more I had that

strange feeling as though I had of a sudden crossed swords with a foe. The girl did not appear to see our mutual glance.

"Louis," she said, turning to him, "may I present Mynheer Dirck Dewitt? Mynheer Dewitt has done me a great service. He rescued my pretty scarf from—"

"Greta," expostulated the man, in no way acknowledging the introduction, "I have told you, time and again, not to wear that scarf on shipboard. It might readily be lost or torn—"

"And it cost ninety guilders," she finished. "I've heard all that before. But since the scarf is quite safe, and the ninety guilders were long ago spent, perhaps you will trouble to say a civil word to Mynheer Dewitt."

Sulkily the man glanced toward me. Sulkily he bowed, and with ungracious gesture held out his hand.

My own right hand's knuckles, as I now noticed for the first time, were "barked" by a rap they had received in my tumble over the rail. I was foolishly glad of the excuse the accident gave me.

"My hand is scarce fit just now," said I, "to shake any one's."

"Your left hand, then," he insisted, noting my reluctance.

"I fear it might bring bad luck," I returned flippantly, making no effort to touch his fingers.

"As you wish," he growled. "Come, Greta."

They went below. I followed the girl's stately figure out of sight as they vanished. Half ashamed of my own churlishness toward the man, I was none the less strangely elated over having actually met and spoken with the wonder woman, his companion. I could not dismiss her from my mind.

Then, like a blow in the face, came the thought that she was doubtless his wife. What concern, then, of mine were her beauty or her glowing charm? Heart-sick, I moved away.

"I will see her no more—think of her no more," I vowed.

And, by way of keeping my high resolve, I went straight to the captain.

"Captain Stein," said I, as I entered the skipper's cabin, "what are the names of the woman and the man with whom I have just been talking? You must know whom I mean, for you passed as we stood on the deck together."

"I know," he nodded. "I know all about them. They are of Amsterdam. The man is Louis Van Hoeck. A fondness for the dice-box has ebbed his fortune; and a duel with an official of the states general makes Holland too hot for his comfort. So he is off to the colonies to mend both fortune and fame. The lady comes with him right unwillingly, I am told. But as she is all alone in the world save for him, and as his scanty fortunes are hers, she has no choice."

"I scarce wonder," I assented. "For a woman, it must be cruelly hard to leave all old ties, even to follow the fortunes of the husband she loves. And—"

"Husband?" snorted Captain Stein. "Louis Van Hoeck is not the fair Greta's husband, man. She is unmarried. Though with such a face I wonder she's escaped the yoke. Van Hoeck is her brother."

"Her brother?" I cried with a wild, unreasoning joy. Then:

"Captain, this is the most wondrous glorious voyage I ever made!"

CHAPTER IV.
DISASTER.

I HAVE scant experience with women. Most of my rather eventful life has been spent among men. Therefore, I fear I proved but an awkward, shy wooer in the weeks that followed. But what I lacked in polish I assuredly made up in ardor and persistence.

For, out of my waking hours, few were spent far from Greta Van Hoeck's side. Looking back, I can see that my courtship must have afforded vast merriment to our fellow passengers.

But I console myself with the thought that no sighing swain be he ever so *Romeo*-like has ever wholly escaped some ridicule at the hands of the sane portion of mankind.

"All the world loves a lover." Perchance! But of a surety, all the world loves a laugh quite as well.

As I say, I dogged Greta's steps wherever she went or sat. Alternately tongue-tied and voluble, I must have made a sadly eccentric companion. Yet, it seemed to me, my presence was not wholly distasteful to the girl.

Indeed, my vanity told me that daily she and I drew the closer together. There was a growing intimacy between us, as intangible as it was sweet.

To most men who have a halfscore of such pretty affairs to their credit, this may seem an old story. To me it was the most miraculous thing in all life.

Nor was my joy lessened by the sulky displeasure wherewith Louis Van Hoeck viewed our ever-increasing companionship. For the sake of peace, and not to pain the girl by a clash, I avoided her brother when I could. For my own temper is ever quick, and I believed his to be still quicker. Given this fact, on a foundation of mutual instinctive dislike, and it would have taken little to strike the spark.

So matters went, until one moonlit night when we were sailing up the coast of what was later to be known as the Jerseys—at that time a southern shore of the New Netherlands. Another few hours would see us safe in New Amsterdam Harbor.

Greta and I were leaning over the rail, watching the phosphorus dancing along in our wake until it merged into the moon's water-track. We had fallen silent, after the manner of young folk at such times. It was she who first spoke.

"This is the last of our golden evenings," she sighed. "To-morrow we enter the *real* world again. It is hard to take up the busy workaday life once more, is it not?"

"It will always be golden to me, even as this voyage has been," I made foolish answer, "if you will let me see you as often. Will you?"

"You will have your own work to do. Women must stand second to work."

"No!" I protested.

"You are interested in your—work?"

"Much," I answered.

"It means much to you?"

"It means—it did mean—everything to me," I returned.

"*Did* mean?" she exclaimed. "Are you already weary of it before it begins?"

"No. It means as much as ever. But—something else has grown to mean infinitely more."

My huge palm closed over her white little hand as it lay lightly on the rail. The avowal that for weeks had filled my heart trembled now on my very lips.

But, though she must have known—as I believe every woman must always know—what was coming, yet, womanlike, she strove to put off the inevitable moment. Even as a hungry cat will pause to play coquettishly with a mouse ere despatching it.

Drawing her hand slowly from beneath my grasp, she said:

"This great 'work' of yours that means so much? You have once or twice spoken of it. Yet you have never told me what it is. Will you not tell me now?"

"It is of tedious and dry detail," I evaded clumsily. "'Twould not interest you."

She read the evasion in my voice, and it spurred her languid curiosity to eagerness. "Tell me!" she demanded.

"'Tis a long and stupid tale," I countered; "and I would far fainer talk of—you!"

Even to this glorious girl, and in the very acme of my wild infatuation, I could scarce bring myself to babble of the secret that meant so much to me—to the king to America. Intuitive caution held me back. But she would not have it so.

"'Tis a secret," declared Greta. "And you deem me unworthy to hear it."

"No!"

"But, yes! I am all very well for an hour's idle chat, for the sighing of false compliments, for the pastime of a long voyage. But when I ask to enter into the house of your plans and ambition, the door is slammed in my face. 'Tis as I said: we women are ever crowded out of a man's life by what he calls his 'career.'"

"Greta, you wrong me cruelly! You have no right to say—"

"It is true," she said coldly; "I have no 'right' in the case. Forgive me for not sooner understanding that. And—Good night, Mynheer Dewitt."

She made as though to move away. In my crass ignorance of women, I was frantic.

It seemed to me I had insulted—wounded her; that I was a ruffianly brute, unfit to speak with so rare and sensitive a creature; that I had forever ruined my chance of winning her love.

"Greta!" I cried in utter misery. "Greta! You are wrong! There is nothing I would not do for you. Nothing I would not tell you. Ah, do not go! The world is so lonely away from you!"

She hesitated. Then, with what I deemed an almost divine forgiveness, she came back to where I stood and looked confidingly up into my face.

As the moon shone down upon her it seemed to transfigure the girl, and to give her a new, unearthly beauty.

"Tell me," she said softly; "what is this strange work to which you are bound?"

Why was it, I wonder, that at the moment there flashed to my mind, by some odd vagary, the memory of a time-stained colored picture that had hung in my mother's room in the little old Plymouth house?

The picture represented a bearded giant to whose arm clung a fair, bewitching woman, looking up into his troubled face with a very anguish of appeal. It was entitled "Samson and Delilah," and beneath it had been printed the text:

"When she pressed him daily with her words, and urged him so that his soul was vexed unto death, he told her all his heart."

Impatiently, I put the vagrant memory from me as unworthy to be dwelt on in connection with so high a spirit as Greta Van Hoeck. The moonlight was in my brain. The girl's eyes were drawing my very heart to my lips. Laugh at me, you who have never known the love of woman!

"My work," I said slowly, "is of a sort that would bring my head to the block were it to become known in New Amsterdam. I say this, not to disturb you, Greta, but to show you how fully—how utterly—I trust you. Here is the story in as brief a space as I may compass it. King—"

A man had come up from the cabin. Now he caught sight of us and swaggered forward. It was Louis Van Hoeck.

I saw that he had been drinking. Also, that the liquor had rendered him quarrelsome.

His surly gaze rested on us two a moment. And he saw that I had again imprisoned Greta's hand, also that my bent head had brought my face very near to hers.

At the sight, he ripped out an oath and stepped between us. Greta, after one startled look at his angry visage, shrank back. At the head of the cabin gangway she paused an instant, then moved out of sight.

It was not the first time I had observed her dread of her brother's brutal temper. But now the sight of her fear aroused in me a reasonless anger. I wheeled upon the frowning man. But before I could speak, he growled out:

"Is the Van Hoeck family so lowered by poverty that any down-at-heel adventurer dare force his low attentions on my sister? I have endured enough of this. What I have just seen shows me my endurance has gone much too far. In a word, *canaille,* if I catch you addressing my sister again, or so much as looking at her, I shall cane you. Is that quite plain?"

Rage turned the white moonshine scarlet around me. Yet, by mighty effort, I forced myself to sanity.

"Mynheer Van Hoeck," I said calmly, though my voice shook with fury, "I overlook your coarse threat for the love I bear your sister. As her brother, you are, I take it, her legal protector. To you, therefore, I herewith make formal request for the honor of her hand."

It was a stiff, stilted speech at best. Yet, as a man of honor, I deemed this the time to make it.

The effect on Van Hoeck was scarcely what I had hoped. He glared at me in silent contempt for a moment, then replied thickly:

"And here is my one answer to your request!"

Drawing back his arm as he spoke, he struck me across the face with one of his heavy buckskin gauntlets.

That was quite enough. Down smashed my worthy resolutions to be cool. Acting before clear thought could prompt or check the impulse, I struck out in rage.

My clenched fist caught him flush in the face, and he fell to the deck in a cursing, sprawling heap.

On the instant, he was up again like an angry cat. Snarling, mouthing, he flung himself at me with drawn sword.

So sudden, so deadly, was his attack, I barely had time to whip out my own blade to meet it.

There, wordless, murderous, on the deserted section of the deck, we fought. The hate of weeks had come to a climax. Forgotten were Greta and my good resolves. Forgotten was all, save that I and mine enemy were at last sword to sword.

Back and forth we moved, lunging, thrusting, parrying. The white light of the moon flashed blue from our crossed, grinding blades.

He was agile, wiry, venomous—a splendid swordsman. Better, at mere skill, perhaps, than I. But fury gave me strength, and my clean life stood me in good stead.

Seldom has contest seemed to me more equal.

The steel rang, grated, and whined in the war-song of the ages.

Panting, slipping, advancing, retreating, ever seeking an opening for a fatal thrust, we strove like madmen.

Teeth bared, eyes agleam, bodies tense and unnaturally alert, we circled about each other like two mastiffs who await a chance to gain the death-grip.

Our pliant swords described wide arcs of light. As they clashed, sparks sprang from them. Oh, it was fine to be a primitive, savage man just then, and to feel myself opposed to a foe worthy of my mightiest prowess!

I thought I saw an opening. I lunged fiercely. He sought to parry. My blade missed him, and our bodies came together with a thud. At that same instant our sword-hilts "locked."

For a moment we heaved and panted, striving to tear loose our weapons and to resume the life-and-death battle. We were so close together as we struggled that I could feel the man's hot, rum-laden breath on my face. Then—there came a startling interruption to the combat.

CHAPTER V.
THE STAND AGAINST COWARDS.

THERE was a confused babel of shouts from below, a sound of many running feet, of screams. An acrid gray cloud burst from the companionway. Van Hoeck and I fell apart. Our swords were free, but we made no further move to use them.

Pallid and aghast, we stood listening to the most awful sound that can greet the ears at sea. The sound of voices roaring:

"Fire! The ship is on fire!"

Up from below swarmed passengers. From rigging and deck quarters flocked the crew. Even the helmsman deserted his post; and the Stadtholder, steerless, came about with a jerk that nearly swamped her.

What use for my dull pen to describe that scene? The air was full of smoke, of clamor, of almost tangible horror. The passengers ran idly to and fro, questioning, screaming, lamenting.

The crew were in little better case. The mate, who was on deck, did what he could to preserve discipline, but demoralization reigned.

Nor could the panic-stricken ones be wholly blamed. Consider our position: miles from shore, in a flimsy wooden ship, low-laden with casks of wines, gunpowder, and spirits. And the ship afire! The spirit or powder casks must soon be reached. And then!

Captain Stein had not appeared on deck. With one or two of the braver sailors he was still below, fighting against hope to keep the fast-spreading flames from the hold. (I later heard that a drunken sailor smoking in his bunk had started the trouble.)

The sailors on deck, as soon as they could organize their panic-stricken members in any way, shoved through the confused mass of passengers to where the life-boats swung.

Down came the boats from their davits, onto the deck, where a score of hands seized and lifted them over the rail. There was no effort to lower them into the water in orderly fashion. Indeed, the task was impeded by the wild eagerness of each member of the crew to be near enough the rail to jump into the boats the moment they should touch water.

That way madness lay. And the mate saw the peril. Struggling to the rail, he leaped upon it. He had snatched up a boat-hook and was whirling it above his head.

"*Back!*" he roared, "back, you cowardly swabs! Passengers first! Starboard watch, detail six men to bring up provisions and water. Bo's'n! Stand by to—"

He got no further. A forward surge of the fear-mad crowd caught him and shoved him bodily into the sea.

At that moment Captain Stein and his handful of singed, blackened fire-fighters came reeling up the companionway. Behind them, through the hatchway, burst a swirl of black-red flame.

Stein's glance took in the whole situation. He flung himself among his frenzied men. Had he arrived a moment earlier his authority might perchance have availed. But the sight of the flames had robbed the crew of their last vestige of sanity.

Bellow orders and gesticulate as he might, the captain could do nothing to stem the tide.

Boat after boat splashed into the water below, each bound now to the ship only by light hempen hawsers. And the crew made for the port gangway, where two or three of them had hurriedly affixed a companion-ladder.

Stein beat his way to the ladder-head and flashed out his cutlas.

"Get back there!" he screamed. "Passengers first! The cur who comes in reach of my hanger will get a carved skull for cowardice."

But the men, like frightened sheep, could not be stayed. True, those in front sought to back away from the short, whizzing blade. But the press behind them was too great. One red-headed Flanders man in the first rank of the fugitives was pushed forward just too far.

Down swept the captain's hanger, and down went the red-headed man beneath the slash. Yet, falling, he managed to raise himself to his knees, with the snarl of a hurt beast, and lunged viciously upward at Stein with a curved sheath-knife.

The captain's knees doubled, and he sank down across the body of the fallen sailor.

It had all happened with lightning speed. And, at the captain's mishap, the crew hurled themselves toward the gangway again.

But, quick as they were, one passenger was quicker. Louis Van Hoeck, sword in hand, cleared at a bound the two prostrate bodies and stood in the gangway, facing the men.

His lips were drawn away from his long teeth in a wolfish grin. His lean, tall body was crouched as if to launch itself upon the sailors.

"Now then!" he laughed (and his laugh was not good to hear). "Who is the first to hunt for safety past my sword-point? "

His cold, jeering fury, as well as his sudden advent on the scene, momentarily checked the rush. But only for an instant. Again the human wave rolled forward.

Yet that moment's respite had given me the time I needed to spring to Van Hoeck's aid.

There, side by side, we two enemies, who so lately had striven for each other's deaths, stood with bared blades, awaiting the onset.

And it came.

The men threw themselves madly upon the frail human barrier that stood between them and safety. It is a scene I do not even yet like to look back on.

I had fought before, but never like this. It was like trying to stem the stampede of a herd of infuriated wild beasts.

Yet, fierce as it was, the fight was brief. We two were skilled swordsmen. The wide rail on either side of us made the open gangway a niche where swiftness and skill could accomplish far more than in the open.

After the first rush, the men reeled back from the area of our fast-flying blades. And in the space between lay five bodies.

Van Hoeck was for dashing among our baffled foes and wreaking useless vengeance. But with one hand I forced him back to my side by main force, while with my sword arm I still menaced the doubtful, baffled crew.

"Quarters, all!" I shouted, taking advantage of their indecision. "Now, then, two men to enter each boat and to steady it while passengers descend! *So!* Now the women. Next, two of you pick up Captain Stein and lower him into a boat. Now the men passengers and last, you sailors. In order there!"

My orders, given one at a time, were, to my surprise, obeyed as men are wont to obey whom sea-life has taught the habit of dull routine. Cowed, dazed, the crew worked as efficiently as though no danger threatened.

We let them pass us, two by two, until the boats were manned. With drawn sword, Van Hoeck guarded against the boatmen's pushing off prematurely from the burning ship.

Next, the women passengers, Greta among them, were helped in safety down the shaky ladder. Then Stein, not only still breathing, but perfectly conscious, was lowered. The men passengers and the crew followed.

The fire had gained such headway I dared not risk sending below for provisions. At any minute now the flames might reach the spirit-casks, or even the powder-kegs in the after-hold.

There was no time to waste. Shore was not many miles away. The night was calm, save for a light breeze. So provisions were not really needed.

As each boat filled I ordered it cast off and propelled out of the danger zone. At last every shallop and life-boat was full and had pushed away from the vessel's side. The dingey alone remained.

"You first!" I ordered Van Hoeck, motioning toward the little craft.

He glanced at me. In the moonlight our eyes met. I read no lessening of his former hatred despite the fact that we two had fought side by side and saved the lives of all on board.

"You first!" I repeated.

He shrugged his shoulders, slipped his sword back into the scabbard, and ran down the ladder. Into the dingey he sprang, cast off the rope, and, holding the tiny boat in place by means of his grip on the ladder, waited for me to follow him.

The flames were now bursting from every opening, and the deck floor was stinging hot under my feet. The smoke was so dense I could scarce see a yard in front of me.

I turned to grope my way down the ladder. As I did so, the portion of deck on which I stood rose straight into the air, carrying me with it as though I had been of a feather's weight. The rending, roaring sound of an explosion deafened me.

I felt myself whirled through space, millions of miles, the whole world around me agonizingly bright with myriad-colored lights. Then I sank into a cool darkness.

And I slept. Or died.

And after a time I dreamed. A strange dream. First I smelt Mayflowers strong in the air that had so lately been areek with smoke. Then I opened my eyes. I seemed to be lying in a boat of some strange description. Dawn was paling the sky. Above me, bathing my throbbing head, was a girl.

"Greta!" I murmured dizzily.

But it was not Greta. The face above mine was almost as dark as an Indian's. The eyes—large, luminous, soft—were alight with tender pity.

At her breast the dream-girl wore a mass of Mayflowers. A spray of them fell away, and dropped into my hand. My fingers closed about it.

I had a strange sense of rest, of utter peace. I was content to lie still, looking up into that sweet, dark face with its glorious eyes.

"You are very beautiful!" I whispered. Then I fell asleep again.

CHAPTER VI.
I Drop in From—Nowhere.

FROM the dream and from the long dead sleep or brain concussion of which it was a part, I awoke at last, after what seemed endless centuries.

I opened my eyes, eager to see again that dainty little face with its great eyes. And I drew in my breath for a scent of the Mayflowers.

Poetical actions both, with direfully unpoetic results.

For the deep breath I took brought me only the pungent smell of waterside shipping and of city streets. The opening of my eyes gave me no vision of a girl's moonlit visage crowned by shimmering hair.

Instead, leaning above me were half a dozen men, all talking in Dutch. Behind and over them I saw the raftered ceiling of a large room. A wizened man in black was feeling my pulse.

"He is coming to his senses," said the man with professional unction."The heart-beats are growing strong and normal. See, the color is returning to his lips. In a few moments at most—"

"What's that he is gripping in his other hand?" asked a deep voice.

Some one, I felt vaguely, began to loosen my unconsciously clenched fist. In another moment my fingers were opened. I heard another voice say in surprise:

"'Tis a spray of Mayflower, your excellency!"

"Mayflower!" echoed the deep voice. "The man was cast up by the sea. For weeks he had voyaged on the Stadtholder. Whence could he find a Mayflower? They grow not on the waves. Nor anywhere else that I know of save in our southern pine woods here in the New Netherlands."

"'Tis all savoring of mystery," commented a voice I knew. "Two nights ago the fellow was hurled into the air by the explosion whereof I told your excellency. I stood in the dingey, at the passenger-ladder's foot. The explosion knocked me into the sea and I had great ado in getting back into the boat. I scoured the near-by waters in vain, searching for him. Yet, this morning, he appeareth, full clad, and in dry clothes, lying senseless at the doors of the White Hall. 'Tis wholly past comprehension."

The White Hall! Surely I was not still in London! No, for these folks were speaking Dutch. And the last speaker was, past doubt, Louis Van Hoeck.

Then I remembered. Governor Petrus Stuyvesant had built near the Battery, in New Amsterdam, a State house which he named the White Hall.

Then I was in New Amsterdam! But how came I there? When the Stadtholder blew up we were far below Coleman's Point.

Now, no explosive known could hurl a man a dozen miles or more and lay him unhurt on a door–step, drying his sea-drenched clothes in the process.

Truly, as Van Hoeck said, the affair was "savoring of mystery"!

Yet, oddly enough, my reawakening mind dwelt far less on this phase than on the fact that a spray of Mayflower had just been found in my hand.

Back with a rush came the memory of that strange moonshine dream. Of the dainty girl whose tender eyes had looked down into mine, whose soft, cool, little hands had bathed my raging head.

The Mayflowers at her breast—the fallen spray of blossoms over which my hand had closed. Was it no dream? But if not, how came I to be—

"His eyes are open!" boomed the deep voice. "Lift him a little."

An arm was slipped under my neck and I was slowly and gently raised to a sitting posture.

I looked about me. The room was large and furnished in a rich, if tasteless, luxury. Through the open windows I could see the Battery foot, the low sea-wall that girds the southern point of Manhattan Island, the shipping, and the glitter of the waters beyond.

Save for Louis Van Hoeck, the men about me were strangers; stolid-looking burghers all of them. I wondered from which member of the group had issued that deep, rough voice of command. Then my eyes fell upon a chair of state at one end of the apartment. In it sat a most remarkable figure.

A man, heavily built, bald of head; harsh, arrogant, and ruddy of face. He was clad in blue velvet jacket, white puff shirt, and breeches of dyed buckskin, caught at the knees with huge bunches of gaudy silken ribbons.

An odd, almost laughable feature of his appearance was that from one of the silk-decked knees protruded a polished black wooden leg, banded heavily with silver.

And by this I knew him. The man in the chair of state was "Old Silver Leg"—in other words, his excellency, Petrus Stuyvesant, Dutch Governor of the New Netherlands, and one of the most strikingly picturesque figures of his day.

Stuyvesant! The man I had crossed the seas to outwit; the human lion whom all the colony feared! And at last, in this queer fashion, we were face to face.

Rising, and leaning on a gold–headed cane, he came stumping down the room toward the couch where I sat.

"Mynheer Dewitt," said he, "my compliments!"

I stared stupidly at him, my head still thick.

"You—your excellency knows my name?" I muttered.

"All New Amsterdam," he replied pompously, "knows the name of the brave man who saved the Stadtholder's passengers from fiery death. The man whose pluck and coolness made possible their escape. The man who, having saved all, himself stayed aboard the blazing ship, until—"

"Your excellency!" I intervened, in common fairness, "Mynheer Van Hoeck was first to spring to the gangway, to hold back the crew. I did but follow his example."

"Captain Stein saw all," returned Stuyvesant. "I have ever found him a truthful man, and I accept his version. The more so as it is backed by other witnesses."

"But," said I, "Van Hoeck it was who—"

"Who did a daring deed," assented Stuyvesant, "for which I give him full credit. But," he added dryly, "brute courage, unbacked by a cool head or common prudence, goes not overfar. When the rush was checked, he was for charging, sword in hand, among the beaten men. That would have robbed his fellows of their last hope of safety. It was *you* who withheld him—who gave the calm orders that meant safety. New Amsterdam—Holland itself—thanks you, *mynheer.*"

As I bowed my embarrassed acknowledgment of his deep-voiced praise, I caught a sidelong glimpse of Louis Van Hoeck. He was eying me with a cold, concentrated fury.

"And now," continued Old Silver Leg, as if relieved at having got rid of his speech of gratitude, "perchance you can clear up this little mystery. You were aboard an exploding fire-ship two nights ago. The boats hunted high and low for you. Not finding you, they deemed you dead, and they made their way hither. At dawn to-day you were found lying outside this White Hall of ours. There is no bruise nor wound upon you. Your clothes are dry. How explain you that?"

"I do not explain it, your excellency," I answered. "My last recollection—my last lucid recollection—is of being whirled aloft by the explosion's force. Then I awoke *here.*"

The Governor's keen little eyes, under the gray, shaggy thatch of brow, were studying me closely.

"Your last 'lucid' recollection?" he quoted suspiciously. "What mean you by that?"

"I—I had strange, impossible dreams," I answered uncomfortably. "So indistinct and unreal are they in my confused brain that I fear I cannot voice them. Nor would the idle fancies of a stunned man be worth your excellency's hearing."

"Was *this* an 'idle fancy'?" he queried sharply, picking up the Mayflower spray. "Such blossoms as these grow only on land, and usually not overnear to the shore. How did you come by it?"

A new spasm of dizziness overcame me as I strove to rise to my feet. Brain and body alike reeled drunkenly. I heard Stuyvesant's voice, as from a great distance, repeating:

"How did you come by it?"

"It—it was in her girdle," I heard myself answer weakly. "As she leaned over me, this spray fell into my hand. I—"

"He is delirious, your excellency," I heard the black-clad doctor whisper amid a buzz of wondering interest that swept the room. "It were best to let him rest a while ere you force him to further talk."

His words roused me, and in anger I shook from my senses the lethargy of weakness that had been stealing over me, a weakness that had made my tongue babble about the fantom girl, in spite of my guardianship.

"Your excellency," I said, less thickly, "I am a clerk by profession. May I hope to find service in your official household? 'Twas with that hope I crossed the seas. I will do diligent work—"

"And I shall prove Holland is not ungrateful for what you have already done," answered Stuyvesant with ponderous graciousness. "It hath ever been my aim to surround myself with men who were honest, brave, and quick of resource. The combination is rare. Yet, your actions show you possess it, far more than any written recommendations could attest. And, by the way, I suppose you have such recommendations?"

"My effects," I evaded, "were all aboard the Stadtholder. I saved naught."

"True! True! Consider yourself in my personal service. When you are stronger, we will talk over details. Come, *mynheers!* The council is at an end. Dr. Beekman, see that your patient is made comfortable in one of the sleeping rooms."

The burghers, led by Stuyvesant, filed solemnly out.

Louis Van Hoeck followed. As he passed my couch he muttered under his breath to me:

"There is an old saying that when a fight is interrupted, it will one day be resumed. The law here makes dueling punishable by death. But—there are other ways."

I scarce heeded him. For, with all my feeble strength, I was engaged in stooping over to pick from the floor a certain withered spray of Mayflower.

CHAPTER VII.
I Play My Part.

A HUDDLE of crooked streets, sprawling east and west from the Hudson and the East rivers; two water-side thoroughfares; the Bowling Green and the Battery to the south; the old wall cutting off the city to the north. And there you have a picture of New Amsterdam as it was in these early days of mine.

North of the low wall (and of the lane running alongside it, which folk call the Wall Street), the growing town was already spilling a fringe of scattered houses, like fingers stretching out toward the distant villages that lay between New Amsterdam and far-off Haarlem.

Straight to the city's north ran the shady Bouerie Lane; through field, farm, and woodland, until, above, it ended in Petrus Stuyvesant's own country residence.

Up this lane, one day, a month after my arrival in New Amsterdam, I was riding, on my way to see the Governor, whose secretary I was newly become.

Through the pleasant May weather I cantered easily along. At a turn in the lane I came upon a merry group of equestrians on their way back to the city from a day's picnic on Haarlem Heights. Four or five officers from the fort—a few rich burghers' sons and daughters and—Greta Van Hoeck!

A horse had wedged a stone in its shoe. The group had halted while the rider sought to hammer loose the obstruction.

They saluted me gaily as I rode up. Returning their greeting, I reined in beside Greta. She had been chatting with two officers, and now turned, with tolerant good humor, to reply to my salutation.

The rider of the horse with a stone in its shoe called on one of his comrades for advice. The other officer rode with his fellow to the spot, leaving me for the moment alone beside Greta.

I was not so much at ease as I had been wont to be on shipboard. Since my convalescence, my work had kept me close in attendance on his excellency. At such rare intervals as my duties had permitted me to see Greta Van Hoeck, I had been pained and puzzled to note a subtle change in her.

True, we had never met alone. For, ever she was surrounded by a bevy of admiring young Dutchmen; and I could scarce get a word with her.

But it had seemed to me, even then, that she put me on a different plane than when we were together during those wondrous shipboard evenings. I could not define the change, but it hurt me. I was resolved to steal this moment of *tête-à-tête* to learn wherein I had offended her.

"Well, Master Secretary," laughed she, meeting my appealing glance with a level gaze as I drew up beside her, "your new dignity actually does not prevent you from speaking to a poor maid whom you knew in less favored hours? "

"Less favored hours? The most favored of my life!" I retorted. "For, did I not see you—and see you alone—every day?"

"Fair words! Fair words!" she mocked gaily. "And I am crushed beneath such honor from the Governor's own secretary!"

"Greta!" I protested miserably. "Why will you laugh at me? Cannot you see—"

"Cannot I see," she finished, "how grand a personage you are become? The Governor swears by you. He has made you his secretary, even over the head of mine own brother who came to him so highly recommended. And poor Louis, forsooth, must content him with the office of your assistant. Truly, I am honored at your condescension in deigning to notice me."

"Greta," I exclaimed, "you have no right to speak so! You know it is cruelly unjust. I ask only to be near you—to—"

"To tell me, perchance, of the Moon Maiden who leaned above you and showered Mayflowers into your hands? Oh, look not so glum! The tale has gone abroad. It has made you quite a hero in the eyes of these placid little New Amsterdam damsels. Who was she, Dirck?"

"The maid of my dreams?" I asked. "The woman whose face and voice are ever before me? "

"Aye. Who—"

"Men call her 'Greta Van Hoeck,'" said I. "But I call her—"

"The trick of speech is still yours," she declared. "It brings back to me those long, weary days aboard ship."

"Long? Weary? Would we were back there!"

"Nay, let us be doubly grateful we are not!" she cried. "Even the New World has enough gaieties to make one glad to forget—"

"To forget those we once fancied we cared for?" I queried bitterly. "*I* am not so fortunate."

"No?"

"No!" I repeated. "Our voyage seems to have been to you a dreary season wherein even so stupid a wight as I served to pass the time a bit the less tediously. To *me* it meant more. More than you know or would care to know. Moonlight spells 'madness.' Yet, I would the awakening were less sharp."

I made as though to ride on. But, womanlike, she sought to stay a victim who seemed about to pass beyond her capricious reach.

"Dirck!" she called softly.

At the old, sweet note in her voice my resentment died. Again the mist of infatuation blinded me. I halted, and reined back beside her.

"I have seen you so seldom," she said, lowering her eyes. "Since we landed, you have almost seemed to avoid me. And after all your sweet protests, too! I feared you had but sought to lighten a long voyage by toying at mock love. Can you blame me that I feared to show my own heart when I thought—"

"Greta," I panted, "I was wrong! Brutal! Forgive me!"

She flashed her dazzling smile into my sorrowful, eager face.

"Let there be peace between us!" she commanded. "And, in token thereof, you shall tell me the secret that was on your lips that terrible night when—"

"I—I cannot!" I stammered.

Full oft since that evening of moonlit madness I had fiercely rebuked myself for the weakness that had led me to the partial divulging of my great mission.

"I cannot!" I repeated wretchedly. "Ask me anything else. The secret is not mine. If it were—"

"If it were," she interposed, "I wonder if it would still endanger your life, as you then told me it would? And if the king—"

"Hush!" I begged, with a startled glance toward the others.

"Tell it to me!" she pleaded, her eyes alight with cajolery, her lovely face perilously close to mine. "Tell me—*Dirck!*"

Again that wild intoxication mounted to my brain like strong drink. But, with a struggle that left me trembling, I cried again:

"Oh, I *cannot!* I—"

She must have seen that, strong as was her spell, my resolve was at last stronger. For, with a short, hard laugh, she flicked me lightly across the brow with the tassel of her riding-whip, as she rode off after the rest, murmuring:

"Perchance the little I already know might make rare telling. *Au revoir,* Master Secretary!"

I do not know why it is, but women can say things that sting and that worry me ten times worse than could any words from another man.

I rode on toward the Governor's home in anything but a happy frame of mind. On shipboard I had half believed that Greta returned my love. Since our landing she had dropped the dear old manner. To-day, for a moment, she had resumed it, and had set all my heart-strings to throbbing again—only to leave me with a mocking smile and with something very like a threat.

The peril conjured up by her parting words troubled me little, so far as I myself was concerned. As to its possible effect on my mission, that was quite another matter.

I had been working hard, day and night, to prepare the right sort of material for my report to the king.

While I had succeeded in some ways even better than I had dared hope, yet I did not wish to forward the report as complete until I could find out, past doubt, the way a certain large and terribly important element of the New Netherlands population would accept a change to English rule.

This element was—the Indian population. Across the East and Hudson rivers, and to the north above Haarlem, the land still teemed with savages.

The Dutch had more than once clashed with them. Under Governor Kieft, Stuyvesant's infamous predecessor, there had been a massacre of the helpless Indians who dwelt beyond the Palisades.

True, a peace had later been patched up, and Stuyvesant's just laws had done much to pacify the avenging savages. But—who can read the Indian mind? Even I, who had spent much of my youth among them, scarce understood their ways.

It might be that they were at heart loyal friends to the Dutch, and that they would resent British conquest by sending fire and tomahawk through every settlement of new-arrived Englishmen.

Or, if they still hated the Dutch, they might prove mighty allies to King Charles, in the event of a British attack upon the New Nether-lands.

I must find out their attitude to my own satisfaction before sending report, and announcing that all was ready for our scheme's completion.

But how could I hope to study the situation? What chance had I, seated at a secretarial desk, to feel the pulse of this great, lurking element in our problem's solution?

I knew there were disaffected savages—Indians who resented Stuyvesant's order that liquor and firearms must not be sold to them. But how large or how small a percentage of their people these ever-threatening malcontents represented I could not guess.

My broodings were interrupted as my horse, from long habit, turned in at the wide gateway at the private drive that led up to Stuyvesant's mansion. I entered the Governor's study to find Louis Van Hoeck already at work over a sheaf of papers. One or two clerks were in the room, and Stuyvesant himself was stumping up and down, dictating a peppery letter to the ever-meddling Holland states general.

I went over to my desk and settled down to my routine work.

Outside, the bees were droning drowsily in the honeysuckle. Inside, the only sound, between the harsh-grunted sentences of Stuyvesant's dictation, was the scraping of quill-pens.

Seldom have I been present at a duller, stupider, more commonplace scene. Then, in the wink of an eye, came the change.

Something whizzed into the room, through the open window, with a funny little whistling sound, struck with a click against no less important an obstacle than Governor Petrus Stuyvesant's own sacred wooden leg, and clattered to the bare floor.

Everybody jumped up. I was first to reach the spot where, on the boards in front of the amazed Governor, lay a long arrow.

"Indians!" bawled a nervous clerk. "An attack!"

"Peace, fool!" growled Stuyvesant. "You will have all the women-folk in the house screeching about us like a brood of peafowl. 'Tis no attack! The sentries, else, would have set up a hullabaloo ere now. Give me the arrow, Dirck."

I had picked up the missile, and now handed it to him.

"H-m!" he muttered, unrolling a strip of birchbark that was wound close about the shaft. "As I thought! I have heard of this sort of message. 'Tis no attack, I say," he consoled the still trembling clerk. "See, the arrow-head is blunted."

We crowded about him as he proceeded to stretch out the white birchbark sheet. On it were scrawled, in charcoal, a few laboriously inscribed words in very bad Dutch. The Governor, amid a general hush, read aloud:

> EXCELLENCY:
> I am your friend, for I sell my bearskins to your traders. But my people do not love you.
> The murder of our women and children by Kieft is burned into many hearts. Let your guard be sleepless. For my people swear to repay.

I glanced out of the window. Meadows and tilled fields rolled away on every side.

The nearest "cover" was a tongue of woodland that ran out into the fields to westward almost a furlong distant.

From within the shelter of this the red-skinned "friend" must have launched his odd, anonymous communication.

The room was instantly alive with confused comment. Stuyvesant, smiting his silver-shod leg on the floor for silence, at length restored quiet.

"Perchance 'tis a silly, practical joke by one of our own graceless boys," he commented.

"Pardon, your excellency," said I. "This is a blunted *war*-arrow. The braves guard these weapons carefully, and neither give nor barter them. No boy of the colony could have procured *it.*"

He looked at me in grudging admiration.

"You talk sense," he observed. "But where got you your knowledge of the different sorts of Indian arrows?"

"I have told your excellency," I answered boldly, "that this is not my first visit to America. As a runaway lad, I once traveled from Massachusetts Bay to the Delaware with a party of trappers. We lived for months among the savages. I picked up a knowledge of their ways and a smattering of some few dialects."

"So? I had forgot. Have you means, then, of guessing whether this arrow came from the tribes that dwell behind Breucklen or Haarlem or the Palisades? "

"I take it the sender was a brave of the tribes living beyond the Palisades," I answered.

"Why?"

"It was the Palisade Indians that Governor Kieft assailed. And that assault is spoken of in the screed you hold."

"I see. You are right. I would this had not happened. Have I not enough to vex me, with the states general at Holland ever interfering, the burghers of New Amsterdam grumbling, and the Swedes on the Delaware quarreling with our traders? And now this new menace!"

He was speaking to himself rather than to us. Presently he turned to me again.

"Since you have proven so apt in Indian lore," said he, "what is your opinion? Is this warning important or—"

"Your excellency," I made reply, "an Indian seldom plays a joke. Nor does he risk being picked off by a sentry merely to shoot useless arrows through an open window. I take it the warning is not only genuine, but of real import. The sender is probably a hunter whose living is made by trading in skins with your people. Should the colony be destroyed, his livelihood would cease. Hence the message."

"It is good sense," the Governor agreed, his head bowed in thought on his chest. "Good sense. You have a level brain, lad. What suggestion can you make?"

All at once I saw my longed-for "chance" had come. I saw, too, that it involved fearful danger.

"Your excellency," I replied slowly, as though pondering my words, "some petty tribe may be mouthing threats. In which case we are safe enough. On the other hand, there may well be a conspiracy that runs through all the tribes west of the Palisades. In that event, New Amsterdam already lies in the hollow of Fate's hand."

"Tush, man," he broke in, "I know that. Don't preach a sermon. I asked—"

"There is but one way of learning the truth," I continued. "Send some one into the wilderness disguised as a trapper, and let him gather what information he can from the redskins."

"Gather information?" scoffed Van Hoeck. "More likely lose a scalp."

"*Much* more likely," I gravely agreed. "Yet should he escape alive, his news would be of value to the colony. Mynheer Van Hoeck," I went on maliciously, "perchance you will volunteer for the service. It ought to mean promotion—either in his excellency's service or in a better world."

"Peace!" cried Stuyvesant, checking Louis's angry retort. "Dewitt is right, as he has a way of being. Lad," he went on, addressing me in gruff friendliness, "there is but one man I know who could carry so ticklish an expedition to possible success. But, as it means dire risk of life, I am loath to ask it."

"There is no need of 'asking it,' your excellency," I retorted. "I beg you to let me volunteer."

The grizzled old warrior stamped his wooden leg in approval.

"Good lad!" he bawled. "And your reward shall be—"

"Your excellency," I interrupted (unconsciously using almost the same words as I had employed toward King Charles), "my reward shall be the serving of my country."

As I made the ambiguous speech the others applauded loudly. But Louis Van Hoeck remained silent. His silence and the strange smile that played about his thin lips vaguely alarmed me.

CHAPTER VIII.
Near Neighbor to Death.

THE forest—the forest that I loved! Mile upon mile of tumbled green, the big hills everywhere, and at their feet the fire-blue mountain lakes.

And through the mighty midsummer silences I strode. My bearded and bronzed face, my once dandified costume changed for the coarse fur garments of a trapper; my court rapier discarded for a long musket and hunting-knife—few at casual glance would have taken me for a New Amsterdam official.

For weeks I had roamed the greensward. Westward for many miles from Hudson River I had wandered. Here and there I had boldly entered Indian camps, chaffering for skins and tobacco, and winning safety by vague hints that on a future trip I might be able to smuggle to the braves some of the firearms and fire-water that Stuyvesant had declared contraband.

I had learned much. The tribes that occupied that vast tract of the New Netherlands, nowadays known as "the Jerseys," hated the Dutch. There was much talk of a descent upon New Amsterdam.

Daily the confederation was strengthening.

One element was lacking to make it perfect. That was the doubtful attitude of the Arareeks, a powerful northern tribe who held the Pomp-i-ton region.

Should the Arareeks favor war on the Dutch, the whole country west of the Palisades would be united. And Stuyvesant's best efforts could scarce save the city from attack—perhaps from destruction.

Thus it was that I had at last turned my face northward to visit the Arareeks. I had learned all I needed to know, save the exact feeling of this tribe toward the colony. When I should have determined that my work would be done.

I could then return to Stuyvesant with full information. What was infinitely more important, I could send a complete report to King Charles and set in instant motion the machinery for making the New Netherlands an English province.

I was resolved to tell Stuyvesant the whole truth as to the sentiments of the Indians. Not only because I had pledged myself to do so, but because my plans included no massacre of innocent people.

It was enough for me to know the savages would welcome any change from Dutch rule. I did not wish to see a peaceful city harassed uselessly by hatchet and flame.

I had tramped long that day. I was very tired. I know I was in the country of the Arareeks. But just where lay their chief's village I could not guess. Reaching a lake's edge, I threw myself down for an hour's rest.

The soft whisper of the trees and the hum of the myriad invisible tiny forestfolk all blended into a drowsy lullaby note. I had meant only to rest. Instead, I slept—slept like a log.

From heavy slumber I entered at last the lighter, less dense realms of dreamland. It was a troubled journey through the shades. The thing that worst annoyed me was the fact that something restless and rather heavy was moving about on my chest.

I aroused myself enough to give an impatient twist to my pectoral muscles. The slow, irritating motion ceased at once. But the light pressure was not removed. Indeed, it seemed to concentrate on one spot.

I moved impatiently once more, half opening my eyes. My sleepy motion brought forth a sharp, whirring sound, dry as a locust's note. The sound came from somewhere very near.

I stared, still barely half awake. Then all at once I became the wakefulest, if most motionless, man in all America.

There, on the summit of my chest, just within range of my downcast eyes, coiled a rattlesnake. The creature was as thick as my wrist.

He had doubtless been crawling across my inert body when my sudden movement had startled him and awakened in his brain the rage that is such reptiles' second nature.

Coiled compactly, his flat, arrow-shaped head reared twelve inches or so in air, his long rattle spinning like an angry bee's wings—he had already drawn back his slender neck for a blow at my defenseless face.

It is a moment on which I do not enjoy looking back.

A bite on leg or arm from any of our American serpents can usually be healed by means of ligature and cautery. But a bite on the face or body cannot be ligatured, and is too often apt to be fatal, unless a surgeon is at hand.

I realized all this. I knew something of rattlesnakes; enough, at least, to be certain that the swiftest move of my hand or body in an attempt to dislodge the monster would not be one-tenth so quick as the stroke of that deadly head.

So, helpless, I awaited my fate. A bare three seconds, at most, had passed since I had opened my eyes upon the horror. They seemed to me three lifetimes.

So, here was the end of my youth, my high hopes, my life!

I watched the slowly, back-drawn venomous head with a queer, almost impersonal, interest.

I knew the creature was preparing for his stroke. So I had seen such a snake strike at a quivering rabbit in the New England hills.

The head poised, I closed my eyes. As I did so the air about me split into a thunderous roar.

Instinctively my eyes flew open. There was the serpent, still coiled and with upraised neck. But—I could not yet understand—*the head was gone!*

It was an odd, gruesome sight. I gaped at it, wondering if I were delirious from fear.

Then, as I stared, the neck slowly sank. The great thick coils relaxed. The body that had a moment before been so instinct with murderous life rolled limply off my chest onto the ground.

I sprang to my feet. I could not, in my dazed condition, even yet understand the simple miracle that had saved me.

Then my wondering eyes fell upon a canoe scarce fifty feet out in the stream. In it sat an Indian, whose slender fingers still grasped a smoking rifle.

And, all at once, I knew. The savage, paddling near shore—perhaps to investigate my own sleeping presence there—had seen the snake and fired.

The ball had carried away the reptile's head. It was a beautiful shot. A half inch to either side would have caused a fatal miss. Had the ball passed six inches lower it must have buried itself in my body.

To score such a mark called not only for wondrous shooting, but for a nerve of chilled steel. So much hung upon failure that the coolest marksman might have been pardoned for trembling.

The setting sun streaming across the lake was in my eyes, turning the canoe and its burden into a jet black silhouette. I raised a somewhat shaky hand above my head in the "peace sign."

Then I called out, in the Delaware dialect and in the flowery language of redskin courtesy:

"A thousand thanks! You saved me from the 'Creeping Death,' O brother! My life lies at your feet."

The Indian had picked up the paddle that lay across the canoe's thwarts and, with a few long, easy strokes, brought the craft to shore.

There had been no reply to my florid speech of gratitude. So I tried once more, this time using the "Trader dialect" that passed current among the Five Nations and many of the tribes to southward.

"Brother," said I, "I owe you my life. Accept—"

The Indian stepped ashore and faced me, interrupting my halting speech with a laugh of silver.

"Twice have you called me 'brother,'" came the unexpected greeting, in Dutch. "And both times in a language you can scarce speak. Why not use your own native tongue? And"—with another laugh—

"why not say—*'sister'*?"

It was a woman. Yes, and no Indian, though darkly sunburnt and in native dress.

But all these details, as well as my own ludicrous mistake, were swept from my thoughts by what a second glance told me.

She was the "dream maiden" who had saved me from the sea, and from whose girdle that mystic spray of Mayflowers had fallen!

CHAPTER IX.
THE WILDERNESS WOMAN.

I LOOKED at her—long and in silent amaze. She returned my gaze—at first in cool surprise, then doubtfully, at last in dawning recognition.

"The—the dream," I muttered, foolishly enough, "the maiden of the Mayflower dream!"

Her grave little face, with its childlike eyes, broke into a slow smile that made me think of a sunshine rift after a gray day.

"Herr Dirck Dewitt," she said in mock solemnity, "you are very welcome to the Arareek country. But I scarce expected to see you as a trapper. When last we met, you had more the look of a very wet man of fashion."

"You—you know my name?" I faltered.

"'Twas writ on a bundle of letters that fell from your jacket into the boat that night," she answered. "We found them—later."

"Later?" I echoed. "After you had saved me? It seems I am twice in your debt for the poor gift of life. Twice, out of empty space, have you come in a boat to save me."

"'Twas my father who saw you in the water that night," said she, "and who picked you up. He brought you back to your senses. Then, when you sank into a heavy, trancelike sleep of pain and exhaustion, it was he and our Indian boatman who laid you at the threshold of the White Hall in New Amsterdam."

"It was they who—"

"'Twere not well for my father to be seen by the folk of *any* city," she answered sadly. "That is why he dared not do more for you. But he made sure your life was in no peril ere he left you."

"You speak much of your father's goodness to me," I said, "yet—yet—it was *your* face that bent above me in the boat that night—*your* hands that bathed my bruised head."

"You were senseless," she protested. "How can you know? You opened your eyes but once. And then—"

"And then," I made answer, "I saw *you*. The Mayflowers—"

I broke off in my bewilderment.

"It somehow seems so natural—so much a part of my dream—to be speaking with you again," I went on, "that I half forget the strangeness of it all. A month or more ago, when I was cast into the Atlantic Ocean, you were there and rescued me. To-day, when I was in still more dire plight, fifty miles from that ocean, you once more come to my aid. How chance you to be here?"

"It is my house," she answered simply.

"But the Atlantic?" I insisted. "Is that, too, your home? Or—"

"My father," said the girl, "can have no home save the wilderness. His friend—under the same ban as himself and sharer of our exile— fell ill and longed to see England again at whatever risk. We arranged for a Dover-bound sloop to meet him a mile off the Southern coast. We had rowed him to the sloop and were returning when an explosion shook the sea. We rowed near to the fragments of a ship. There, floating unconscious, we found you."

I wondered more and more. She wore the dress of an Indian. Her long brown hair lay loose in waving ripples. Her soft skin was tanned dark. Yet she had the voice and speech of a gentlewoman. She spoke of her father as an exile who dared show his face in no city.

"Tell me," I begged, "can I do naught for your father? I have some small influence at New Amsterdam. And—"

"No," she answered, with a little shake of her head, "the Dutch are not his foes. I thank you none the less."

"But," I insisted, "you said he dared not be seen in New Amsterdam."

"There are English in New Amsterdam," she replied; "yes, and Dutch burghers, too, to whom five thousand pounds were too rich a reward to be missed. He would be seized—"

"Your father?" I repeated, amazed. "But surely no man in the colonies is important enough to have a price of five thousand pounds on his head?"

"Nevertheless," she declared, "that is the sum King Charles of England has offered for his capture, dead or alive. Oh, in England the very name of Goffe—"

"What!" I cried, aghast. "*William* Goffe, the regicide?"

"The martyr!" she corrected me, her eyes flashing.

"Forgive me," I made humble amends. "I did but use the general term. I crave your pardon."

Europe and the colonies, too, had been scoured by British agents in vain search for this man. Well did I recall his history.

A stanch Puritan, Goffe had been one of the judges who had condemned to death Charles I, the King of England. Later, he had served right valiantly as general in Cromwell's army.

At the time of the Restoration, Charles II had shown scant mercy to the foes of his slain father. Against Goffe in particular his vengeance had been unremitting.

It was known that the "regicide" and his friend Whalley had fled to America. There all trace of them had long since been lost.

And this "dream maiden" was Goffe's daughter!

At my confused apology her frown relaxed. Now, at a thoughtless question from me, it was replaced by a glance of suspicion.

"And William Goffe," I exclaimed, "is *here*—in this wilderness?"

"Yes," she made answer. "There can be no harm in telling you. You have not the face of an informer or a seeker for blood-money. Yet, if you were English instead of Dutch, I should sooner go dumb to my grave than tell you as much as I have."

Somehow it was hard to lie to this clear-eyed, slender girl whose head came scarce so high as my heart. Nay, for some unexplained reason, I could not even deceive her by letting well enough alone. I must needs blurt out like any guilty schoolboy:

"But I *am* English."

She stared at me uncertainly.

"Your name," she murmured, in doubt, "is not—"

"I am English," I repeated, "or rather, American."

"An exile?" she queried hopefully.

"No," I said.

"Not not a king's man?"

"Yes," I admitted. "I am in this very wilderness to-day on a secret mission for King Charles."

Why I said it, I don't know. In the case of Greta Van Hoeck, the secret had once been half dragged from me by mingled witchery and moonlight. At another time I had wholly resisted her coaxings.

Yet I had been feverishly in love with Greta. Now, this wilderness woman, whom I most assuredly did *not* love—whom I scarce knew—was making it impossible for me to hide my heart's secrets.

Let him who deems me weak remember I knew little of women. Also let him look into eyes like the dream maiden's and still resist their spell—if he can.

The effect of my words upon the girl was electrical.

Dropping her empty rifle and catching up my own gun, she coolly presented the weapon's muzzle at my chest.

"A spy?" she queried.

Still bewildered, I could only nod.

"The only secret mission that could bring a spy of King Charles to this part of the wilderness," she declared, "is the search for my father and a craving for the price set on his innocent head. You tracked him here. I, in my folly, have confirmed you in your search. Oh, that any man could stoop so low!"

"No!" I cried. "You are wholly wrong —wholly! I—"

"The man who rescued you from drowning," she went on, a sad irony in her voice, "the man whose daughter has even now stood between you and death! But why waste words on such a creature? You are my prisoner, Master Spy! One move, except at my order, and I pull trigger. You have seen a sample of my shooting."

The humor of the thing slowly dawned upon me. Here was I, a giant, who could crush an ordinary man at a single blow. Here was she, a fragile wisp of a girl, scarce eighteen years old at most. Yet she was very determinedly making me her captive.

I had much ado to keep my face straight.

"I am indeed your prisoner," I replied. "Will it please you to place me on parole?"

"Parole?" she flashed. "One does not trust the word of spies! You will march in front of me to the canoe. If you turn or attempt to escape, I shall draw trigger."

Solemnly I moved down the bank to the waiting boat.

"Halt!" came the frigid orders of my captor. "Now enter the canoe. Go to the stern and sit down. Pick up the paddle."

I followed instructions with cringing meekness. I seated myself in the stern, paddle in hand. She stepped into the birch-bark craft and took her seat in the prow.

"Now," she resumed, still covering me with my own rifle while she laid her empty weapon in the bottom of the canoe, "paddle! You *can* paddle, I suppose?"

"A little," I said. "In which direction?"

"To the left—around that promontory. When we round that we will be in sight of the village. Paddle me thither. You sought for my father. You shall find him—in the midst of two hundred loyal Indian friends. So I doubt me if your discovery will ever bring you the coveted five thousand pounds."

"Can you show me no mercy?" I groaned.

"None!" she returned firmly. "For injury to myself I would most freely forgive you. For harm to my blameless father there is no forgiveness. You came here to seek him. Very well! You shall have your wish."

"But will he not order his redskin friends to put me to death?" I whined.

"Probably," was her cold reply. Yet I saw a little shade of trouble cross her face.

"'Tis humiliating," I sighed, "to be made prisoner by a mere girl. And with my own rifle, too. I am half tempted to upset the canoe and—"

"At your first movement to either side," she warned me, "I shall fire."

Without further words, I submitted. Presently my long paddle-strokes brought the light canoe around the promontory. On a knoll above a cove, scarce a quarter-mile distant, I saw a cluster of huts and tepees.

At last I was in touch with the chief Arareek village. The girl, without turning, whistled long and shrilly. The note must have been a signal, for a number of Indians appeared from amid the huddle of lodges and started down to the water-edge to meet us.

From the largest hut I saw two tall figures emerge. One was that of a young Indian, scarce thirty years old at most, clad in the garb and insignia of a tribal chief. The other was a venerable man, dressed in black European clothes and with a snowy beard that fell well-nigh to his waist.

As we drew near to the village, a great black-crested loon rose from beneath the lake's surface a bare seventy feet from us.

The girl saw him. Her fingers twitched on the rifle.

"Pardon," I suggested humbly, "but I would not advise you to try a shot at him. You see—my rifle is not loaded!"

"*What?*"

"I drew the charge during this morning's thunder-storm," I continued shamefacedly; "and neglected to reload."

"And—and you *pretended*—"

"No, no!" I protested. "I was your prisoner I am. Have I your leave to land?"

The canoe prow grated on the pebbly beach. The white-bearded man had been scanning me closely from under his arched palm. Now, as our eyes met, he hastened to the brink, both hands held out to me in eager welcome.

"My dear, dear boy!" he cried. "To think of our meeting again after all these years!"

As I returned his hearty grip, I glanced over my shoulder at the girl. Her sunburnt face was scarlet with mortification.

"*Oh!*" she gasped, encountering my amused gaze. "I hate you! I *hate* you!"

CHAPTER X.
The Future of America.

WILLIAM GOFFE turned to the young chief at his side.

"Macopin," he exclaimed, "chance has thrown a welcome guest our way. This is a friend of other days who once aided me right loyally. Accept him as your own friend for my sake."

The chief, with a kindly dignity, raised his hand to his brow; then extended it, palm upward, to me.

"I greet you," he said in excellent English. "Our poor home is yours."

Even as he spoke his eyes strayed past me and rested for a moment with strange tenderness upon the girl.

"You have already met my daughter, I see," said Goffe. "Blanche, did he tell you he and I were olden friends? "

"No, sir," returned the girl shortly. "Nor did you mention it when we picked him up in the ocean." And she made as though to move onward to the huts.

"Picked him up in the ocean!" echoed Goffe, detaining her. "I do not understand."

"It was this gentleman," she went on, trying to master her chagrin, "whom we—whom you—rescued from the debris of the burning ship."

"No," cried Goffe. "And yet—well, 'tis not strange I did not recognize him in the moonlight. The man we picked up was smooth-shaven and wore his hair in court fashion. Now, in forest garb—"

"Yet *you*, Mistress Goffe," I put in, "recognized me to-day when you met me, bearded and in trapper dress."

"It fell to my lot," she evaded coldly, "to dress your hurts that night while my father minded the helm. He scarce had a glance at your face. I was unable to avoid seeing it plainly and for a long time."

"Young eyes," supplemented Goffe, "see more than old ones. By daylight I can still make shift to use mine with the best of them. But after dark I find my vision sadly wanting. A step toward old age, I suppose. Yet," he went on, "the papers that fell from your pocket in the boat bore the name 'Dirck Dewitt.' That is a Dutch name. And you were an English Colonist in the days I knew you."

"You knew Mynheer Dewitt?" asked the girl, curiosity overcoming indignation. "You knew him and called him 'friend'? And yet you did not know his name?"

"Names counted for less at that crisis than deeds," returned Goffe. "Whalley and I had but just smuggled ourselves into Boston. Every man's hand was against us. We made our way to the hills above Hadley, in the Massachusetts Bay colony. The hue and cry was at our heels, a price on our heads. We hid in the caves above Hadley village."

"I remember," she murmured, pressing his hand. "'Twas the year before I came out from England to—"

"To turn your back on comfort and home and share an old man's exile," he finished gratefully. "Whalley and I hid in the caves. And there we were like to starve, for we durst not enter the village. One day a settler's son, hunting among the hills, found our hiding-place. He learned our sorry plight, although he asked not our identity. And daily for a month he brought us food."

"It was well," approved the young chief, Macopin, with a grave nod.

"We had long chats with him in those days of hiding," resumed Goffe. "And ere he left that part of the country he arranged to have provisions and clothing and arms sent to us. I have never forgotten. And to-day I meet him here—hundreds of miles away from the caves of Hadley. It is rare good fortune."

"Months later, sir," I said, "I went through Hadley again. There I heard a strange tale of an attack by the Pequots upon the villagers during my absence. The folk were ready to fly in panic, when you appeared among them, sword in hand, led them to the rout of their savage foes, and then—vanished. An old Cromwellian soldier in the village recognized you as General William Goffe. It was thus I learned the name of the man who had so oft and so entertainingly talked to me."

"I am sorry," whispered a penitent little voice in my ear as we all moved up the slope, toward the huts; "I am sorry I said I hated you. And—and I am sorry I called you a spy."

She was so little, so childlike, so appealing, I had much ado in refraining from lifting her up bodily and kissing her, as I might have done to some winsome forest baby.

"Mistress Goffe," I answered gently, "it was *I* who should be craving pardon for the scurvy trick I played you about the rifle. Believe me, I wish it *had* been loaded—"

"If you talk that way," she interrupted, her momentary penitence giving place to a flare of spirit, "I shall be sorry, too, that it was empty. Or that I fired my own rifle at a mere snake instead of saving the charge for a better purpose."

As I replied lightly I caught the eye of the young chief, Macopin, fixed on us in a troubled, almost lowering, look.

It was at the camp-fire that night when Goffe, Macopin, Blanche, and I sat together before the chief's own hearth, that I spoke openly of my errand and of all the hopes and plans that were mine.

Goffe, to whom I had broached the subject before supper, had vouched for Macopin's loyalty and wisdom. He loved the handsome young chief, so lately raised to the head of his tribe. And he bade me profit by his counsel and aid.

So it was that I told him my story. Goffe sat upon a felled log, across the fire from me, listening gravely and tugging sometimes at his long beard.

Blanche sat at his feet, her head against his knee, the firelight playing fitfully across her eager little face. Macopin, in his place at the end of the hearth, heard me in grave silence, his eyes now and again straying furtively toward Blanche.

None interrupted until my tale was done. I described my interview with King Charles, my journey across sea, my employment with Stuyvesant, the object of my wilderness wanderings, and outlined my reasons for believing that England's present rule of the Colonies would mean America's best welfare.

When I had finished there was a brief pause. Then Goffe spoke.

"The idea is good," he declared. "It is feasible, and it will unite all the Atlantic colonies. Who can lay what that union may not mean in future ages? It is for the future of America that you are working, Dirck."

"The future of America," repeated the chief slowly. "The words mean much to you. And, since I am your brother, I offer you my aid. But what is the 'future of America' to me and mine? To the people who for countless centuries have ruled this land? The future to us stretches out dreary and barren as a rainy sea. The white man's gain must ever be our loss. And one day our homes shall forget the very name of 'Indian.' Still," rousing himself from his gloomy reverie, "what must be must be. He is a fool who stands up against the tornado of destiny. Do you ask any help?"

I nodded, distressed at the bitter hopelessness in the savage's tone.

"Then," he went on, "in a small way I can aid you. That you reached this spot at all, through so dense a mass of the tribesmen who are hostile to white men, is a miracle of fortune. You could scarce count on as good a venture during your return journey. I will go to New Amsterdam with you. My presence will serve as your passport through my people. I will even appear before your governor to confirm your tale of their hostility and to vouch for the Arareeks' neutrality. Is it well?"

"It is well," I made answer. "From my heart I thank you."

Blanche sighed softly to herself. At the slight sound Macopin turned quickly toward the girl, seeming to divine her thought.

"It grows wearisome for you," said he, "to dwell ever in the wilderness, far from the laughter and social pleasures that are a part of cities and of youth. If it is your wish, and if your father will grant consent, join our expedition. My mother shall go along to care for you. At New Amsterdam you shall meet other maids—yes, and men, too. And, perchance, their amusements and innocent follies may serve to make good holiday for you."

The vision that rose to my mind, of the wild forest girl, tanned, loose-haired, in her half-Indian garb, moving among the prim, capped-and-kerchiefed damsels of the Dutch city, was dispelled by the eager, childlike joy wherewith she greeted the suggestion.

Her father gave reluctant consent. To hide his pleasure at the happiness he had afforded her, Macopin turned to me.

"You speak of the report," he said, "that you are about to send your king. How shall you get it to him? A packet thus addressed, despatched on a New Amsterdam ship, would—"

"Give me credit for a scrap of judgment," I interposed, nettled by what I chose to think his superior tone. "That was arranged ere I left England. The packet is to be addressed to 'Mynheer Troup, Cronstadt, Haag.' 'Tis the name of a secret agent of England's Dutch ambassador. Troup will bear it to the ambassador, who hath royal order to send it by courier direct to his majesty. One week from the day the report reaches him a British war flotilla, under Colonel Nicolls, will leave Southampton for 'special service.' That 'service' will carry the flotilla straight across seas until Nicolls casts anchor off the Battery fort."

"And," the chief persisted, "your report. You have it safe?"

"Naturally. 'Tis complete now, save for my news of the Indians. So

I dare not leave it where prying hands can touch it. 'Tis locked safe in the drawer of my desk in the White Hall. And—"

"In a *desk?*" cried Macopin, almost lifted out of his customary grave calm. "In a house where many men congregate?"

"And why not?" I asked crossly. "The desk is locked."

"Locked!" he almost groaned. "Are there none who can force locks? Or is it past reason that your governor, in search of some paper of import, should bethink him that such paper might be in his secretary's desk, and order the desk opened?"

"'Tis most improbable," I scoffed; nevertheless, feeling a little chill of apprehension.

"Also," he pursued, "you spoke of a foe. One Van Hoeck, with whom you fought, and whom later you supplanted as secretary. His hate might well set him to searching for cause against you."

I smiled in lofty contempt.

"None in New Amsterdam suspect me," said I. "They deem me a zealous supporter of Stuyvesant. Why should they search the desk of such a man?"

He lifted his black eyebrows, but made no reply. And at the moment a vagrant thought turned me white.

Greta Van Hoeck knew I was not what I seemed. She had wit. She might readily piece together what I had told her into a fabric of suspicion that would set her brother on my track.

In a breath I banished the thought as unworthy. Greta would surely never sink to so vile an action. No woman could bring herself to put in jeopardy the life of a man who had never harmed her. To bolster up my wavering self-complacence, I continued:

"Chief, I am not wholly a fool. I have taken what precautions were needed. I am seldom tricked."

He made no answer; but rose and, walking past me, moved toward his hat. Then, as if changing his mind, turned back and approached me again. In his hands were a little bundle of letters and a purse.

I recognized them as my own purse and as the letters that Goffe had picked up in the boat the night of my rescue and had that very evening, restored to me. Both had been in separate outer pockets of my tunic.

"Where—where found you these?" I demanded in open-mouthed

amaze.

"I took the liberty of removing them front your pockets as I passed by you just now," he answered quietly. "You see, the best and wisest of us may sometimes be 'tricked.'"

"But—"

"Be glad that I am not Van Hoeck, your enemy," he continued, "and that these papers are not your report. I ask your pardon for playing so idle a trick upon a guest. But for all of us it is well never to underestimate a foe."

Goffe's hearty laugh dispelled my tendency to anger.

"Macopin," he explained, "is a medicine man as well as a chief. Thus from babyhood he has been trained in sleight-of-hand. Be not angry at him, Dirck. The lesson will do you no harm."

Impulsively I held out my hand to the young chief.

"You were right, sir. And your rebuke is just. I spoke like a school-boy, and you reproved me more gently than I deserved. I ask your friendship."

"It is given," he exclaimed, his grave face lighting with kindly feeling. "And now let us make ready for the morrow's journey. For I am none too easy in my mind concerning that same report of yours."

And a tinge of his own uneasiness once more stung me like white hot iron.

CHAPTER XI.
Two Women.

THE "levee" of Governor Petrus Stuyvesant at the White Hall, New Amsterdam, was in full swing.

The great council-room was filled with burghers, officers, and women, all in such extremes of fashionable attire as the sober Dutch colony afforded.

For these monthly levees were the chief social features of New Amsterdam life. He who was not bidden thereto might as well regard himself as an outcast from colonial society.

As I entered the room, clean-shaven, my hunting garb exchanged for a coat of peach-blow satin, white silk small clothes and hose, gold-buckled shoes, and a throat-fall of Mechlin lace—my advent caused a right gratifying little stir throughout the company.

It was my first public appearance since my recent return from a "perilous journey through the hostile wilderness," as the governor's congratulations worded it. Also, I was known to be in high favor with his excellency because of the results of that same journey.

For, according to him, it had been my intervention alone that had prevented the Arareeks from joining the anti-Dutch federation. So I was, for the instant, a local celebrity.

We had reached New Amsterdam the previous day. Macopin, his mother, and Blanche had been lodged in solemn state in a suite of apartments at the old tavern facing upon the Bowling Green.

After making hasty visit to the governor and telling him the result of my trip, I had gone in guilty haste to my desk in the secretarial-room of the White Hall, had unlocked it, and rummaged for the packet holding my report to the king.

With a sigh of relief, I found it untouched. Macopin had accompanied me. With a slight gesture, I showed him that the seals were still intact. He made no comment, but moved away and looked out of the window.

I had worried foolishly over the matter ever since the chief's warning. Now the reaction was so keen I doubt not that it must have shown in my face. For, glancing up, the packet in my hands, I found that Louis Van Hoeck, from his own desk in the far corner, was eying me with evident interest.

"Some good fairy," he sneered, "has placed a parcel of wish-gold in your desk while you were gone? You gloat over yon packet as though—"

"Some routine papers I had mislaid," I answered coolly, "and which I rejoice to find again. For," I added, with perfect truth, "I wish to send them by to-morrow's ship to Holland."

I sat down and plied my pen right vigorously, completing my report. Then, resealing it and addressing it to "Mynheer Troup, the Cronstadt, Haag," I put it back in my desk and turned the key.

Van Hoeck, who had been writing busily, looked up again.

"I, too, am writing for to-morrow's post-ship," he said. "But I knew not that you had so important correspondence with Holland. I understood—"

"'Tis of personal import alone," I said lightly, pocketing the desk key. "Now I am off to get shaven and find change of clothes. A good night's rest will freshen me for to-morrow's levee."

I left the room, chuckling to myself at my former fears as to the report's safety.

My work was done.

As I entered the great room, next day, for the levee, Stuyvesant beckoned me across to him.

"This frill-and-folly gathering will end in an hour or less," said he, "and I have called a council meeting here at the levee's close. I forgot to speak of it to you. Also, make Chief Macopin remain for the council. Our deliberations may impress him. He and the maid you brought along will be here presently. Invitations were carried to them last night by my own orderly."

I moved away, and found myself the center of a youthful group that clamored for news of my forest exploits. As I talked at random, answering questions and parrying repartee, Greta Van Hoeck's eyes suddenly met mine amid the maze of faces. To my secret wonder, the sight no longer filled me with the old madness of infatuation. Ere I could analyze my change of feelings, she spoke.

"Louis tells me," said she, "of your triumphal entrance to the city yesterday. He says you bore as captives a veritable Falstaff army of tatterdemalions. An Indian chief, in full war-paint and wampum—"

"Indian chiefs," I interrupted, "do not wear war-paint on friendly visits. And wampum is—"

"And a hideous old witch of an Indian squaw," she continued, unheeding; "also a ragged, tousled-haired gipsy wench who—"

"Who thanks you most humbly for the description," spoke a clear young voice at my elbow.

Blanche and Macopin had entered the room unnoticed, and had reached my side just in time to catch Greta's words. I went scarlet with mortification, and others in the group looked genuinely horrified. But Greta's face changed not a whit. Gazing down at Blanche with a cool superiority, she said:

"I scarce thought you would hear me, Mistress Goffe. For I did not suppose you would come to the levee."

"Why not?" asked Blanche innocently. "One goes to all sorts of promiscuous places when one is holiday-making."

"I meant—" began Greta, a shade less composedly.

"Oh, pray do not apologize," smiled Blanche; "you knew no better."

A suppressed titter ran through the group. Greta's rose-and-cream complexion deepened a shade or so, and her eyes sparkled. Yet she made one more daring effort at superiority.

"I meant," said she, "that, coming from the wilderness, you would feel sadly out of place in such an assembly as this."

"I do, indeed," agreed Blanche sweetly. "In the wilderness rudeness to a guest is an unpardonable offense that is never committed."

"Your wilderness rules," snapped Greta, losing all her coolness when most she needed it, "seem as out of place in civilized society as does your wilderness costume."

"*Civilized* society?" echoed Blanche doubtfully.

"Yes. 'Tis doubtless your first visit to—"

"Oh!" cried Blanche, with a little laugh. "How stupid of me! You were referring to New Amsterdam social gatherings as 'civilized' society? I see now. We always regarded New Amsterdam as an outpost of civilization, you know."

"You in the wilderness regarded—"

"Oh, no. I was thinking of mine own dear old home—London. When last I appeared in what you call 'civilized society,' 'twas at the royal palace in London, at a state ball. I bethink me now of a certain gawky Hollander—a Dutch embassy attache—who came to the ball and roused much mirth and some pity by his boorish, provincial ways. In that gay, polished atmosphere he seemed like a stray donkey in a flock of peafowl. Poor man! His name, *mejuffrouw,* if I recall aright, was Van Hoeck—Louis Van Hoeck."

Greta's face was purple. Scarce would I have recognized the lofty beauty of old in this baited creature. But Blanche was as cool and unstirred as a Damascus blade—and as deadly.

"How strange;" she went on amusedly, as though changing a tiresome subject—"how strange is the effect of weather upon different women's hair! This morning's rain, which has tightened *my* locks into ringlets, seems to have dragged *yours* out into stringlets. I have been walking about this funny little town of yours to-day. 'Tis a quaint village, with its fifteen streets and its hideous squat houses. 'Twas laid out after the pattern of Holland cities, I am told."

"If you like not our ways, and if you scoff at our homeland," stormed Greta in a last flash of resistance, "why come you here?"

"At the invitation of Mynheer Dirck Dewitt," returned Blanche. "I and mine protected him from stinging reptiles and treacherous beasts in the wilderness. I had foolishly hoped he might be able to do as much for *me,* here. But—"

"Oh!"

In that monosyllable of utter impotent fury Greta Van Hoeck gave up the futile struggle. She strode away, glaring to left and right, at faces whose covert amusement seemed to madden her tenfold.

With a smile of utter innocence, Blanche turned to me.

"Was it not vastly amusing?" she asked.

"Yes!" I groaned. "It was—not! I have fought ere now for my life, and at various times I have encountered sundry other perils. Solemnly do I assure you that I count them all as naught compared with the battle I have just witnessed."

"'Witnessed' is the correct phrase," she answered; "for I note you took no share in it."

"I was afraid," I admitted. "Frightened past words. Ne'er again can I boast that I know not fear."

"And yet—"

"Spare me," I entreated. "You have done enough slaughter for one day. Turn not the sword-edge of your tongue upon a helpless man."

We had moved somewhat apart from the rest, into the embrasure of a window.

She looked up at me with an utter change from her former bright, icy mien.

"I have made you suffer," she said softly. "I am sorry."

"Nay," I cried reassuringly, "I was but in jest. Surely you understood that? The only 'suffering' I felt was that my guest should have been thus spoken to under the Governor's own roof. Yet what could I do? A man I could—and would—have challenged. But a woman—"

"You do not take my meaning," she broke in. "I made you suffer, I fear, talking to her as I did. You love her. Is it not so?"

Through my surprise at the simple, direct question ran again that same vague wonder. For, all at once, I knew I did *not* love Greta Van Hoeck. Indeed, I marveled—infatuation being fled—that ever I had fancied I loved her.

But how could I tell this to another woman? Perchance it would have been the correct thing to say. But I could not do it.

"There is no bond—no tie whatever—between Juffrouw Van Hoeck and myself. She regards me as the dust beneath her feet."

"I fear she does," sighed Blanche, "and, if she cared not for you ere this, she *loathes* you now."

"Now? But why now any more than—"

"A woman would understand," she answered, as though unable to explain to any one so stupid as a mere man. "She hates you. Saw you not the backward glance she cast as she hastened across the room toward her brother? You witnessed her public humiliation. You were its indirect cause. She—"

"She went across to her brother?" I interrupted, looking about me. "I see them not."

"They have left the room," said Blanche, without even turning to look. "Be on your guard, Master Dewitt! Neither of them loves you. From what I can read of faces, those two are not content to hate passively."

"Why said you that I—loved her?" I queried.

"Because, as we came into the room, I heard a burgher remark: 'Yonder is Secretary Dewitt singeing his wings once more at the flame of the most arrant, heartless flirt that ever crossed seas.' And—"

"Who said that?" I demanded hotly. "No man shall speak thus of me and—"

"I will not tell you," she retorted. "Nor shall you rage like any stage hero when you are supposed to be entertaining me. Fie, man! Where be your instincts as host?"

"Forgive me," I growled, half penitent, "I—"

"And now," she went on, "tell me who some of these gaudily clad folk are. Or—first," she corrected herself, glancing out of the long north window, "tell me the names of the places where Macopin and

I wandered this morning. For example—yonder twelve-foot wooden palisade, with its sharpened stakes and its two gun-mounted turrets. Is it a fort?"

"No. 'Tis the city wall. Northernmost boundary of New Amsterdam's actual borders. The lane alongside it is the Wall Street, and—"

"Then, to northward," she went on, "we came upon so pretty a lane, with a stream running alongside it, and girls washing clothes in the water. Look! From here you can see the linen drying on the hillock just below the lane. 'Twas like a quaint old picture."

"I know the place," I answered. "The maidens of New Amsterdam do all the city's washing there. At the path's foot is the ferry to Breucklen. The ferryman comes when summoned by a horn hung below on the bank, and, for three stivers, rows one across to the Breucklen shore—an hour's journey if the tide runs strong."

"We passed the ferry on our way back from our walk. We came along a crooked way that bent in half-moon fashion. A laughable street—"

"The Parel Straat (the Pearl Street)—our largest highway," I said. "Saw you the fort, with its twenty guns, by the Battery sea-wall? The church behind it is St. Nicholas's, where the Very Rev. Everardus Bogardus—"

"And there, just before the end of the Parel Straat, we saw a most horrible city jail!" she broke in, with a shudder. "With gallows and stocks reared in front of it. A gruesome sight. There!" she concluded. "I think I have wooed you from your black temper. I will force you to play guide chart no longer. Here comes Macopin. He does not look happy."

CHAPTER XII.
Mine Enemy.

THE chief moved toward us, crossing the room with its fast-thinned crowd, and moving with a regal grace that made the others look like yokels.

He still wore his native garb, though Blanche, on reaching town, had exchanged her half-savage costume for a simple gown and ker-chief.

"Brother," he asked as he reached us, "did you send your report by the post-boat that sails to-day?"

"I did," said I, "as I told you I should. I placed it in the post-bag an hour agone. It is on its way to the ship, doubtless, by now. The vessel sails at noon sharp, since the tide serves at that hour."

"A moment since," rejoined Macopin, "I saw the port messenger come here for the post-bag. It is but five minutes' walk to the ship. In ten minutes or so, if the sailing hour is not changed, the report should start on its journey overseas. And your work will be done."

I fancied I detected an odd note in his deep, grave voice; but I replied:

"Yes, the work is done. I trust the packet's wrapper will not tear during the voyage. For, underneath the covering whereon is inscribed Troup's name and dwelling-place, the inner parcel is addressed to King Charles himself. Yet, why should I worry? 'Tis safe."

Macopin scarce heeded me. Turning to Blanche, he said:

"The guests are leaving. And the council, to which I am bidden, is assembling. Perchance it would be well for you to return to the tavern."

His almost expressionless voice seemed ever to take on a subtle gentleness when he addressed the girl. I wondered at it; for, to Indians, women are usually inferior beings, unworthy of regard.

The last guests departed, curtsying or bowing low to his excel-lency as they backed through the wide doorway. Presently the doors were closed, and Stuyvesant stumped pompously across to the chair of state that had been drawn up at the head of the long table.

A long-faced clerk rose and droned forth the council roll, each member replying and taking a seat at the table as his name was called.

"De Hart, Leisler, Loockermans, Phillipse, Steenwyck, Van Cort-landt, Dewitt, Van Hoeck," intoned the clerk. Then he halted, and said again:

"Van Hoeck?"

As the second call came Louis slipped into the room. His thin face was flushed, his eyes shining with a strange glow.

"Here, master clerk," he replied, settling into his place and smiling across at me. I had seldom seen the man smile. Never at *me*. And the expression carried about as much friendliness as an oath or a kick.

Macopin, who had left my side a little earlier and had been strolling aimlessly about the corridors, now came in and seated himself respectfully on a stool near the window.

Stuyvesant looked up with a glower.

"Mynheer Van Hoeck," he rasped, "when I do men the honor to admit them to my council, I expect them to show their appreciation of that honor by being punctual. Pray do not force me to speak of it again."

"I crave your excellency's pardon," returned Louis, his sallow face betraying no such sullenness as it usually showed when he was crossed. "My sole excuse was that I was vigilant on your excellency's business. I beg leave to lay before this council a most urgent—"

"Later, man! Later!" snapped the Governor. "Who are *you*, to take precedence of your betters? Sit down, I say! You shall be heard in due time."

Reluctantly, Van Hoeck took his seat. Yet, though twice snubbed, he gave no sign of feeling the rebuff. That queer inward elation seemed still to buoy him up.

Stuyvesant was in one of his harshest moods to-day. 'Twas ever so in wet weather. Perhaps he suffered from neuralgia. Perhaps, as men whispered, at such times he felt a tingling and ache where his lost leg used to be. In either case, on these occasions he was about as pleasant a companion as a sick bear.

"Now then, *mynheers*," he said, after the routine business had been attended to, "we will take up the case of Heeren Meyln and Kuyter. These men now lodge in the city jail, by my warrant. They protested formally against certain features of my just rule. When I bade them tear up their silly petition and ask my pardon, they threatened to carry the matter before their high mightinesses." (The recognized title of the Holland States General.)

"I explained to them," boomed Stuyvesant, in growing wrath, "that to complain against one's Governor is high treason. I added that if I really believed these two men really intended to lodge complaint against me to their high mightinesses, I would hang the pair of them from the highest tree in the New Netherlands. Then clapped them into jail until their senses should return."

He, paused, glared about him from under his beetling brows, then went on in stiff formality:

"I have set this lamentable case before you, gentlemen, that I might learn your full and unbiased opinion of the matter. Well, well!" he shouted, as none replied. "What say ye? What say ye? Are ye all dumb? This is a council of free speech."

"I move that the council, as a whole, indorse his excellency's wise and merciful action," piped a fat-faced man far down the table.

The motion was gravely seconded and carried. Stuyvesant nodded grim approval, then began to sort out his papers in evident search for some document.

"Master clerk," he demanded, "what did you do with the notes you took on Secretary Dewitt's expedition among the Indians?"

"'Tis in my office, your excellency," replied the clerk. "I will go fetch it."

"While we wait," decided Stuyvesant, glancing around the board in search of some new cause for ire, and chancing to meet Louis Van Hoeck's eager gaze, "while we wait, we will e'en hark to this precious 'most urgent' business of Mynheer Van Hoeck's: Speak up, man! And make it brief."

Louis arose and walked toward the table's head, until he stood beside the Governor's chair. A red spot blazed in each of his yellow cheeks.

"Your excellency," he began, drawing a thin packet from inside his coat, "I am no informer, but I have the interest of Holland and of the New Netherlands at heart. And when I see those interests imperiled by a spy, I deem it my duty to speak out."

"What's all this pother about 'spies?'" snorted Stuyvesant. "And what is that thing you're sticking at me? What, is it, I say?"

"A paper that I entreat your excellency to read," answered Van Hoeck. "It tells its own story far more eloquently than could I. Read—and judge for yourself the fate that should be the writer's."

I half rose from my feet. My throat was sanded with utter terror. For, even at that distance, I easily recognized the packet he held. Its gray parchment covering, its oblong form, the untied tape and broken seals that had bound it—all were as familiar to me as was my own name.

It was the packet containing my full report to King Charles. His majesty's own name stood forth upon the inner covering, to be seen so soon as the inner wrapper should be removed.

Mine enemy had bided his time, and at the last he had bested me. I guessed the story. Greta, in her blind rage, had gone straight to Louis with the tale that I was on secret business, whose discovery spelled death. She had doubtless repeated my mention of the king.

With such a clue to go upon, Louis could not but have remembered my ill-hidden eagerness over the packet in my desk. From the mail-pouch he had abstracted that packet. He had broken the seals, learned the contents of the report and had brought the damning evidence straight to Stuyvesant.

Now, too, I understood his smile, his refusal to take offense. My life was forfeit. I could feel the rope about my neck.

Yet I was not minded to die so easily. To have staked heavily and then to lose without an effort was not in any man's nature. Forcing myself to cool self-control, I strode forward.

"By your excellency's leave," said I calmly, reaching for the packet that Louis was seeking to force into the Governor's hand, "as your secretary, permit me to take charge of this bit of correspondence, whatever it may be."

"Good lad!" approved Stuyvesant; "you are ever taking bothersome details off my shoulders. Glance over the thing and give us the gist of it."

My outstretched hand had touched the precious packet and my fingers had almost closed about it. But before I could secure my grip Van Hoeck had snatched the treasure back with a cry that was almost a screech.

"Hands off!" he yelled. "Hands off! You—*spy!*"

Here was my chance. Simulating righteous rage, I whipped out my sword and sprang at him.

"No man shall call me that vile name and live!" I shouted.

I hoped by a lucky blow to strike the packet from his hand and to seize it as it fell. But he was too quick. His own sword was out in a trice, and in his left hand the paper was held safe behind his back.

A bellow of outraged dignity from Stuyvesant, and a full dozen men had thrown themselves between us.

"Dewitt! Van Hoeck!" gurgled his excellency, almost speechless. "Zounds, black guards! What mean ye by drawing blade in our own council chamber? I have hanged men for less. Lay your swords on the table, both of ye. You are under arrest!"

"Is a true man to stand by meekly when he is called a spy?" I raged.

"The charge is truth!" yelled Van Hoeck, in far more genuine fury. "I hold the proof of my words."

He brandished the packet before Stuyvesant's face.

"Read it!" he implored.

Then I made my false move. Misjudging the distance, I gave a clutch at the packet. My face must have shown my wild eagerness. For, as I missed the hold I sought, Stuyvesant's loud rage gave place to a sudden grim calmness.

"Back all!" he ordered. "Dewitt, return to your place. Van Hoeck, give me the packet. There is something wrong here. I mean to learn what it is."

Held down in my chair by a half-dozen stalwart burghers I could but watch in cold despair as slowly the Governor tore open the horrible document and glanced at its inner covering.

CHAPTER XIII.
Fate Tosses the Dice.

THEN my taut muscles relaxed. I had thrown the dice—and lost. The game was in Fate's hands now. I was beaten.

Stuyvesant had broken the inner wrappings of the packet and had gathered up the loose sheets of writing. He was already poring over the first page, his near-sighted little eyes close to the paper.

My captors, when they found I no longer struggled, eased their grip on me and watched Stuyvesant's purpling face for further developments, as he read on in silence.

Louis Van Hoeck, between two men who still held him, was watching me with a cold, malignant triumph, such as few men could bestow on their worst foe.

The others waited breathless the bursting of the storm that grew and gathered so fast in Stuyvesant's tempestuous countenance.

Macopin alone showed absolutely no concern. With true Indian stoicism he sat gracefully on his three-legged stool, looking with civil interest down through the long window into the Paid Straat below.

'Twas no concern of his what might befall me. That was very evident. He had warned me. I had vaingloriously chosen to disregard his warning. Now, what cared he that I must pay full rates for my folly?

I sat there, trying to brace myself to be cold and brave when I should be denounced by Stuyvesant and dragged off to the gallows. I am glad to remember it was less the thought of my forfeited life that gripped at my icy heart just then than a crushing grief at the failure this discovery would cause to all the high hopes and ambitions I had formed for my dear country's future.

I had played for an unborn nation's welfare. And I had lost. What mattered my petty life compared to that numbing blow?

And thus—while Stuyvesant glared his incredulous, infuriated way through page after page—endless centuries of time seemed to drag on. It was by no means the lightest part of my anguish, to realize that my folly in half telling a woman a secret that was not mine to tell, had caused my downfall.

There was a deathly, tense silence throughout the room. A stillness broken only by his excellency's stertorous breathing, and by the crackling of the successive sheets of paper as he turned them.

At last—after an eternity—the Governor finished the last page and looked up from the reading. His face was empurpled, apoplectic, even to the crown of his bald head.

His eyes bulged like those of a man in a fit. The great veins on his forehead stood out black. I have never beheld such rage.

His gaze swept the room, then presently rested on me.

"Dirck!" he mumbled, almost incoherently.

I rose to my feet, folded my arms and looked him in the eyes. Macopin should not tell his fellow savages that a white man flinched at facing death.

Stuyvesant gulped, sought for words, then cried, in a spasm of half-inaudible anger:

"Dirck! I did wrong in ordering you to throw down your sword! I should have let you spit the cur like a trussed fowl!"

"Your—your excellency!" I babbled, my stoic calm knocked to flinders, my brain in a whirl of crass amazement. "I—I do not understand."

"Nor does any decent, loyal man!" he bellowed. "Lad! Know you what is in this packet you struggled to take—at my command — from this scum of the Dutch canals?"

He pointed a wrath-shaken forefinger at Louis Van Hoeck, as he put the question. Louis, utterly aghast and dumfounded, managed to sputter:

"Your excellency! You have read it, and yet you—"

"Peace!" boomed Stuyvesant. "Gentlemen," he went on, trying to steady his voice, and wheeling to face the curious burghers, "I will enlighten you in a very few words. Mynheer Louis Van Hoeck is a man who came to me highly recommended. I gave him a post of honor in my own official household, as you all know. And I treated him with all kindness. How hath the beast repaid me?"

"Your excellency!" protested Van Hoeck. "In showing you that report I did but what seemed my duty. I—"

"Listen, gentlemen!" thundered Stuyvesant, silencing him with a fierce gesture. "I have done all this for Louis Van Hoeck. In payment here is what he hath written, and which—by what twist of a disordered brain I know not—he hath chosen to beg *me* to read ere he sends it to Holland:"

"*I* wrote it not, your excellency!" shouted Louis. " 'Tis in his own hand writing, and signed with his own name.

"If I have cause to bid you again to be silent," snarled the Governor, "a squad of the fort guards shall enforce the order. The whole thing is in your own hand, Van Hoeck, and signed by you. Whom you seek to involve by the charge of 'spy' I know not. Nor do the words of a discredited informer like yourself carry a feather's weight. Listen, gentlemen, and I will read this noble screed to you."

I stood agape. I doubt me if any could have said which looked the more thunderstruck—Van Hoeck or myself.

I felt in a tangled nightmare through which I could see no light. Then Stuyvesant, his great voice still shaken by ground swells of passion, read:

To their High Mightinesses, the States General, at Amsterdam, Holland. From their humble and loving servant, Louis Van Hoeck. Greetings and these:

Pursuant upon the secret arrangement entered into between your High Mightinesses and myself, before my departure from Holland, I have joined the service of Petrus Stuyvesant, your Governor of New Amsterdam.

I have watched him closely, as, you bade me, and have studied the sentiments of the people toward him. I have also been enabled to look into the most private phases of his government.

I find in brief that all your High Mightinesses' ideas concerning the man were well founded. More, the half has not been told you. Arrogant, brutal, unjust, grasping, he is the most hated man in New Netherlands.

The poor hate him for his haughty contempt of them; the rich for his unjust curtailment of their rights and privileges. The arbitrary laws he has enacted for the restriction of trade have cut down commerce here, antagonizing the Indians, and have checked exports and turned away much wealth from your colony.

I respectfully suggest the immediate recall and public disgrace of this ignorant, incompetent tyrant. Subjoined, you will find full reports, proofs, and specific incidents in support of what I have here outlined. Your obedient subject and employee,

LOUIS VAN HOECK.

Stuyvesant, dropping the letter as though it were some venomous thing, picked up the first of the attached sheets and began to read it.

But I did not hear. Sick, weak, trembling at my escape, I turned away from the table and leaned against the window embrasure, seeking to revive myself with deep breaths of the cool, damp sea-wind.

How my deliverance had come—by what miracle—I could not guess. I could not understand one detail of the suddenly twisted, apparently impossible situation.

For the instant, it was enough for me to know not only that the noose was lifted from around my throat, but that America's future was not yet shattered; that there might even now be hope of my wondrous plan's success.

As I stood there, trying to get control of my racked nerves, and breathing wordless thanks to God for my deliverance, a low, almost inaudible voice beside me whispered:

"Brother, have I done well?"

I glanced about. The only person near me was Macopin. Still seated stolidly and gazing into the street he did not seem aware of my presence. Yet, looking closely, I saw his thin lips move ever so little.

And again I heard that soft whisper:

"You bore yourself bravely—for a white man."

"Macopin," I muttered, almost as low as was his own voice, "I—I do not yet see how—"

"The tall maid with the corn-silk hair and the pink face," he continued, "went to her brother in rage. I heard not their words. But they went from this room together. And I followed. To the post-bag the man went. They drew out your report, tore it open and both read it. Then Van Hoeck thrust it into his bosom and came hither."

"Yes?" I whispered.

"I had seen him place a packet of his own into the bag earlier this morning. From the care he used, I judged it was of value. I took it forth, passed him in the hallway, and took back your packet."

"He allowed you—"

"Brother," he answered, with faint reproach at my stupidity, "did *you* 'allow' me to take your letters and purse when we met at my Pomp-i-ton village? Yet I took them. And you knew it not."

I bowed my head in acknowledgment of my own denseness. And he went on:

"I took from him your packet. Yet, loath to make him lose so good an impression on the Governor, I wrapped the broken covering around *his* packet and replaced it in his coat. That is all."

"But mine? My report to the king?"

"I placed it in another wrapping and wrote on it the name and place you had spoken of—'Mynheer Troup, the Cronstadt, Haag, Holland.' And I slipped it into the post-bag just as the messenger came from the ship."

The boom of a small cannon sounded far to southward.

"The Staaten Eiland block fort saluting the post-boat's departure!" I murmured. "Heaven be praised! The ship has sailed. And my report is aboard it! Macopin, how can I ever thank you?"

"Hush!" warned the Indian. "His excellency is finishing his reading."

I straightened up and faced back into the room. Stuyvesant was rolling out the final sentences of the last page. From him I looked at Louis.

Van Hoeck was crouched stiffly forward in his chair, his eyes glaring, his lips twitching. He looked like a man in the throes of a fit.

I verily believe he was for the moment incapable of conscious thought or action. Bethink you how this must have struck him:

He had written, sealed, and posted a report to the States General, whose secret agent in America he was. Then he had taken from the post-bag mine own report to King Charles; had opened it, read it, and thrust it inside his coat. When he had drawn it forth a few minutes later it had changed by miracle to his own packet. Yes, had changed, although the outer wrappings were still the same!

Remember (you who read these lines as I pen them a half-century later), this was the age when witchcraft and "demoniac possession" were believed in as thoroughly as were any natural phenomena.

The fear of the supernatural was graven deep into his twitching face, and had so seized upon his very soul as to paralyze him. Thus he had sat inert, stricken, while his report to the States General was read aloud by the States General's bitterest foe.

"Old Silver Leg" seemed to take the same grim pleasure in reading Van Hoeck's detailed denunciations as does a cross child in biting on a sore tooth. And it had much the same effect on his choleric temper.

Finishing the last page, Stuyvesant folded the collected sheets neatly, replacing them in their wrappings; then, with a mighty wrench, he tore the parcel in two.

"Gentlemen," he remarked, "in case there be among you any more snakes in the grass—spies of the States General—let me herewith express my contempt for them and for you."

Dropping the torn papers to the neatly sanded floor, he ground them under his silver-hooped leg.

"I am Governor of the New Netherlands!" he roared, lionlike in his wrath; "I am master of life and death in this colony. And I stand accountable to no man—to spies nor to their high mightinesses themselves! Understand that, one and all! I am as a father to you all, while you remain my dutiful children. To him who conspires against me, I am as the hand of vengeance itself. Louis Van Hoeck, stand up!"

The wretched informer looked piteously at the Governor and even strove to obey. But the temporary paralysis still gripped him and the numb limbs refused their office.

Two officious burghers hauled him to his feet. He hung limply between them. In spite of myself, I was fool enough to feel a thrill of pity for the fellow.

Even Stuyvesant noted his plight, and doubtless set it down to helpless, cowardly terror. I alone of them all knew the man had no more cowardice in his nature than has an adder.

"Louis Van Hoeck," said the Governor, "it is the sentence of this council, voiced by me, its Governor, that you—"

Van Hoeck, summoning all his slow-returning strength, drew forth a slip of parchment. It dropped from his palsied fingers onto the table in front of Stuyvesant. The Governor picked it up and glanced at it.

"A safe-conduct from the States General!" he snarled. "What care *I* for that?"

None the less, I noticed that he did not go on to pronounce sentence. Revolt against the States General as he might, neither Stuyvesant nor any other Dutchman of his day dared outrage the sacredness of that body's safe-conduct.

To relieve a situation's embarrassment, the Governor turned to me.

"Dirck," he said, "once more I wish I had let you kill the cur. The safe-conduct protects him and makes him immune so long as he may care to tarry in the New Netherlands. I would you had slain him ere he produced it. Has your loyal clever brain no suggestion of a way out of this muddle?"

All at once, and before I could reply, Louis Van Hoeck became galvanized into life. Lurching forward, he shook an accusing arm at me.

"Excellency!" he cried wildly, "if I be discredited or not, I brand this man as a traitor! As a spy in the pay of England's king! You *shall* hear me!"

CHAPTER XIV.
"A WOMAN SCORNED."

THE man's vehemence, breaking, as it did, through the helpless paralysis that had so enveloped him, struck upon us all with an uncanny force. Louts took advantage of the second's astonished pause to shout again:

"There has been witchcraft! Vile, black magic, that has turned the spy's report in to the strange words you have just read! He *is* a spy! I ask—I *demand*—leave to prove it."

Stuyvesant, recovering from his amaze, broke in:

"Tush, fool. You are caught fairly in a trap. Why increase your baseness by seeking to drag an innocent man into the toils? Dirck Dewitt, too, of all men. At his life's risk he hath proven his loyalty and honor."

Right as I felt myself to be in the course I had taken, yet hot shame filled me at the Governor's rough words of praise. But I had scant time to reflect on them. For Louis again cried:

"I do not ask you to take my unsupported word—"

"The word of an informer!" scoffed his excellency. "The word of a hired secret agent of the States General! We thank you, *mynheer,* most deeply, for not insisting that we accept it as truth."

"It *is* truth!" yelled Louis. "And you shall hear me!"

"'Shall' is an odd word," said Stuyvesant coldly, "to use in speaking to your master. Let us have an end of this! Leave my council chamber and—"

"No!" declared Louis. "I appeal to your own law, which says: 'Every dweller in the colony shall have, on demand, the right to free speech.' I have a complaint to make, a formal charge to bring. As Governor of the New Netherlands, your own decree forces you to hear me."

"Else there will be a new grievance in your list for their high mightinesses?" sneered his excellency. "It is well. You have cited my law and have appealed to my justice. No living man shall say that Petrus Stuyvesant waived righteous law and justice, even in dealing with so low a thing as yourself. Speak on, but be brief. The room's air will be the sweeter when you are gone."

"Your excellency," I interposed, rising and bowing formally to the Governor as Louis made as though to begin, "as I understand it, this maniac accuses me of certain unknown crimes. He hath already publicly shouted to you all that I am a 'spy.' And I have been forced to endure the term. The justice of the New Netherlands is made for honest men as well as for knaves. I, too, ask a hearing."

"I protest!" fumed Van Hoeck, "I—"

"Speak on," said the Governor kindly.

"Your excellency," I resumed, "I am the victim of this man's charges. Here is no case for the law's slow course. If my accuser be indeed insane—as seems most likely—I ask that he be confined, for the safety of the town. If he be sane, then I entreat that you waive the laws against the duello, and let me vindicate mine honor with drawn sword, as becomes a brave man. 'Tis the only adequate redress."

Yes, I know how foolish, how braggart and futile was my dramatic appeal. I knew it then. I knew, too, that the plea would not be granted.

But I was playing for time. The ship bearing my precious report to King Charles had left port. It had passed Staaten Eiland, as the cannon's salute had told me. But if, indeed, there were any chance for exposure I wanted that possible exposure to come too late for the vessel to be recalled.

In another hour or less, the fast-sailing post-ship would have gone too far on her journey for the swiftest of our local craft to overhaul her and bring back the mail-pouch.

"Dirck!" exclaimed Stuyvesant in cold reproof, "'tis incredible that you, my secretary, a stanch upholder of my laws and authority, should make so gross a demand. Youth's blood is ever hot. And for that reason I excuse your words. Rest assured that justice shall avenge you as readily as could your own sword."

"But your excellency—"

"Know you not," he kept on, "that our laws provide amply for such cases as this? 'If a citizen,'" he quoted, "'bring criminal charge and fail to sustain the same, and if it can be shown that his charge was prompted by malice and without what seemed good evidence, he shall be punished according to the eighth clause of the statute regulations.' So runs the law. And, even a States General safe-conduct cannot intervene in the case of a criminal offense. Let Van Hoeck have his say. He will punish himself far more certainly than you could avenge your honor. Louis Van Hoeck, the council will hear you. Speak!"

Louis, wriggling, mouthing, cursing under his breath, had listened with mad impatience to the wrangle. Now, steadying himself with manifest effort, he began:

"Your excellency cites the law. Be it so. I, too, cite it, the law governing witchcraft. To-day I found a document that proved a man here to be a spy in England's pay. I bore that document straight to your excellency. It did not leave my person. By the time it reached you, it was miraculously changed to a lying report supposed to have been written by me to the States General."

The fellow was not only recovering his strength, but his subtle wit as well. I saw the trend of his words. Not only did he plan to ruin me, but to reinstate himself with Stuyvesant by denying all knowledge of the incriminating report he had written to their high mightinesses. It was clever—clever, past doubt.

Nowadays, when folk are for the most part beginning to believe that witchcraft does not exist, Van Hoeck's talk of black magic might well raise a laugh. But those burghers of an earlier age looked from one to the other in troubled doubt.

"I ask you all," resumed Louis, "to use your own good sense. Had I penned a scurrilous screed against the Governor, would I have been insane enough to thrust it upon him and to beseech him to read it? Doth the panther implore the hunter to slay her?"

The burghers whispered excitedly. Van Hoeck had made an impression. Stuyvesant's angry face had changed from wrath to perplexity.

There were wit and logic in Louis's claim. Even *I* had to admit that. There was no shadow of reason why he should knowingly have shown Stuyvesant his letter. Van Hoeck saw the effect of his words, and hurried on:

"I came here from the Vaterland to cast my lot with this colony, and to do all in my poor power for the colony's advancement. I was so happy as to receive appointment on the Governor's own staff. Had I been an agent for his enemies the position would have been an ideal one for the purposes of spying. The longer I could continue to make adverse reports to the States General, the longer my pay from them would have continued. Should I have been lunatic enough to rob myself of *both* employments by showing his excellency such a report? I ask not that you consider me too *honest* a man to play so foul a part, but that you give me credit for a grain of intelligence."

"There may be something in what you say," vouchsafed Stuyvesant grudgingly. "Proceed with your charges."

Van Hoeck squared his shoulders. He was himself again—subtle, shrewd, deadly.

"Before high heaven and before this council," said he, "I accuse Dirck Dewitt of being the paid spy of Charles, King of England. I accuse him of having come to New Amsterdam for the purpose of learning this colony's weaknesses and of making report on them to his English master. I accuse—"

"Your excellency," I burst in, "grant me leave to answer this man with cold steel."

"Peace, lad!" ordered Stuyvesant; not unkindly. "'Tis hard, I know, to sit and listen to such vile lies. But have patience. He will bring himself his own punishment. Go on, Van Hoeck. Make as swift an end to your charges as you can."

"I accuse him," proceeded Van Hoeck, as though reading from a printed page, "of having drafted that report and of placing it this day in the official mail-pouch whence for the good of the colony I abstracted it.

"This man wrote to England's king a detailed account of every condition here, of the Indians' hatred toward us, of the easy conquest England could gain should she send a force while your excellency is at odds with the States General and while the people at large are so discontented with Dutch rule."

"Is that all?" queried Stuyvesant in frigid politeness as Louis paused.

"Not quite. From the letter that accompanied the report I gather he is an Englishman; that he went to Holland from London, assumed a Dutch name and identity, and through the connivance of the British ambassador there was enabled to—"

Stuyvesant's great laugh shook the air.

"You overshoot, Mynheer Van Hoeck," he cried. "'Twas a very pretty batch of charges as it stood. Why weaken it by claiming him a newly emigrated Londoner? Do Londoners speak Dutch with no trace of accent? Do they know the Indian dialects and the art of 'forest running'? Next you will say he is King Charles in disguise."

"I speak," answered Louis, "not of mine own opinions, but what I read in black and white, in his own handwriting, over his own signature."

"And *now,* have you done?" asked the Governor. "Or is there more?"

"I have done. I have accused the so-called Dirck Dewitt of being an English spy. The charge stands."

"Not yet," corrected Stuyvesant. "There remain two trifling formalities. One is the taking of solemn oath as to the truth of what you have said. Second, to establish proof thereof. We await your convenience. But, ere you commit yourself to oath, let me remind you that perjury is here punishable by death."

Van Hoeck's reply was to walk to the bronze lectern where lay the council Bible. With his hand on the sacred volume, he said solemnly:

"I, Louis Van Hoeck, do hereby swear on the blessed Book that to the best of my knowledge and belief the charges I have just made against the man calling himself Dirck Dewitt are in every respect true, and the whole truth, so help me."

I think no one, observing the man, could have wholly doubted his sincerity.

There was an instant's awed silence. Then Stuyvesant drew a long breath.

"'Tis done," said he gravely. "Mynheer Van Hoeck, for your immortal soul's welfare as much as for that of your mortal body, I trust you have told what you deem to be the truth. 'Tis a fearful thing at best to call upon the Creator to witness our spoken words. And now," more briskly, "to the point. Your proofs, man! You promised us proofs of your monstrous assertion. Produce them!"

Van Hoeck hesitated.

"My chief evidence," he said, "was the document itself. It has vanished, and another screed has been magically substituted for it."

"So your whole proof hangs upon the doubtful assertion of witchcraft?"

"No. Else had I not dared press the charge. I beg to call a witness."

"A witness?"

"My sister. The Juffrouw Greta Van Hoeck, who is known to your excellency."

A stir of excited interest swept the room. I turned sick. Not with fear, though hope seemed to be stranding me on the shoals of despond, but at the thought that any woman—Greta least of all—should be called upon to take away a man's life.

My first shock passed, my senses rallied. Why, of course, I was safe. The girl who had once so infatuated me, would surely not now help bring about my utter ruin? Then I remembered her face as she had turned from us that morning. And once more a dull doubt oppressed me.

Ere leaving London I had gone one evening to the Globe play-house to witness Master Congreve's right turgid drama, "The Mourning Bride." A tag in this stage-play—that had most vastly caught the fancy of the audience—now recurred to me. 'Twas a couplet that ran:

> Heaven knows no rage like love to hatred turned,
> Nor Hell a fury like a woman scorned!

"It is well," agreed Stuyvesant, after a moment's frowning reflection. "Let the Juffrouw Van Hoeck be summoned. No!" as Louis started for the door, "stay where you are, *mynheer.* There shall be no chance at collusion. We will hear the lady's story independently.

"Clerk," he went on, "seek the Juffrouw Greta Van Hoeck, and beg her with my sincere compliments to attend us here with all convenient speed. It may be she hath not yet left the White Hall, but is waiting below with the rest for the rain to abate, ere venturing home."

"Your fate," whispered Macopin, as the clerk bustled out on his errand, "hangs on a thread."

"On a woman's mood," I corrected.

"Are the two so different?" was his only reply as once more he turned to his inspection of the rainy street below.

CHAPTER XV.
I Stand Condemned.

AN exclamation from one of the burghers drew all eyes to a spot on the floor where Stuyvesant had hurled the torn, crumpled sheets of Louis Van Hoeck's epistle to the States-General.

The little pile of crushed paper—near which no one chanced to be standing or sitting—began to exhale a thick cloud of smoke. Presently, as all looked on, it broke into a light blaze.

"Witchcraft!" cried Van Hoeck.

And "Witchcraft!" "Sorcery!" "Magic!" echoed the rest in awe.

Stuyvesant, hard-headed old warrior though he was, eyed the tiny conflagration almost with fear.

"Van Hoeck is no fool!" muttered Macopin to me, under his breath. "When all were listening as your Governor gave orders to the clerk to go fetch the maiden, I saw your enemy drop a spark from flint-and-steel on to the paper."

But the burghers, who had seen nothing of that, quickly caught up Louis's exclamation of "witchcraft!"

"'Tis as I said!" declared Van Hoeck. "'Tis all a bit of Satan-work. The paper was made and writ on by no mortal hand. Its work accomplished, it returns to the fiery element whence it came."

To a less excited audience, even in that age of ignorance, this wild theory might have brought smiles. But all were keyed up by the events that had just transpired; and all, I think, were more than half-ready to give credence to the idea.

Stuyvesant advanced cautiously and poked at the smoldering pile with the point of his wooden leg—sniffing the air as though for scent of brimstone.

At that moment Greta Van Hoeck was announced.

As though ashamed of their twinges of supernatural dread, the councilors drew themselves up; and prepared, like spectators at the theater, to relish this newest sensation.

Stuyvesant, with limping courtliness, advanced to meet the girl, bowed low, and, taking her by the hand, led her to a chair.

"*Mejuffrouw,*" said he, "accept our thanks for obeying the summons to this council, and our regrets for the unpleasing necessity of forcing you to appear in so sad an affair. Will you do me the honor to answer a few questions that I must put to you?"

Shyly the girl consented, glancing about her as though vastly impressed at finding herself in so lofty a company. Her look and manner evidently flattered the burghers. I could see that these things, coupled with her beauty, predisposed them strongly in her favor.

"*Mejuffrouw,*" began Stuyvesant, "did you, or did you not, see a packet that was consigned to this morning's post-bag?"

"I did, your excellency," she answered, as though in surprise at the question.

Her voice was respectful, yet strong and full of the nameless magnetism that had once so thrilled me. Indeed, I wondered that the sound of it now left me so cold.

"What was the nature of that packet?" pursued Stuyvesant.

"It was enveloped in an outer cover of gray parchment," she returned, "bound with tape and seals, and superscribed to one Mynheer Troup, the Cronstadt, Haag."

"Did you open the packet?"

"No, your excellency. But," she added, with apparent reluctance, "it was opened in my presence."

"By whom?"

"By by my brother, Louis Van Hoeck."

"If it please his excellency," spoke up bluff Oloffe Van Cortlandt (he in whose honor, a few years later, Cortlandt Street was named) "if it please his excellency, may I inquire how Mynheer Van Hoeck chanced to be meddling with the post-bag's contents?"

"I can answer that, Mynheer Van Cortlandt," said Greta. "I had told him my suspicions of a man in his excellency's employ. He had seen that man prepare with great care and secrecy a document for over-seas. For the sake of his duty toward the colony's welfare, he—"

"Quite so!" interrupted Stuyvesant. "He opened the packet? In your presence, *mejuffrouw?*"

"Yes, your excellency."

"And you read with him its contents?"

"Yes, sir."

"Was that also 'for the sake of duty toward the colony's welfare?'" queried Macopin, with so much the air of an innocent child seeking information, that even Stuyvesant had not the heart to reprove him.

Greta flushed and turned her back upon the impassive Indian—awaiting the Governor's next question.

"Pray describe to us the nature of the packet," said Stuyvesant.

"Its inner covering of silk," she continued, "was addressed thus: *'To His Most Christian Majesty, Charles II, King of England.'*"

A wave of sensation swept the council. All leaned forward. The girl paused, visibly embarrassed.

"Please continue," prompted Stuyvesant.

"Your excellency," she pleaded, "I am loath to describe the contents of the document. Is it needful?"

"I fear so," said the Governor.

She drew a deep breath; then, as though forcing herself to a painful duty, spoke rapidly, in a low tone, that was scarce audible through the room.

"The packet," she said, "was a report of the various defenses of New Amsterdam; the supposed feelings of the burghers; the traders, and the Indians toward your excellency; and a list of the force of armed men at your command. A letter, accompanying the report, said that the New Netherlands would collapse at a touch from England's finger, and that Holland's rule here was already tottering to a fall. That is the gist of letter and report. I cannot recall the exact words."

"Was there a signature?"

"There was, your excellency."

"Whose?"

"I beg your excellency—"

"*Whose?*" shouted Stuyvesant.

"Mynheer Dirck Dewitt's."

"Was the document in his handwriting?"

"I know not his handwriting, your excellency. My brother, who is familiar with it in official work, said it was Mynheer Dewitt's."

"May I ask another question?" put in Van Cortlandt. "The *juffrouw* has said she had reason, beforehand, to suspect Mynheer Dewitt. I beg to know that reason."

"Sirs," exclaimed Greta, her white hands clasped, her eyes wide with appeal. "'Tis most painful to me to be forced to speak of this. Cannot it be avoided?"

"The truth," returned Stuyvesant, "is seldom other than painful. Yet I know of naught that has ever been gained by avoiding it. Pray answer Mynheer Oloffe Van Cortlandt's question."

Again, as though compelling herself to hurry through a distasteful topic, Greta replied:

"We crossed from Holland on the same vessel with Mynheer Dewitt. One night, in boastful mood (when in jest I had been taunting him, as a foolish maid will) he declared that he was bent upon a secret mission here, whose discovery by your excellency would cost him his head. He also spake vaguely of King Charles. Then, as though he feared his boasting had carried him beyond prudence, he ceased speaking. Nor did he ever again revert to the theme. I suspected, and—in due time I told my brother."

"In 'due' time?" echoed Macopin, with that same stupid, innocent air of seeking difficult facts. "Does that mean this morning?"

"Yes!" she flashed.

"And your suspicions came not to a head in all the months that lay between?"

" 'Tis hopeless, seeking to make a savage understand my motives," said the girl, appealing to Stuyvesant.

"Not at all," gently contradicted Macopin, as he slouched back to his favorite post overlooking the street. "There be many serpents in our own villages. I have studied their ways."

Stuyvesant, luckily, did not hear. He was standing, head bowed, features working convulsively, absorbed in his own bitter thoughts. Suddenly the Governor lifted his face, and I saw with dismay that the fierce little eyes were full of tears.

"Dirck!" he called, his big voice thick and shaking. "Come here, lad!" I went up to where he stood beside the lectern.

"Lad," he went on, "I know men. Yes, and women, too. These stories—Van Hoeck's and his sister's—agree marvelous well, and they can scarce have rehearsed them. Yet, somehow, I am loath to believe. Nay, I will not believe that you are a spy in the pay of Holland's foes. Van Hoeck has taken oath. I call upon you to do the same. And, Dirck, I will accept your oath ahead of his. For a man with eyes like yours, could not commit perjury. I know enough of faces to vouch for that."

Again, a lump rose in my throat at his simple trust in me.

"Lad," he went on, "lay hand upon the Holy Bible, and swear that Van Hoeck's story is a lie. I command it!"

I drew back. Stuyvesant stared at me in dull disapproving wonder. Even yet he did not understand.

I have, at various times of my life, described this scene to friends of mine. Some of them have scoffed at me, saying:

"Pooh! There were a dozen ways for you out of the dilemma!"

But when I have pressed them to point out to me one of these "dozen ways" they have straightway fallen to talking of other matters. One man—his late majesty, King Charles II of England—said to me:

"Why did you not take the oath, dolt? What is one perjury, more or less?"

I know not what I should—or might—or could—have done. I knew only that I could not perjure my soul for the sake of saving my neck. And I stood stupidly silent.

"Come! Come, lad!" fumed Stuyvesant. "The oath! Take it, I say!"

"Your excellency," I made quiet answer, "I cannot."

He sat down heavily, staring at me, while the deep color ebbed from his face.

"I had sooner believed it of mine own son!" he groaned at last.

Then, all at once, seeming very old and weary, he beckoned the captain of the provost guard.

"Lodge him in the city jail," he ordered briefly. "I will send you the death warrant. Hang him at sunrise."

A soldier on either side of me, I passed from the room amid a tense, pall-like silence.

As the door closed behind me the stillness was broken by a silvery laugh from Greta Van Hoeck.

"The ship, at all events," I told myself, "has sailed past recall. *I* shall die. But—through me—America shall one day live!"

CHAPTER XVI.
A Voice in the Night.

THE day's rain had culminated in a thunderstorm that sounded like a continuous roll of artillery. In my unlighted cell of the city jail I sat on a hard bench, dully watching the opposite wall as the almost constant flashes of lightning brought its whitewashed surface into view.

Some former occupant, with a pleasant taste for humor and art, had scrawled upon it with a bit of charcoal a sketch of a gallows-tree.

There, gazing at the wall, had I sat since noon, with none to break in upon my solitude. I had no means of knowing what time it was. For there were scarce a dozen watches or clocks in all New Netherlands.

Time was told from sun-dial and hourglass. Nearly all of us, on any clear day or night, had learned to guess the hour to almost a nicety by glancing at the sky.

I had no further need of time. Presently—or in a few hours at most—gray dawn would creep in through the bars of my window. Then would come sunrise and a tramp of feet. And I should be led forth to my death.

When one is under thirty, be he ever so brave, there is scant joy in stoicism at such a thought. I tried to make my tired mind dwell on other themes—on America's glorious future, on the doom that was advancing upon this smug, ill-managed Dutch colony, on my own luck in Macopin's having despatched my report ere the crash had come.

But, ever, my thoughts would swing back, against my will, to the creaking gallows-tree in front of the jail and to a vision of the gaping crowd that would surround it at sunrise.

Not noble or uplifting reflections for a man's last hours? Perhaps not. There is little enough about me that is noble, as you may have guessed ere now.

There was an instant's cessation in the roll of thunder. Thence came a flash of lightning so vivid that the shadow of my criss-crossed iron window-bars stood black and distinct against the white of the wall.

I half started up. For, in that instant of blinding light, my dazzled eyes seemed to behold a black profile silhouetted upon the wall, in the midst of the bars' pattern.

The silhouette was of a face—a daintily featured little face—crowned with a mass of loose hair. At the next flash it was gone.

Convinced that the whole thing must be a hallucination, bred of tired vision, I nevertheless strode to the window. A second vivid flash showed—nothing! Nothing but a fleeting glimpse of the town's wet roofs, blue white in the glare, between the bars.

I was turning back heavily, when, on the very echo of a crash of thunder a woman's voice called my name. I halted, mystified. No one but myself was in the cell.

My nerves must surely be going to pieces, since I heard the voice of a girl and had seen the shadow of her face up there twenty feet above ground!

I had convinced myself of my error and had resolved to keep my brain calmer when the voice came again. And now I located it just beneath the ledge of my window.

I pressed my face against the bars. By the next flash, I saw a ladder, rising to within a yard of the sill. And on its summit, crouched a little rain-drenched figure.

"Quick!" cried the voice again. "I cannot wait. I may be seen from below at any moment. Can you hear me?"

"*Blanche!*" I here gasped. "Blanche Goffe! I—"

A crash of thunder that seemed to rock the whole island drowned my words. On the recurrent hush she called:

"Louis Van Hoeck will visit you. Show no violence. Hold him in talk for a few moments. As long as you can. Do you understand?"

"Yes!" I exclaimed. "But—"

A guard crossed the courtyard below, as the girl began to speak again. Darkness swallowed everything. When the lightning flashed once more she and the ladder had vanished.

Still half-doubting my senses, I continued to lean forward, my face thrust against the wet bars, and stared downward.

Whether I waited thus for one minute or ten I do not know. I was aroused by the click of a rusty bolt, and a stream of yellow light poured into my cell.

I wheeled about. On the threshold stood Louis Van Hoeck. Water streamed from his mantle and broad-leafed hat. Behind him a turn-key swung a lantern.

In my high-strung condition, my old hatred flamed up afresh and I was minded to leap at Van Hoeck's throat. My muscles were tense for the spring, when, like a sweet echo, came the memory of Blanche's odd warning:

"*Show no violence! Hold him in talk!*"

My sinews relaxed. I dropped limply, despairingly on the bench, my head in my hands. Every line of my huddled body must have bespoken fear and desolation.

Van Hoeck gazed at me a moment, then came further into the cell.

"Have you brought me a reprieve?" I whined.

He laughed shortly, and exclaimed:

"Would *I* be chosen for such an errand?"

With a sigh of heartbroken resignation I curled into a closer, more miserable heap, and buried my face in my hands.

I did not at all know why I had received those orders from Blanche. But since she had risked life and limb to bring them to me, the least I could do was to obey.

My cringing attitude seemed to decide Van Hoeck on some course.

"I shall not need you," he said to the turnkey. "Leave your lantern here and wait for me outside."

The man obeyed. As the thick door swung shut behind him, I grew tense once more with the longing to hurl myself upon mine enemy and take brute vengeance on him for my undoing.

But sanity restrained me. Even should I overcome him, the sound of our struggle would be certain to reach the turnkey just without, who would promptly bring a dozen men of the watch to overcome me. So I decided upon following Blanche's command, and "hold him in talk."

"There is no hope of pardon?" I asked. "If I might make personal appeal to the Governor—"

"The Governor!" repeated Louis. "Scarcely! However, all appeals to the Governor must pass through the hands of his secretary. And—since noon to-day—*I* hold that high office."

I made no comment. He went on: "It is in my official capacity I am here. I have been thinking. It seems to me that to-day's 'wonders' savor less of witchcraft than of your malice. It was *you* who somehow changed the two packets, one for the other. Am I not right? "

"How could I?" I answered. "Since you declared in open council that your letter to the States-General never really existed, but was an invention of the Evil One?"

"Why play with words?" he sneered. "There are none to hear us. You changed those packets. Therefore, you must have secreted the one you wrote to the English king. Where is it?"

"Where is it?" I repeated. "I do not understand!"

"No?" said he. "And yet you are wont to be shrewd enough. Listen to me: You have that report somewhere. Give it to me or tell me where it is."

"But *why?*"

"It will aid me much with his excellency and banish his last doubts of my word."

"And," I cried, "you expect *me* to do this for you? "

"At a price. Yes."

"What price?" I asked, genuinely curious. "My life is already forfeit. What can you offer me? A pardon?"

"No," he admitted, "but, as secretary to his excellency, I can get your sentence of hanging changed to the soldier's death of shooting. Is that no consideration?"

"A great one," I assented. "But what assurance have I that you will do it."

"My promise," he replied.

"Mynheer Van Hoeck," I laughed, "as a member of a race of wise business men, you surely must see how absurdly inadequate the collateral is."

He flushed angrily.

"I could have you searched," he declared, "and—"

"And you thought of that," I finished, "but you remembered I was stripped and searched when I entered jail. Also you have no doubt carefully hunted the council-chamber, before coming here."

From his start of surprise, I knew my guesses were correct. Still, remembering Blanche's warning, I sought to prolong our talk.

"Come!" said I. "We may even yet strike a bargain. If I tell you, on my word of honor, exactly where the packet now is, will you swear that I shall be shot instead of hanged?"

"Yes!" he cried eagerly.

"Then," I made reply, "I assure you, on my sacred word, that the packet (directed outwardly to Mynheer Troup, and, on the inner wrapping to his majesty, King Charles II) is safe in the post-bag aboard the ship which sailed from here for Amsterdam this morning."

"It is not so! It *cannot* be!" he shouted. Yet, looking in my eyes, he saw I was speaking truth.

"How—how did you—" he began.

"That was not part of our bargain," I returned. "I agreed only to tell you where the packet now is. I have kept my word."

"His excellency must know at once!" he stormed. "Our fastest vessel shall be sent after the post-boat, and—"

"My dear secretary," I mocked, "pray learn more of port affairs if you wish to serve his excellency with any sort of competence. Not a ship in our docks could be manned and victualed for such a voyage in less than three days at the very least. That would give the post-boat a four-day start. Ere your pursuing ship could reach Amsterdam, the packet would be in King Charles's hands. And you know it."

He glared at me nonplused, his yellow wolf-fangs bared. The door opened and the turnkey reentered.

So significant are the things that catch our attention in moments of stress, that I suddenly found myself staring at the prison employee's feet. When he had last left the room I had noticed that a pair of heavy military boots clumped beneath his long soldier-cloak. Now, he was barefoot. And his feet—

"You think you have tricked us all finely!" growled Louis, not hearing the entering of the turnkey behind him, "but you lose, not only your own life, but your hopes as well. For the town shall be so strengthened against any possible approach of the English—"

I laughed outright.

"My friend," said I, "the defenses here are already as strong as a disunited colony can make them. To render them stronger, or the garrison larger, would require a full twelvemonth. Ere that time—"

"Ere another twelve hours," he cut in, "I shall at least have the joy of watching you hanged."

"'Shot,' I think you meant to say," I corrected, monstrous polite.

"No, hanged by the neck, until—"

"But our bargain?"

"One does not keep bargains with—"

He got no further. The turnkey who had stood silent and impassive in the shadows behind him, calmly reached out, caught him about the throat by both hands and held him thus.

Louis, with a terrible, convulsive struggle, sought to wrench himself free, to cry out. But his windpipe was clutched fast, and he might as well have fought in the grip of a grizzly bear as in that of the two sinewy hands that held him.

There was no sound, no turmoil. The turnkey simply maintained his grip. Then, suddenly, with a movement so swift as to baffle the eye, he shifted one hand from Van Hoeck's throat to the latter's face. And I saw he held in it a cloth which exhaled a faintly sweetish smell.

A gasp or two, and Louis's head fell limp. The other relaxed his hold. Van Hoeck slid silently to the ground.

"He is not dead," said the turnkey quietly. "There is no time to lose. Put on his hat and cloak. Pull the hat-brim over your eyes. *So!* Now give me the lantern and lock the door behind us. Come!"

"Macopin!" I exclaimed, as I obeyed the curt directions.

Then I stumbled over the body of a half-clad man in the corridor. It was the *real* turnkey, bound and gagged, and deprived of his coat and helmet.

Down the stone stairway we went. On reaching the ground floor, Macopin turned sharply to the left, instead of going forward into the main hall where lounged several officials and a squad of the town watch.

The Indian made for a small passageway which led direct to the jail's courtyard. He plodded along with maddening slowness; shoulders bent, feet striking the ground with flat, springless tread.

Thus ever pottered the lazy turnkeys on their tours of duty. The chief was a born actor, and he must have used his eyes well, to acquire that shuffling gait and lifeless carriage.

We were in the shadows, at some distance from the central torch-flare that lighted the hall. Macopin took pains to swing his lantern so as to throw its beams anywhere except on our faces.

One or two of the loungers glanced at us as we made for the passageway. What they saw could not have aroused any suspicion. A little earlier, Louis had come to the jail. A turnkey had been assigned to show him to my cell. Now, apparently, the same turnkey was conducting him out of the jail.

As we entered the passageway, the watch-captain called civilly to me:

"Mynheer Van Hoeck, 'tis a vile night. Will you not wait with us until the rain slackens? A mug of hot-spiced *schnapps* and a seat by our brazier will perchance ward off a quinsy or a lung fever. Join us, I pray."

I was hard put to it for a reply. Rallying my wits, I growled hoarsely, yet, with as near an approach to Van Hoeck's usual querulous tones as I could copy:

"I am already stricken with so heavy a cold from my wetting, that I fain would get me to bed. Good night."

"The courtyard lies an inch deep in mud," he protested, rising and coming forward. "Turnkey, what put it into your blockhead to pass the herr secretary out *that* way? Is he a tradesman, to be sent forth by the postern? This way, Mynheer Van Hoeck!"

Officiously, he ran back, caught up a torch, and came forward again.

Here was a pretty tangle. While my cloak and wide-leafed hat were ample disguise to deceive any one who might gain a momentary glimpse of me as I slipped through the shadows, yet the first full ray of the torch must show the most casual onlooker that my broad shoulders and huge bulk did not pertain to Louis Van Hoeck's lean body.

On came the officer. The other bystanders, as a token of respect to the new secretary, had risen. I gathered myself for a dash through the passageway and the postern-door. Yet I saw the almost certain futility of such a move. For, a sentry paced the courtyard, and at its outer gate an armed guard was always stationed.

No man dashing forth at a run, could reasonably hope to pass these two. Assuredly they would fire on me. And, as certainly, the gate would be swung shut, trapping me like a rat in a blind drain.

Macopin had already reached the postern door, unbarred it, and thrown it open. A swirl of wind, bursting through the drafty passageway, caught the wide hat I wore and whisked it from my head.

The light from the watch-captain's torch fell full upon my face. He gasped, stupidly, as at a ghost. Then, dropping the torch with a yell, and whipping out his sword, he bellowed:

"'Tis Mynheer Dewitt! An escape! At him, lads! Take him alive if you can."

Forthwith, the whole watch-squad, the captain at its head, launched itself upon me.

CHAPTER XVII.
FLIGHT.

IT was not a wholly pleasant situation. A few feet behind me was the open postern door; Macopin at its threshold. In front of me the watch-captain, sword drawn, his men crowding close after him.

And I—stripped of my petty disguise—unarmed—helpless—caught as easily as a muskrat in springtime. I have been in happier positions.

Do not fancy, please, that we all remained thus grouped, like actor folk in a stage play.

From the instant my hat blew off, disclosing me to the watch-captain, to that when I sprang to the postern-door with the whole shouting, swearing pack at my heels, was a bare second or so.

To the postern I leaped. Better to be shot or overcome in the open courtyard than here in this passageway where a man might not have scope to use his strength.

As I made my dash, the watch-captain had already seized me. I left my cloak—Louis Van Hoeck's cloak—in his grasp; and, striking a backhand blow as I jumped, sent him staggering backward against his foremost followers.

The instant's pause and confusion thus caused in the confined space gave me chance to reach the door. And I sprang out into the dark courtyard, Macopin at my side.

The chief clanged shut the door behind us. Then, seizing my arm, he dragged me to one side. We found ourselves beside a gun-rack—that rested against the eight-foot courtyard wall.

I needed no further counsel. A spring brought me to the rack's summit. I reached up to seize the wall-top and drag myself over.

But Macopin, who was again at my side, drew me to a point two or three feet below the spot where I had been about to seize the wall. A flash of lightning showed me his reason for this precaution.

The wall's broad top was everywhere surmounted by spikes and shards and broken glass. Had I mounted where I first intended, my clothes and flesh must have been terribly lacerated, but at the place to which he had directed me the chief had thrown a thick, doubled blanket over the wall's capstone, to break the sharpness of the obstacles.

Over we went, one after the other, dropping lightly into the mud of the lane outside. Our whole maneuver had taken almost no time.

Yet, quick as we were, a guard had already fired at us; the door had been flung open, and a dozen armed men had rushed out from the jail. Now, from the main entrance, poured city watchmen into the lane. As we touched ground, a slender little figure, rising apparently from nowhere, joined us. Even in the pitchy gloom that followed the lightning glare I knew her.

Blanche, Macopin, and I were all trained "forest runners." To us, from long travel-nights in the wilderness, darkness was almost as day for all practical purposes. Light we were of foot, swift and noiseless of motion, and well versed in the art of concealment.

Yes, and we surely needed our utmost skill in all these qualities during the half hour that ensued. Doubling, crouching; now running, now lying moveless in a dark corner; the pursuit sometimes far off, sometimes passing almost over our moveless bodies—so went the time, until at length we found ourselves near the riverside bushes where now Cortlandt Street ends. There we halted.

I was sadly out of breath. Neither of my comrades showed sign of fatigue. With Macopin this was but natural, but it irked me that a fragile-looking girl like Blanche Goffe should have more endurance than a giant like myself.

We halted, I say, and listened. The pursuit had died away. We were for the moment safe.

"I owe my life to both of you!" I cried. "How can I ever hope to thank you for your great goodness to me?"

"Goodness?" echoed Macopin in genuine surprise. "Why, you are still, in a sense, the guest of my tribe. I could not have left you to die, even if I would. Else had I been shamed before my people. But," he added, distressed, " 'twas a bungle at best. Never have I been in a condition whereof I was less proud of myself than when we were caught in that passageway. 'Twas, for the minute, almost—almost—*dangerous.*"

He seemed abashed at making such a confession. I agreed; struggling to repress a smile:

"Yes. It was—*almost* 'dangerous.' And now—"

"There is a canoe moored at the edge of this copse," he went on. "You two will take it and paddle across to Pavonia Village, under the lower Palisades. From there, strike inland along the route the maiden knows. At Hak-en-Sak Hill you will await me."

"But *you*—" I began.

"I cannot come, yet," he made reply. "Your escape is known. If, on the morrow morn, it is learned that I, too, am missing, your Governor will suspect me. And, from what I know of him, he is quite capable of carrying fire and sword to my tribe in search of you."

"But—"

"True, he and his soldiers would never reach the Pomp-i-ton country alive," explained Macopin, "but their march would stir up instant war with the tribes through whose territory they must pass. And that would mean useless bloodshed."

"Then you are going back to—"

"To the tavern. There shall my mother and I be found on the morrow. When we learn of your escape, we shall find excuse to leave the city. Await us on the Hak-en-Sak Hill. We will be there ere nightfall. In the canoe are provisions. Two horses are tethered for you on the far bank."

"Should we fail to find that Hak-en-Sak Hill in the darkness?"

"You *must* find it," he replied quietly. "It is a peace hill and sacred. There, and there alone, in all that region shall you be safe. Should you meet with a war party or with Hak-en-Sak hunters elsewhere, you would most surely be taken. For they hate the white man. And, in such captivity, even *I* could not help you. Good-by, my brother."

He had slipped away noiselessly into the gloom before I could answer. At the head of the path, a furlong back, a torch appeared. A search-party were evidently about to hunt the river edge for me.

Blanche and I stole noiselessly down to the water and found the canoe. The storm had whipped the waves high and I had much ado to hold the frail little craft steady while Blanche boarded it.

Then, taking my own seat and paddling furiously to keep the canoe's prow into the wind, I started out from the shadow of the shore.

Westward I drove the boat, straight into the very teeth of the storm, taking advantage of every momentary lull to shift my course northerly toward Pavonia.

By the time the searchers had reached the bank, we were well out into the stream. And, even the lightning flashes, in that mass of tossing waters, failed to disclose us.

For a full half hour my long, steady paddle-strokes battled with the waves. The rain was slackening. Yet it and the spray drenched us to the skin.

At length, as we reached midstream, a mile or so to north of our starting point, the storm fell dead with the bewildering suddenness of a tropical tempest.

The last roll of thunder died away far to eastward. The rain ceased, and through the rifted clouds the full moon butted its way. The sweeping wind sank into the lightest of summer breezes.

I rested on my paddle, amazed at the change. To town-bred folk our plight even then was far from comfortable. Our clothes were soaked. Despite Blanche's constant bailing, there were several inches of water slopping about our feet in the bottom of the canoe.

But to man and maid accustomed to forest life these were minor troubles. There was a calm loveliness in the moonlight night around us that made one forget wet clothes and tired sinews.

Heading straight for Pavonia I struck into an easy, fast stroke that sent the boat spinning along with scarce an effort. Blanche set to work bailing again and presently the canoe was dry.

I looked at her as the moon fell on her little sunburned face with its huge eyes and tangled masses of wet hair. She was little, so elfin-pretty! And, for *me,* a comparative stranger, she had endured such discomforts and perils!

I felt as I might if some child had hoarded all its sweetmeat-money and, with the sacrifice, had bought me a gift. She had done so much for me! And I, in return, had done for her—*nothing.*

It is not pleasant for a grown man to know himself hopelessly in a woman's debt. I recalled my mad infatuation for Greta Van Hoeck and its bitter outcome that had gnawed so sore a rift in my heart—or my vanity. Then I remembered how this forest maid, who owed me nothing, had risked all for me. And the contrast stung me like white-hot iron.

Blanche must surely care for me, I mused. One does not cast safety to the winds for the sake of a casual acquaintance. I was probably the first civilized man, except her father, whom she had seen in years. And—she had learned to care.

The thought brought no balm to my vanity. Instead, it saddened me. What had that dead, seared heart of mine to do with love? How could I requite the simple, beautiful affection of this forest maid? And yet—

My life was lived. (What blighted youth of twenty-six is not far surer of this than is the most miserable man of sixty?) I had loved—and had worse than lost.

My romance days were past. Yet Blanche had twice risked life that I might live. Did I not owe her such poor reparation—such paltry reward—as lay in my power to give?

A long sigh—a resolute turning of my back on the past and on what once I had dared to hope—and I set my face resolutely to this new task.

I raised my gaze to Blanche's face. Her own eyes were shadowy—half-seen, half-hidden—under her crown of dusky hair.

"Mistress Goffe—" I began.

The words stuck in my throat. And my soul turned sick at the duty that now lay before me.

CHAPTER XVIII.
I Play the Fool.

SHE looked across at me in real concern.

"You're ill?" she asked. "Your voice is so—strange. The strain has been too much for you?"

"No," I returned, irritated, as man must ever be when sentiment is mistaken for sickness.

"Then—" she began.

But I took tight hold on all my new-formed resolutions and made the plunge.

"Mistress Goffe," I said, "you have done more for me than any woman—or man, either—whom I have known. I owe you life, safety, freedom. Again and again you have—"

"*Mynheer,*" she protested in embarrassment, "for what little I've had the good luck to do for you, I've already received a wearisome amount of thanks. Have done, I pray. Or—"

"I cannot have done," I replied, "and I beg you to hear me out. I have known so few women! The first with whom I was thrown to any extent befooled me, betrayed me, and cast me away with a laugh. The second is yourself—who have done more for me than any mortal can repay."

"*Mynheer!*" she exclaimed impatiently. "To what end do you—"

"Blanche," I broke in, resolved to make an end to a scene that was fast waxing ridiculous in its pompous stiff speeches, "I am for the moment a fugitive. Yet I have lands in the Massachusetts Bay Colony and a fair inherited sum of money in the Boston Counting House. And, when England seizes the New Netherlands, my future should be comfortably assured."

"My compliments, sir," she answered with mock demureness, "upon your excellent and well-merited prospects. I am honored that you deemed me fit to hear such holy confidences."

"Blanche!" I cried. "You have no right to make jest of me. If I prate of my obligations and of my worldly estate, 'tis but to lay before you honorably the facts that lead up to something of far vaster import."

"And, pray, sir," she asked in genuine curiosity, leaning forward again to scan my face, "what may be the wondrous climax to which this preamble leads?"

She spoke with the unsuspecting frankness of a child whose inquisitiveness and whose patience are piqued. Yet, in my fatuous folly, it seemed to me she *must* understand. I felt she was encouraging me as far as maidenly diffidence would permit. And at last I came to the point.

"Blanche," I said, with what imitation of fervor I could muster, "I beg you will do me the undeserved honor of becoming my wife."

(I have set down the foregoing dialogue with merciless accuracy that each and all of you may realize what an imbecile an ordinarily sane man at times becomes. I flinch, yet, at the memory. But if I played the fool, I was most assuredly and most bitterly to pay the price. As you shall presently see.)

For a second or two after my declaration the girl sat moveless, staring transfixed. Then to my puzzled chagrin she threw back her head and—over the still waters rang peal after peal of sweet, tempestuous, unrestrained laughter.

I tried to tell myself that the mirth was bred of overtaxed nerves; perhaps even of joy at my proposal. But even then a chilling doubt began to possess me.

"I fear," said I stiffly, "that you scarce grasp my meaning. I had the honor to request your hand. To—"

"Oh, you made it *quite* clear!" she panted, weak with laughter. "I understand. Have no fear."

And again she laughed, in that odd, almost hysterical fashion.

Of a sudden she ceased; and, as she tossed back the wave of soft hair that fell over her forehead, I saw that her face no longer bore the faintest trace of mirth.

Instead, it was as cold, as hard, as a December lake. Yes, and as beautiful, under the white moonlight's play. Her dark eyes were ablaze with a light that for the moment startled me.

"Mistress Goffe," I muttered, "I—"

"Peace!" she ordered; and if her voice was as sweet as a silver bugle it was also as sternly commanding. "Peace, dolt! Have you not insulted me cruelly enough, without—"

"Insulted you?" I gasped.

"Yes. Though I doubt not your dull brain deems it a compliment. You announce to me, coolly, that you feel yourself somewhat in my debt; and that you purpose to wipe out the obligation by granting me your most worshipful self in marriage. *Oh!*"

"I said naught of the kind!" I flashed back. "You have no right so to distort my words."

"What else, then, meant you?" she demanded. "In dry, set speech you declare yourself my debtor for the saving of your life—a service I would as blithely have rendered to a trapped puppy. You next explain how excellent a match you are for a fugitive's poor daughter, and—"

"I did not! I—"

"And you conclude your remarkable oration," she pursued, unheeding, "by graciously consenting to marry me. And I risked life to save such a man! To win for myself the first insult that man ever dared offer me! For it is an insult. The blackest of black affronts to any woman's pride. Are you too stupid, even yet, to see it?"

"I am," I answered, her scornful words stinging me as if they were as many whips. "Never yet have I intentionally offered insult to any woman. Least of all to you. I did not say I was worthy to wed you. I but begged for that great honor—"

"Do not add hypocrisy to the heap! I am not a child nor an imbecile," she replied.

"Is it an insult for an honest man to ask a maid to wed him?" I asked hotly.

"Aye! When *love* doth not force the words to his lips!" she retorted. "When such a man seeks to pay a debt by offering me a loveless marriage he insults me. When he urges that he 'begs' it as an 'honor,' he turns hypocrite."

"Oh, if a *man* could but speak so to me!" I growled deep in my throat.

"Righteous rage!" scoffed she. "Another form of hypocrisy. And the very worst form. For it is self-deception."

"You have no right," I repeated, "to misjudge me so. I—"

"Misjudge you?" she repeated. "Now, Heaven forbid! Listen to me, Master Dirck Dewitt. You have asked me to be your wife. Why?"

"Why? Surely—"

"Yes, *why?* There are but four recognized motives that can make a man ask a woman to marry him: love, money, influence, and—a, home. I have no money. I have no home. I command no influence. All that remains is love. Look me in the eyes. Do you love me?"

"I—I—"

"In the eyes. *Tell* me!"

As on that former day, the lie withered unspoken when I looked into the clear, fearless depths of those strange eyes. I could not speak.

"Do you love me?" she insisted.

"I—"

"The truth?"

"N—no!"

The denial spoke itself, without my conscious will. I could have bitten out my tongue for saying the word.

There was a moment of wretched silence.

Then, all the anger and life gone from her young voice, she said quietly:

"You have proven me right. You love me not. Yet you asked my hand. Was that no insult?"

She paused. And, again, my reluctant answer came:

"Yes."

"And, in seeking to make me believe you loved me, were you not then playing the hypocrite?"

"Yes. I—I—Blanche! I *do* love you! I *do!*"

(Laugh at me, ye wise ones. Laugh till your sides ache. I blame you not; even though I can hear you chuckle: "Not only no hero, but a fool as well!")

How it came about I know not. I suppose I shall never know. But, as I looked, soul to soul, into those eyes of hers, I all at once knew that I loved her. That I had loved her since the moment her face had bent over me in divine pity, that first night in the boat.

In that flash of self-revelation I saw now why I had been able to resist Greta Van Hoeck's later blandishments; how, under the rays of real love, my infatuation had melted like mist before the glow of the rising sun.

I loved Blanche Goffe. I loved her with all the heart and body and soul of me. And, blind fool that I had been, never had I so much as suspected it until I had just now looked into her truth-compelling eyes.

Somewhere, in an old fable, I once read of a well of truth; and that those who gazed into its depths saw their own selves as they really were. Now I understood. And into that well I was looking—looking miserably, hopelessly.

At one instant I had admitted, under the spell of Blanche's eyes, that I did not love her. The next second I had been crying out like any gawky schoolboy that I did love her. Then, the mad incongruity of it all struck me speechless.

At my blurted avowal, she drew a quick little sobbing breath; almost as though I had sworn at her. She peered into my face, leaning far forward. Then a black cloud rushed across the moon, leaving both our countenances in a gray blur.

When the cloud lifted, Blanche had sunk back into her seat, a forlorn little heap.

"Shall we go on?" she suggested; and her voice was dead.

"I love you!" I insisted doggedly.

"Please don't!" she begged, with that same little intake of breath.

And I somehow could not continue, in the face of her quiet appeal.

I paddled along, unhappy, furious at myself. She did not speak again. We neared the Pavonia shore.

Leaving the canoe on the beach, we went to where the two horses stood tethered. I lifted Blanche to the saddle, mounted my own horse, and we rode inland.

For several miles neither of us spoke. She was leading the way. Then, catching a faint sound, I looked ahead, more closely. She was crying softly to herself.

"Blanche!" I begged. *"Don't!* Oh, I love you! I *love* you! *I love you!"*

"Do not seek to comfort me with lies!" she implored. "I—"

"It is no lie! I love—"

"It was bad enough without *that!*" she cried. "Mynheer Dewitt, have you not the kindness, the manhood, to drop the painful topic? All is said! If you owe me aught, seek to repay by forgetting to-night's horrible scene."

"As you will!" I said briefly, my pride coming to my aid. "But—"

The rest was never spoken. Something struck me sharply across the throat, and I was hurled violently from my horse to the ground.

CHAPTER XIX.
TRAPPED!

WE had been cantering, at the time, through a bit of tree-lined level road at the top of a sloping hill. The rough road-bed had shone dimly, through patches of moon-shadow. I had caught up with Blanche, who rode ahead.

While I had been saying my final sulky words my horse had taken fright at something I could not see, and had sprung forward a yard or two in advance of Blanche's mount before I could check him.

It was then that I had felt the tug across the front of my throat, and—riding carelessly as I was—had been brushed from the saddle.

An exclamation of alarm from Blanche reached me as I fell. Even before I crashed to earth I knew full well what had befallen me; and I cursed my folly in traveling so heedlessly through a tract of a hostile country.

It was an old Indian trick to bring down a rider by stretching a green withe from tree to tree across a road. Some wandering war-party, I knew, had heard our horses' hoofbeats and the sound of our raised voices, and had halted us in this primitive fashion.

I was right.

Scarce had my falling body struck ground when a half-dozen silent forms had sprung from the shadows and thrown themselves upon me.

As I fought desperately I had a fleeting glimpse of two more savages at the head of Blanche's horse, and of a third who was lifting her from the saddle.

The sight filled me with a maniac strength. What man is there who will not fight tenfold more furiously in behalf of the woman he loves?

I tore away the writhing, half-naked bodies that swarmed over me; I beat them back and struggled to my feet.

It was a Hercules effort. But I did it. I, unarmed, against my forest foes—and it was the love of a woman that gave me the power.

A huge savage, hideous in the war-paint and insignia of a subchief, slashed at me with his hatchet as I struck him from me. I ducked, eluded the blow, and rushed in, gripping him about the body.

The stroke of his hatchet, deflected, grazed my shoulder. The pain of the graze completed my Berserk rage.

Digging my chin into the hollow between his shoulder and neck, I used my arm-hold about the body as a lever, clasping my hands behind the small of his back, and exerting all my mighty muscular power in the pressure.

He was a strong man—as tall as I and heavier—and he fought like a wildcat. He beat at my head and struck fiercely, if ineffectively, with his war-hatchet.

Pressing outward with my chin and drawing inward with my arms, I gave one final heave. No back-bone could stand that strain. Something snapped, and the giant lay limp and helpless across my clasped arms like a shot squirrel.

The rest raised a fearful cry as he tumbled heavily to the ground. A score of weapons flashed out. I wheeled, gloriously drunk with excitement, to face them all.

Oh, I was in fine mood to die—to die fighting, like a wounded wolf on whom the pack turns!

Blanche, as the braves gathered for their rush, cried out a swift sentence or two in the Lenape dialect. She spoke so rapidly that, in my wrought-up state and imperfect knowledge of the vernacular, I could not understand her.

But the others did. They halted a moment, irresolute. She hastened on in her rapid speech. Even at that crisis I envied her her splendid knowledge of the native tongue.

She ceased. Several of the leaders drew together about her for a muttered conference. The rest of the war-party—perhaps forty in all—stood glowering in silent wrath at me, their hands on their knives and tomahawks, awaiting only their chief's permission to fly to the slaughter.

And at my feet between us lay the huddled mass that had so lately been a giant Indian.

At length the powwow ended. Blanche came up to me.

"You understood?" she asked.

"No," I replied; "scarce a single word. I am to die, I suppose. It matters little, if only they will spare *you*. I wish I might have saved—"

"There is no question of death yet," said she. "You slew the son of their chief. They are of the Hak-en-Sak people, and foremost of the tribes to plan war against the Dutch. They were about to avenge their sub-chief's death when—"

"When you cried out something."

"When I told them I am an adopted daughter of the Arareeks, and that you are an honored guest of Macopin."

"That was why they paused?"

"Yes. The Arareeks are a powerful people. The Hak-en-Saks want to stir up no blood-feud with them. They fear, if they kill us, Macopin will find out and will carry vengeance through their country."

"It was wise of you. So they will set us free?"

"Not they. You have killed their sub-chief. They dare not—yet— put us to death or torture. But they will not free us. Instead, we are to be taken somewhere—and held captive until—"

"Until the hunt subsides or Macopin is thrown off the track, and it will be safe to put us out of the way in their own pleasant fashion? I understand."

"Macopin will pass here to-morrow. He will strike this trail, and he will read from it all that has happened as you or I might read a printed page. Then he will assuredly give chase, and—"

"March!" ordered an Indian, stepping up to us.

The braves fell in on every side. For an unarmed man to break past that human wall would have been impossible. Moreover, I owed it to Blanche to take no futile risk, but to bide near her in the faint hope of being at last of some use in case of emergency.

Back we traveled over the lane by which we had come from the river. The moon was low, and the skies were paling before the dawn wind's breath as we once more reached the waterside.

A couple of scouts, sent on ahead, had stolen several small canoes from Pavonia village just below, and were awaiting us at the brink.

"I see the idea," said Blanche. "They know Macopin will follow. And they know that no man may read a water-trail. They are going to take us by boat to some far outlying native village—perhaps to a village of another tribe that is allied to them. I have heard of such cases."

Into separate canoes we were thrust. The little flotilla set forth from land and faced up-stream. Northward through the gray of earliest dawn we went, propelled swiftly, silently.

The bulk of the war-party did not accompany us, but remained on the bank. Our escort consisted of perhaps twelve picked braves.

But, before starting, they had tied us, wrist and ankle, with deerskin thongs; so we were quite helpless.

There is no sense in tugging and mouthing when repose will suit one's purpose quite as well. Were there to be any future hope of escape, that chance would not be strengthened by useless struggles at present. Therefore, in very unheroic, but also very Indian, style I settled back quietly to await events.

Hour after hour the paddles plashed rhythmically into the still water. Hour by hour we moved northward. Around the ever-recurrent headlands of the Hudson's western shore we swept, keeping close to the bank and under the high hills' lee.

A man must needs have been in sorrier plight or in more dire danger than I in order to see that wonder panorama stretch out before him and feel no thrill.

The tall cliffs, the mountains, the lovely green forests, crept past behind us. Above was the blue morning sky, below the sun-kissed waters of the noblest river in the whole wide world.

A hundred times have I traversed that stream, but never without that same feeling of awed delight.

Here and there, in the distance, we saw a Dutch fishing-smack or two. But they were far out of hail. And if they noticed us, they took us for an Indian trading-party bound up-stream from a fur trip to New Amsterdam or Pavonia.

Dawn deepened into morning, and morning into noon. And so sped on the hours.

Around still another jutting headland we swung, and out to where the river broadens into a monster sheet of glittering azure water, more like a great lake than a stream's widening.

I knew the place. It was called by Dutch fisher folk the "Tappan Zee," or Sea of Tappan, taking its name from the tiny fur-trade post on one of its green banks.

We were far above the Hak-en-Sak country by now. An oblique movement of the leading canoe—and we shot across the Zee, transversely, coming to a halt at last in a shallow cove, shut off from the main river by a tall boulder-covered hill.

Beneath this hill, like a wasp's nest hanging to a shed's eaves, huddled an Indian village. The inhabitants ran down to the water's edge to welcome us. Our leader was evidently well known to them, for they greeted him warmly.

He jumped ashore. Gathering the head men of the place about him, he made a brief harangue, pointing from time to time at us.

A few minutes later we were lifted out, unbound, and shoved toward a couple of huts.

"Here we are to stay," said Blanche, "until it is safe to end our lives. They do not bind us or set sentinel over us, because they know we cannot get away."

"Cannot?" I asked. "Why not?"

"They have made themselves accountable to the Hak-en-Saks for us," was her reply. "That means every man, woman, and child of the village is our sentinel."

"And it was through me," I cried bitterly, "that you were captured!"

"Don't!" she said, a brave little smile twitching her lips. "We are good comrades, you and I. We must be, for each is the last white person the other will ever again see. And—it might be worse!"

"Yes," I answered under my breath. "I might be forced to live on without you!"

CHAPTER XX.
A DREAM OF FREEDOM.

MONTH after month—winter and summer again—and still Blanche Goffe and I were captives at the wretched Tappan Zee village.

For all practical purposes we might have been at the north pole. News of the outer world never reached us. Save for each other, we saw no white folk.

We had, at first, made one or two utterly futile efforts to escape. But of late months we had so realized the uselessness of such an attempt that we had ceased to struggle. And now even the sleepless vigilance of our guards had begun to relax.

It had been a strange and not wholly unhappy period. I had been with Blanche daily, and all day. And each hour had strengthened that suddenly acquired love of mine until it was now the only real thing in my whole existence.

Yet I had never spoken of it. Once or twice I had cautiously broached the theme.

But each time that look of troubled fear in her big eyes had choked back my avowal. She did not believe I loved her. By my own forced denial that night in the canoe she must be certain I cared naught for her.

Nothing I could have had the wit to say would have changed that wretched impression.

And I had learned gradually, too, that what I had once foolishly deemed her fondness for me was but the honest, frank affection a girl might have for a brother. Otherwise there must surely have been some sign in all these months of a deeper feeling.

Yet I loved her so absolutely that I tried to make myself imagine I was well content just to be where she was, to see her, to hear her speak, to know she was near me, that she depended on me for companionship.

I *tried* to imagine it, I say. But 'twas a pitiful effort at best, I fear.

One afternoon I sat on the rocks jutting out into the water, idly casting and recasting an Indian bass-rod, in the vain hope of catching some fish big enough to give me a good fight before I should land him. At anchor, a mile out, lay a Dutch fishing-smack, her sails furled. A man and a boy were moving about the deck, working over a net they were preparing to attach from the anchor-rope to a stake in the water, a hundred feet nearer us.

Dressed in native deerskins and bronzed by a year in the open air, I must have looked, to the boat's occupants, like a mere savage.

They were too far away for me to hail. And, had I done so, it would not only have been worse than useless, but would at once have sharpened my jailers' sleeping watchfulness.

As I sat there Blanche came to me. She carried a fishing-rod, and walked with lazy slowness. Scarce nodding in response to my salutation, she seated herself on the rock just below me and began with elaborate care to entangle a snarl in her line.

With moveless lips and bent head, she started to speak. I had to strain my ears to catch what she said.

"Don't look at me," she began. "Don't pay any attention to me. Some of them may be watching. Listen! I have great news. Can you hear me?"

"Yes," I muttered, leaning eagerly forward in another direction, as though to scan an imaginary "bite" from an equally supposititious bass.

"A messenger came half an hour ago," she went on. "I was with the squaws in one of the kitchen tents. And a girl who had been sent to carry food for the messenger told us the tidings he brought. He is from the Palisades tribes."

"Well?"

"The lower tribes have massed, and are in the forests behind Pavonia. They descend upon New Amsterdam to-morrow. It is the attack you foresaw last year."

"New Amsterdam?" I exclaimed. "Tell me, could you gather from the talk whether the Dutch still hold the New Netherlands? Has not Nicoll, with the English fleet, come yet?"

"I am sorry," she said softly, "but the Dutch still hold the city and the province."

I could have groaned aloud. For weary months I had been imagining the British fleet arriving off the Battery, the fall of the Dutch, the Anglicizing of the New Netherlands—the fulfilment of my life-dream. Long ago, according to my rough calculations, the fleet should have arrived. And now—

"I'm sorry," she breathed again compassionately, for she knew how dear this hope had been to me.

"It's all right," I answered. "I am a failure at all I ever attempted. This but crowns my life-task of incompetence. Tell me more, won't you?"

"Governor Stuyvesant has taken nearly every available fighting man," said she, "and has sailed, with seven ships, on an expedition against the Swede colonies on the Delaware. He was to have gone last year, but fear of an Indian attack made him keep his forces in the city. The Indians knew this, and for many months they have tried to prove themselves peaceful and harmless."

"And Stuyvesant was fooled by such a trick?"

"It seems so. He has gone at last to the Delaware. And the tribes mean to enter New Amsterdam to-morrow. They vow they will not leave one stone standing on another or one white man, woman, or child alive. Oh, Dirck, *don't* look so heartbroken over your beautiful plan's failure!" she broke off. "'Twas no fault of yours. You plotted it splendidly. If the English had not the wit to take advantage of—"

"I have ever failed," I said, after a short pause. "And now I am going to start on one final venture. This time, perhaps, I shall succeed. If not, I shall at least not be alive to reproach myself with my last failure."

"Dirck!" she exclaimed, "what do you mean?"

"The Dutch must be warned," I said briefly.

"But you can't—"

"At least I can try."

"But how? It is madness."

"I have been 'mad' before," I returned, "and my madness availed me little. Perhaps Dame Fortune may relent, now that I offer my own life in payment. As to the means for doing this thing, I must think them out. There are always means when the man himself is worthy."

"Dirck," she pleaded, "stop and consider. We are close-held prisoners here. You could not get away. Even if you could steal one of the guarded canoes, there would be pursuit. Before you reached the Palisade headlands—"

I had scarce heeded her. I was studying the clouds to the northward. Now I broke in on her entreaties with the seemingly irrelevant remark:

"There will be a stiff north wind by night. Almost a gale; unless those clouds tell lies."

"I don't understand what—"

"You speak of canoes pursuing me. And one of the long war-canoes with its twelve paddlers could easily overhaul a single man. But sails, before a north gale, can outstrip any canoe."

"Sails? There are no sail-craft here. You know that."

With an almost unnoticeable gesture I pointed to the Dutch fishing-smack at anchor a mile away.

"The fishermen?" she cried. "Is that your plan? But how can you get word to them? It is too far away for you to shout. And—"

"It is all a desperate venture at best," I agreed. "But if I could steal a canoe and get out to that fishing-smack, I could easily persuade them of the danger. Or, if not, I could force them to put on all sail and hurry to New Amsterdam."

"But, Dirck, you could not get a canoe a hundred yards from shore without being seen. A pursuing canoe or a flight of arrows would—"

"After nightfall, then."

"The canoes are always guarded at night. You know that. If white men were watching, you might hope, by forest lore, to outwit them. But no white man—be he ever so clever a forest runner—can catch two sentry Indians off guard. You might possibly overpower them with that great strength of yours. But at first sound of struggle every brave in the village would be upon you."

"You are right," I growled. "Disgustingly right! There is no possible chance to get a canoe."

"And you will be wise and give up this crazy plan?"

"Why, no," I answered, in surprise. "I don't give up plans when once I've made them."

"I know you don't," she sighed in despair. "But I hoped—for *my* sake, perhaps—"

"I had forgotten," I broke in, all penitence. "Here I've been trying to think out a way of saving a parcel of wretched Dutch burghers—and forgetting all about you. I can't go and leave you here. Forgive me for not thinking sooner of it."

Her eyes flashed and she retorted in pretty vehemence:

"We are comrades, you and I, Dirck. And where you go, I shall go. Shame on you that ever you doubted it! I begged you to give up this useless attempt because it seems to me to spell suicide for you. But if you are so pig-headed as to go, you sha'n't go alone."

"Blanche!"

"Oh, there is no peril to *me!* If we are caught the tribesmen will only bring me back to captivity. But they will kill you. It will be the chance they have so long awaited. Now, tell me this wild plan of yours, if you still have one."

Instead, I looked at her, a forlorn hope battling for life in my heart.

"Blanche!" I whispered. "You say you will go where I go. Does that mean—"

"It means," she said coldly, "that if there is a chance of escape I do not wish to be left behind. It means that. No more. No less. Let us understand each other quite clearly."

"I understand," I said quietly. "Forgive me."

A dull silence fell between us. At length she asked, in a collected, businesslike tone: "Have you thought out any plan?"

"How far can you swim?" I returned.

"I don't know. I swam the width of Pomp-i-ton Lake and back without once touching bottom."

"That is nearly two miles in all. Could you swim out to that fishing-smack? With a heavy north wind blowing?"

"I think so," she replied.

"If there is any doubt," I answered dryly, "it would perhaps be as well to reflect on that doubt now, on dry land, rather than to wait until we are a half-mile off shore."

"You mean to swim out to the smack?" she cried.

"Under cover of night," said I. "Their anchor is cast. They will probably fish until morning. If we can reach the boat and—"

"Will they take us aboard? Can you make them believe your story? Can we get clear of the shore without being seen?"

"Let us take up those questions when we get to them," I suggested.

CHAPTER XXI.
Frying-Pan and Fire.

THE wind rose at sunset, as I had foreseen. The night was overcast save for a rift or two in the clouds where a faint star shone through.

These stars showed me that the hour was close on nine, when Blanche and I (who had returned to our fishing after supper as the result of a loudly reiterated and laughing wager as to which could make the heaviest "catch" before midnight) slipped noiselessly into the cool water.

The waves were running high. Their swish on the shingly beach quite drowned any slight sound we may have made.

It was a propitious time. The hunters had returned from a day in the forest, and were gathered about the roaring campfire, eagerly questioning the messenger and discussing the chances of their Palisade brethren's raid.

All the camp was astir with excitement. Vigilance was slack. Nor did any think we would try so foolhardy a feat as to swim out into that wind-tossed river.

Your Indian is a fairly good swimmer. But, as a rule, only in quiet waters. When the wind is up, he believes the storm-spirits are playing over the waves. And, even in a boat, he will seldom of his own accord venture forth among the billows.

Least of all will he dare the storm-spirits' ire by swimming where those sprites are at play. Nor can he imagine that any one else would do so. This fact helped us; as I had hoped it would. And I was grateful, even though it is no easy task to swim in the trough of the Tappan Zee's highest waves.

Out from the shore we glided, Blanche and I, shoulder to shoulder. With the long, easy overhand stroke we swam, making almost no effort, content to husband our strength and to achieve only fair progress.

Our faces turned from the waves that washed sideways across us, we kept on. Little by little we drew away from land, out into the black night.

The girl was a perfect swimmer, and my doubts as to her skill and endurance were quickly set at rest. There was a stirring, glorious sensation in thus breasting the rough waters, side by side with her, facing together outward into the unknown.

The fishing-smack showed no lights. It was quite invisible from the shore. I had known it would be so. And my trained forest eye that afternoon had marked with the most careful precision the boat's location.

At dusk, too, I had glanced out toward the craft again, to make certain it had not shifted its anchorage. To swim through such a wind to the supposed spot and then find the boat gone was a possibility we could not afford to risk.

If you think it was easy to swim in fresh water, with your clothes on, with waves ever slapping the side of your head, and toward no visible goal, you are quite mistaken. Strong as I was, and carefully as I nursed my strength at each stroke, I soon began to feel the strain.

"How are you holding out?" I asked Blanche.

"It is all right," she answered gallantly.

Yet I could catch the fatigue in her voice. And I checked the stroke that had been keeping me beside her.

"Turn over and float," I ordered.

"In fresh water—in this wind?"

"Do as I say," I insisted.

She obeyed. With one hand under her shoulders, and "treading water," I buoyed her up. After a moment of relaxation she asked:

"Is it much farther, I wonder?"

"We must be more than half-way there," I replied. "Are you strong enough to start on again? At any moment they may miss us. Then, when they find no trail leading into the woods, they will take their chances with the storm-spirits and come looking for us in a war-canoe."

We struck out again, and for a time swam on, stroke for stroke, side by side; the waters buffeting us and filling our eyes and nostrils.

We swam thus for what seemed an eternity. Then, all at once, the rhythm of our movement was somehow broken. I turned my head to note the cause. And Blanche was no longer beside me.

Back, ten feet or more, she was lying, strangely huddled, her white, upturned face awash, scarcely visible above the surface in that ghostly light.

With a plunge I was back beside her.

"Blanche!" I cried, seizing her numb hands and drawing her toward me.

"I-I hoped you wouldn't miss me—till—till—it was too late!" she panted feebly. "I—I can't so on. It is a cramp. In both my arms. Oh, *go!*"

"Go!" I echoed. "And leave you to drown, you hero-girl? What do you think I am made of?"

"You *must!*" she gasped. "It all depends on you. "If you stay here with me we shall both go under. The warning cannot be given. I—"

"Blanche!" I cried, a red anger heating my chilled blood. "If you want to practise the feminine vice of self-sacrifice, do so, I pray! But not one inch shall I stir without you. If you refuse to let me help you, you throw away both our lives. Now, choose! And choose quickly! For my own strength ebbs."

"As—as you wish," she murmured, like a worn-out child.

"So! Have your cramped hands power enough to hold tightly to my shoulders? Try it. *So!* Good. Now lie flat, rigid. Hold the fringe on my hunting shirt's shoulders as gently as you can. And breathe as deep and as seldom as possible."

Off I struck again. She obeyed my simple orders, and at first I scarce felt her weight, though it impeded my speed.

"Remember," I warned her, "if you loose your hold, *I* shall stop, too. And it will be the end of us both."

It was no time for pretty speeches. At certain rare crises man is the master. And the most self-willed woman knows it and instinctively obeys him. This, if ever, was such a crisis.

On we went. The light touch on my shoulder grew to a crushing weight. The girl's slender body that I was drawing after me through the water seemed to weigh a ton.

I struggled on, doggedly, fiercely. I was fighting. Fighting the storm-spirits as never had I fought mortal opponent.

Despite my best care, my lungs and throat burned with the water that found its way into them. My muscles stiffened, and every motion was anguish.

Then—my outthrown left arm struck sharply against something hard and rough. My hands both closed upon the obstruction.

It was the stake that bound one end of the fishing-net.

At the other end of the straining net I knew lay the smack.

"We are there!" I panted to Blanche, hanging to the stake and letting my racked muscles rest. "See, over to the right. A bare fifty feet away."

Through the gloom, the fishing-smack was visible, tugging at her anchor and tossing heavily in the waves. The net between us and it was drawn as taut as a bowstring by the force of the pushing water.

"Come!" I said. "One more effort and we will be safe."

"Listen!" she broke in.

My own dense, water-beaten ears had caught no sound but the swish of wind and waves. But, as I harkened at her bidding, I now heard the steady soft *plash-plash-plash* of paddles striking the water in perfect unison.

Glancing over my shoulder as I struck out for the smack, I could see, ever drawing closer, a low, pointed, black shape. It was a war-canoe manned by six braves.

I needed no second vision to tell what had happened. Missing us, and finding we had not taken to the forests, the Indians had jumped at once to the conclusion that we had swum out to the fishing-smack in an effort to escape. And—remembering the smack's location quite as well as did we—they had set out after us.

It was no time for thought, but for the swiftest of swift action. I reached the smack's side, threw one arm over the low gunwale; and with the other, lifted Blanche over the rail. It was a feat that required all my ebbing strength.

The man and boy lay asleep on the little dirty deck. The boy, at the shock caused by my heave, started up.

"Injuns!" he bawled at sight of Blanche.

The canoe was already past the stake. Another two strokes would bring it up to us. Then, instead of being slaughtered or seized in the water, we should meet the same fate on deck.

Blanche safe over the side, I reached down to my belt for the long curved knife I had stolen that night from a momentarily empty teepee. The net's straining rope was close beside me. I gave one mighty slash with the blade, at the same time hugging the gunwale close with my other arm.

Out of the water leaped a brown curving thing; long, swishing, hideous, against the upper sky. Through the air it hissed, its flying ends just missing me.

Up and out it flew, encircling the war-canoe in the grip of an octopus.

"What—what *is* it?" cried Blanche aghast.

"The net!" I gasped, scrambling aboard. "It was strained almost to breaking point, and I cut the rope at this end. Luckily it was not weighted."

I had wasted no time in talking. Barely two seconds after I severed the net-rope, I was aboard, in the prow of the smack, cutting away like mad at the stout, over-taut anchor hawser.

The rope parted with a crack like a pistol's. The boat lurched violently and went floundering, wild among the waves.

The man, aroused by his boy's shout, had jumped to his feet, mouth open, eyes dazed with sleep.

"Injuns!" squealed the boy again; and "Injuns!" roared the man in reply.

He snatched up a blunderbuss from under a bit of tarpaulin. But I was too quick for him. Darting in, I struck his shoulder a blow that sent the clumsy weapon clattering to the deck.

Then, snatching up the blunderbuss, I leveled it at his head.

"Up sail!" I shouted. "Quick!"

Scared, he lurched to the mast, followed by the whimpering boy.

Thrusting the gun into Blanche's hands and running to the tiller, I ordered: "Faster! Up sail!"

Even in his dazed, cowed state, the fisherman was a sailor. And as the smack floundered wildly, the dirty gray canvas was slowly raised. Luckily, the two had been too lazy to clew the furled sail properly to its boom. And the raising was thus the easier.

My hand on the tiller held the smack steady.

In as little time as the telling takes, the wind had caught the half-raised canvas, the smack had careened dangerously and straightened, and we had gathered headway.

Then and then only did I have scope to look about me. Blanche, gripping the blunderbuss, was still leveling it at the trembling, chattering fisherman.

The canoe (its prow and paddles tangled in the meshes and loose ends of the flying net) had lost all power of motion. But the six Indians, working like mad, were fast cutting away the maze of wet strands. In another moment they would be free.

"Take the tiller!" I called to Blanche. "Keep headed due south—straight before the wind. Look to it that she doesn't jibe. So! A point to starboard!"

I had taken the blunderbuss from her as she grasped the helm. Now, kneeling—and resting the gun-barrel on the gunwale, I took careful aim and fired.

In the prow of the white birch-bark canoe a mighty hole was suddenly ripped.

I turned back and faced Blanche again.

"That will keep them too busy bailing to try to follow us," I said. "If there are any other canoes in pursuit, we'll probably have gathered speed enough before we reach them to stow a fairly clean pair of heels."

The sail was up. I had seen to that before I fired. Now, as I was speaking, the fisherman strutted over to me, grasping a long boat-hook. The peril of the loaded blunderbuss being removed, he was brave enough for any ordinary emergency.

"What d'ye mean by this outrage?" he bawled.

"From your speech," I answered gently, "you are English, not Dutch. We two are English folk escaping from captivity among the Indians. We need your aid and we implore it. I had no time to request it beforehand. For which, pray accept my apologies."

"I don't understand no fine gentleman talk!" he interrupted. "Leastways not when it's spoke by a man in Injun clo'es. But I *do* know you've spilt my net an' stole my fishing-smack. An' I'm goin' to take it out of yer hide. An' when we git to Tappan, I'll have ye clapped into jail."

"We are not going to Tappan, my friend," I returned, "but to New Amsterdam. We must reach there with all haste. Later, I will pay you for your lost net and for whatever fishing I have made you miss."

With a growl he sprang at me, boat-hook raised. I stepped lightly aside to avoid his rush. My foot slipped on a greasy bit of deck and down I crashed on one knee, the blunderbuss flying out of my hands.

Before I could recover my balance he was upon me. By a sudden twist of the body I avoided the boat-hook's blow and grappled with the man.

Over and over we rolled on the deck; smashing alternately against gunwale and mast; clawing, panting, heaving.

He was a strong man; but he was no match for me in my normal state. Now, however, spent with my long, terrible swim, I could scarce hold my own against him.

Once, in our tussle, my hand touched the knife-hilt at my belt. A single stroke of that razorlike curved blade would have ended the fight then and there.

But somehow the use of the knife in fair combat has always seemed to me unworthy of a white man. I could not bring myself to stab an unarmed enemy. And so we struggled on.

"Dirck!" cried Blanche. "Dirck Dewitt, I say! Master him quickly and come here! Just ahead there is—"

"Dirck *Dewitt?*" cried the fisherman, loosing his hold on me and staggering back. "*Dirck Dewitt,* did she say? You're—you're never Dirck Dewitt, are you?"

"Yes!" I panted, hoarse with exhaustion. "What of it?"

"If I'd killed or harmed you, man," he gasped, "I'd have wished my hands to wither at the wrist."

Suspecting a trick, yet wholly puzzled, I stared at him.

"My brother," he went on, "was the only Englishman in the Stadt-holder's crew. You saved him an' the rest from bein' blowed to blazes in that fire-ship. I—"

"Dirck!" called Blanche again in wild excitement. "Look!"

Scarce thirty yards ahead of us, and almost in our track, swung a great canoe manned by twenty Indians.

Drawn by my shot, while searching downstream for us, the savages had evidently divined what had happened, and had awaited our coming.

Their canoe lay obliquely before us, held steady by a dozen paddles; while six or seven braves crouched ready to spring aboard as we should draw near enough.

With our headway and the canoe's power of swift evolution, it would be an easy matter to board us, even if in straightway speed the savages' craft were not the smack's equal.

I jumped to the helm.

"What are you going to do?" asked Blanche in dismay, as she released the tiller to me.

"Run them down," I answered. "It's the only chance."

"A fine *chance!*" scoffed the fisherman, close at my side. "Don't you know the second we get within reach they won't *wait* to be run down? Every mother's son of 'em will be aboard us, ready for the massacre. An' we'll stand as much chance against 'em as a witch in a Puritan meetin'-house."

CHAPTER XXII.
My Friend the Enemy.

As he jerked out this highly pessimistic forecast, the fisherman caught the tiller away from me. I gladly released it. Picking up the empty blunderbuss and swinging it aloft, club fashion, I ran to the prow to repel the attack as best I might.

Hopeless as I knew it was to try to stave off the invasion of a dozen or more armed warriors, yet I was minded to sell my life as dear as might be.

Down upon the canoe we swooped. The braves crouched ready for the spring. I held my blunderbuss poised for the blow. I was almost near enough to strike. Then—

There was a wrench that sent me clean off my balance and almost overboard. A dismal creak of tackle and timbers, and—barely out of arm's length from the tensely waiting braves—the smack veered sharply to starboard.

Like a living creature—like a shying horse—the fishing-boat curved outward, swung; and wheeled back upon her former course. We had made a semicircle around the canoe, just too far away for the most daring athlete of its crew to make the intended leap.

As a bit of seamanship, the maneuver was well-nigh unparalleled in my own scant experience. So swift, so uncannily sudden had it been, that even the alert canoemen—braced for the shock of collision—were tricked by it.

"Lie down!" roared the fisherman the same instant. "Lie down, all!"

He crouched under the afterrail as he spoke. We obeyed him; and none too soon.

Over our heads, like a flock of angry hornets, whizzed an arrow-flight. One shaft stuck in the mast. A second grazed the top of my head.

"Are you safe?" I called to Blanche.

"Yes," she answered shakily, drawing out an arrow that had pinned the edge of her skirt to the deck.

"Keep down!" bawled the fisherman. "They're li'ble to fire again. We're all right. We'll get out of range of that birch-bark tub mighty quick now."

"Well, Master Dirck Dewitt," he went on presently, "what d'ye think of me as a steersman? You're a grand man at savin' a crew from panic aboard a burnin' ship. But when it comes to doin' a bit of jugglin' with a tiller, you're not my match."

"If you owed me anything for keeping your brother from drowning," I answered, "I think you have squared the account this night."

"I'm downright glad!" he made answer. "Often enough my brother's told me the tale. An' I've wished I could shake hands with you. Now, tell me what all this means. I don't yet grasp the right of it."

As briefly as possible I told him of our imprisonment and escape; of the news concerning the Indian attack planned on New Amsterdam, and our need for arriving there in time to give the warning.

At the end of my recital, he scratched his head and looked at me oddly.

"If your good lady," quoth he, "will step forward, out of earshot, there's a word I would speak to you in private, Master DeWitt."

Beckoning me beside him at the tiller, as Blanche laughingly went to the prow, he whispered:

"No need in scarin' the lady. But, d'ye know, there's a thousand guilder reward for you, alive or dead, posted on the signboard in front of the White Hall, in New Amsterdam?"

"What?"

"'Tis true. My brother told me of it, an' how he was minded to tear down the placard. *'One thousand guilders' reward,'* it reads, *'for the body of Dirck Dewitt, English spy. This sum will be paid to whomsoever shall bring him dead or alive to Petrus Stuyvesant, Gov'nor.'* That's the wordin'. My brother copied it out. An' they mean it. Trust old Petrus Silver Leg not to forgive nor forget an en'my."

"But surely—"

"Yes, Stuyvesant's away on a war-venture, I know. But there's plenty of Dutchmen left in New Amsterdam who would risk their souls for the joy of feelin' a thousand guilders clankin' in their pockets. An', in Stuyvesant's absence, who d'ye s'pose Silver Leg has left in charge at White Hall? Why, his sec't'ry, this same Master Van Hoeck you just said was your worst en'my of 'em all. He'll show you little enough mercy, I'm thinkin', if once he gets hands on you."

"I'm glad you didn't let Mistress Goffe hear," I muttered. "Then— There is but one safe course. *You* must carry the warning to them."

"Me!" he cried in alarm. "Not me, Master Dewitt. I've a fondness for my own thick neck. An' I'd hate to see it stretched."

"What do you mean?"

"Waal," he drawled confusedly, "you see, old Petrus made a law forbiddin' any one to sell liquor or guns to the Injuns. An' I just happened one day—by an off-chance, you know—to swap a couple of hogsheads of schnapps with a Hak-en-Sak chief for sixty beaver pelts. An' the schnapps, as it happened, turned out to be half water. An' the chief told Stuyvesant. An'—"

"Well?" I queried as he paused.

"Waal," he answered, "I'm no fancy thousand-guilder crim'nal. But Stuyvesant condemned me to hang. An' he's offered two hundred guilders to whoever'll bring me to New Amsterdam jail. So I—"

"So you refuse the risk?"

"I most sure do," he affirmed positively.

"I am doubly glad Mistress Goffe does not know," I said.

"Why? Has she took a fancy to *me?*"

"I mean," I explained, "that *I* will have to go to New Amsterdam and give the alarm. And I do not want her to be worried as to what may happen to me."

"You're—you're goin' into the city? Goin' to run your neck into the noose? Just to save a passel of fat burghers from the scalp knife?" he cried incredulously.

"The fat burghers," I answered, "have innocent wives and children."

"H-m!"

"I wish," I went on, "there were some place where I could leave Mistress Goffe in safety until—until it is all over."

"I can help ye there," he cried eagerly. "My brother lives in Haarlem, right on the edge of the Spuyten Duyvil. The lass can stay with my brother's wife. An' glad they'll be to help pay their debt to you by harborin' her. We'll stop there on the way down an' leave you to foot it the rest of the way to the city, if you're still set on sudden death."

And so it was agreed. I made excuse to Blanche that her presence in New Amsterdam, in case of Indian attack, would but embarrass me. And, unsuspecting, she agreed to my wishes.

Thus it came about that early in the morning I walked calmly through the newly opened gate of the city hall; and so—as my timorous friend the fisherman had so cheerily put it—prepared to "run my neck into the noose."

It was the only thing to do. Yet, when I thought of Louis Van Hoeck being in sole authority in New Amsterdam, I was coward enough to feel a qualm of real fear.

CHAPTER XXIII.
DARING DEATH.

UNRECOGNIZED, in my Indian dress and dense coating of tan, I hurried down the Broad Way toward the White Hall.

Pausing once, I inquired from a passing burgher whether the council sat during Stuyvesant's absence. He told me it did, and that it was probably in session at the moment.

(Folk in New Amsterdam breakfasted at six in those days, and went to bed, for the most part, winter and summer, at sunset. Official business was always transacted in the morning; the earlier the better.)

I had known this was Council Day, and I was relieved that that body held its routine meetings while the governor was away. It would make my task the easier.

Still unnoted (for trappers and Indians were as common sights along the Broad Way as peddlers at that period), I reached the White Hall. For an instant I loitered at the huge bulletin-board near the entrance, with its burden of placards.

At the top of the list I caught my own name in large script, and read the offer of a thousand-guilder reward for my capture alive or dead.

For well nigh a year, as the date showed, it had remained there. Of a certainty, Stuyvesant did not readily forget a delinquent.

I had an odd feeling, as might a ghost who reads the tale of his own death. Then shaking my shoulders angrily, as though to throw off some physical weight, I entered the building and ran up the broad, low stairway at whose head stood the Council Chamber door.

At the latter lounged a sentinel. He was nodding, with shut eyes. Even in my perturbation I smiled at thought of the difference his attitude would show were old Silver Leg at home.

Stepping past lightly, without waking the soldier, I pushed open the door and walked into the room.

About the long table, as of old, were grouped the burghers. At the board's head, a silver chain of office about his lean shoulders, sat Louis Van Hoeck. He was reading from a despatch, evidently just received.

"Whereat," he read in a weary, monotonous voice, "the Swedes did surrender unto us the last of their forts, and did formally make over to me the title to their Delaware River holdings. I trust, by the grace of Providence, to be once more in New Amsterdam on—"

"Pardon!" I broke in. "Hear *me*, gentlemen! His excellency's despatch can wait on my more important tidings. The—"

"Dirck Dewitt! By all that's holy!" roared bluff old Oloffe Van Cortlandt. "What make *you* here, man?"

"Guard, ho!" yelled Louis, jumping to his feet.

"Wait!" I ordered sharply. "My arrest can follow in due time if still you think well of jailing me. I bring news. I—"

"Guard!" bawled Louis again.

A soldier or two ran into the room. Van Hoeck pointed at me, his thin lips parted to give command.

"Hold on!" protested Van Cortlandt. "With due respect, Master Secretary, I beg to suggest that a convicted man doth not run into the jaws of death, of his own volition: if there be not some monstrous strong reason driving him. Let him say his say. I'll warrant it is of import."

Louis turned angrily to the guard again, but a general murmur of assent to Van Cortlandt's plea checked him. As he paused irresolute and glowering, I took advantage of the brief interval to say:

"The Palisade Indians and their allies are massing to attack the city. To-day or to-night they make their raid. They—"

"Tut!" sneered Louis. "Another Indian scare, forsooth! Your cry of 'Wolf!' comes a year late, Mynheer Spy. It served you once. It shall not do so now. Guard—"

"It is the truth!" I vociferated. "Would any lesser thing make me come here? I have dwelt among the savages for months. My tale is true. And I am here at my life's risk to tell it."

"The Indians are our sworn friends, nowadays," scoffed Van Hoeck. "You should have coined a better story to—"

"Gentlemen!" I cried, exasperated. "Will you let this man's unbelief weigh against my solemn warning? Is the safety of your wives and little ones of so slight account that you will neglect—"

"The man's speaking truth, for all he's a dirty spy!" declared Van Cortlandt. "I know enough of human nature to see that. *Mynheers*, our chairman is howling for the guard. Let them be summoned, by all means—to defend our town. What say you?"

Again a murmur of strong assent greeted his words.

"Tell us your tale, Dewitt," Van Cortlandt went on. "And, if it be true, I, for one, shall use what scant power I have with the governor to save you. Speak out!"

In as few words as might be I repeated what I knew. Once or twice an impatient gesture from Louis sought to discredit my narrative. But I could see the others believed.

When I had finished, Van Cortlandt brought his huge hand down on the table with a bang worthy of Stuyvesant himself.

"'Tis the *truth!*" he proclaimed. "Everything proves it. The governor's absence; the redskins' patient cunning in waiting till the town is stripped of its master and its best defenders, the whole account. There is no time to waste. As for a first step—"

"As a first step," interposed Van Hoeck, "I order the guard to lock the returned spy in the city prison. He shall be hanged as quickly as I can find and countersign the death-warrant made out for him by the governor. And—now—"

"Pardon, Heer Secretary," put in Van Cortlandt. "You are not Petrus Stuyvesant, but a mere figurehead. We—the Council of New Amsterdam—have a voice in this.

"*Mynheers,*" he continued, turning to the councilors, "here is a fellow who dares death at the savages' hands and then at our own, to save our babes and women from the scalping knife. Shall we pay such service by hanging?"

"No! no!" broke from a dozen throats.

"Mynheer Van Hoeck," cried Van Cortlandt. "The Council of New Amsterdam has spoken. What is your one voice against ours? You are our acting chairman. Not our master. The man goes free!"

"You shall answer to his excellency for this!" snarled Louis, his face white, his fanglike teeth gleaming yellow under his back-curled lips.

"We stand ready to answer to his excellency at all times, Mynheer Van Hoeck," was the reply, "without reminder from you. We have growled at each other long enough. It is time to see to the defenses and to call out every man who can bear arms."

Van Hoeck had left the table and was whispering to a guard officer. The latter signaled now to the two of his men. And the three approached me.

"Officer!" snapped Van Cortlandt. "What are you about to do?"

"To arrest this man at the Heer Chairman's orders, sir," answered the officer.

"The council has just declared the man free," said Van Cortlandt sternly. "If you lay hands on him you do so in defiance of that council. And, as you well know, disobedience to a council order means a year's imprisonment as well as an hour a day in the stocks. Now, arrest him if you have a mind to the penalty."

The soldiers halted, then slunk back to their places.

"Arrest him!" shouted Van Hoeck. "I command it."

"Pardon, Heer Secretary," mumbled the officer, "but the honorable council's orders must bind us in his excellency's absence."

"Poor Louis!" I consoled Van Hoeck. "If only some one could some time be found who would obey you, what a sublime leader you would make!"

Frantic at my solemnly sighed words and at the laugh they raised, Van Hoeck rushed at me. Several men threw themselves between us. They forced him back to his seat.

Then began a quick session. Hurried orders were despatched and defense plans made. Soon the meeting was adjourned, each man hastening away on special duty.

As I passed down the stairs I caught up with Oloffe Van Cortlandt.

"*Mynheer,*" I said, "accept my deepest gratitude."

"The shoe is on the other foot," he grunted. "Hark ye, lad! I have saved you, for the minute. But you know as well as do I that when old Silver Leg returns, neither I nor the whole council can avail you aught. And he is not a man to forgive a spy. Take my advice: Vanish!"

"I cannot," I replied, "though I thank you none the less."

"Cannot? And why, pray? Art in love with the idea of hanging?"

"Not overly much," I said, "but there are perchance a few other things a trifle more precious than life."

"I have yet to hear of any," he grumbled. "Take my advice and—"

"One of those other things," I resumed, "is the safety of others. You said in council just now that the city is pitifully in need of every man who can be found to defend the place against the Indians. It seems that this is no time for a true man to—'vanish.'"

"You would stay and help us in our dark hour?" he cried. "Us, against whom you came a-spying? We who have offered a reward for your death?"

"I would not," I retorted, "were the choice left to *me*. But there seems to be no choice. Duty seldom leads us by the road we prefer?"

"H-m!" he growled, clearing his throat impatiently. "If there be one thing above another that I detest, 'tis a spy. But—but—hang it, Master Dewitt, I ask the honor of shaking your contemptible hand! Spy or no spy, you're a *man,* sir. And now," he blustered on, ashamed of his emotion, "let us waste no more precious time in palaver. To work!"

It was about an hour later. The whole city was buzzing like a hive of bees. Every one was at some special task.

Women were burying silver and were carrying full water-buckets to the house roofs in the event of the city's being fired.

Old men were cleaning weapons, molding bullets, sharpening swords. Such few men of fighting age as still remained in New Amsterdam were strengthening the wall palings, barricading housefronts and manning the stockade.

All at once a lookout on the spire of St. Nicholas's church raised the cry:

"The Indians!"

"Which way?" demanded a hundred voices.

"To the north!" he answered, pointing.

Half the population rushed to the wall or to the roofs for a look at the invaders.

Out of the woods to the north marched a red horde, nearly two thousand strong. Every savage was armed. Each was in full panoply of war-paint.

Marching steadily, slowly, in compact formation, the Indians calmly approached the flimsy stockade, behind which a ridiculously small body of untrained, ill-equipped white men awaited their attack.

CHAPTER XXIV.
THE ATTACK.

Louis VAN HOECK, as his excellency's representative, stood fearlessly at one of the stone gun bastions of the wooden wall, watching the oncoming host. From every point of the wall bristled weapons.

Through its opening, steel headpieces gleamed. The two cannon were manned, the gate shut and barricaded.

The savages noted these signs of preparation and halted. The stolid faces of their leaders showed a tinge of chagrin. The Indians had looked to catch the town unguarded, with open gates; to fill its streets with murderous braves before the first cry of warning could be raised.

In which case nothing could have saved New Amsterdam from an absolute massacre and total destruction.

Now they found themselves confronted by determined men, fore-warned, ready to die in defense of their homes. The sight of the two cannon and the line of leveled muskets was not reassuring.

There was a brief conference. Then one of the chiefs walked forward with a careless, majestic tread until he stood before the gate.

"What seek ye?" called Louis Van Hoeck.

The chief's hand went up in the familiar "peace sign."

"My brother," he answered in tolerable Dutch, "we come as friends."

"As friends?" I retorted from my position near the gate, and speaking in the Lenape dialect; "wearing war-paint and carrying full equipment of weapons? Is it thus that 'friends' pay visits?"

"Silence, there!" ordered Louis, glaring down at me.

Then to the chief he added:

"If you come as friends, why are you in such numbers, and armed?"

"We hold in two days a solemn conclave," answered the chief, "with the Pequots and the Narr-a-gan-setts from the north. We meet in the plains below your village of Haarlem. It is a sacred festival. While we await the northern folks' coming, we thought to visit your great city. Will you make us welcome for the love we bear the Dutch?"

"We cannot admit you here," declared Louis. "Our governor is away and he would not permit us to receive visitors of honor in his absence. Go back."

"Our people have come far—from beyond the Palisades," answered the chief. "Their canoes lie along the river bank a mile to northward. We cannot, for shame, go back and tell our women we have been refused admittance where we came as guests. Let us camp for the night beneath your walls."

"You cannot!" insisted Van Hoeck. "Go back whence ye came. It is my last word. Must I enforce it with powder and ball?"

The chief's heavy face did not change. He stood silent a moment, then walked back to his fellows. There was another conference.

An order was muttered. The whole two thousand turned and marched obliquely northwestward toward Hudson's River.

"You see," said Van Hoeck to Van Cortlandt a little later, as he descended from the wall, "'Twas a mare's nest. The 'raid' was a mere visit of curiosity. And the wondrous 'peril,' whereof the spy prated, is over."

"I am not so sure," answered Van Cortlandt. "What say you, Dewitt?"

"Indians do not come to conclaves—nor on peace visits—in war-paint," I replied.

"Pshaw! 'Twas a ruse of Dewitt's to gain a pardon," growled Van Hoeck, "which a soft–hearted council gave him against my better judgment."

"The danger is *not* over," I insisted. "Mynheer Van Cortlandt, since the secretary is so dull, I beg you to see the city remains under arms. Look yonder!" I broke off, pointing westward.

Down the river in solid phalanx moved a fleet of war-canoes, each full of Indians.

"To the shore! To the Battery foot!" yelled Van Cortlandt. "'Tis a flank movement."

But it was not. As our soldiers ran westward down the narrow lanes that led to Hudson's River, the canoes passed by without so much as veering to landward.

Below the Battery fort they paddled, and straight to the south. Nor did they pause until they had reached Staaten Eiland. There they dis-embarked.

"Now, what make you of *that* move?" demanded Van Cortlandt of me.

"I do not know," said I, sore puzzled. "But I counsel you not to relax guard."

"'Tis simple," here contradicted Louis. "They need provisions. The game has all been cleared out of our woods to far north of Haarlem. On Staaten Eiland there are still plenty of deer and bears. They go for a hunt and a feast."

The burghers near-by nodded in approbation of the theory. The news spread through the town that all danger was past. And the good folk looked at each other shamefacedly at memory of their fright.

I went to the nearest tavern. There I ate, then flung myself on a bed and slept like a log. I had known no slumber for thirty hours and I was exhausted.

I had a disgusted feeling of anti-climax. On the morrow, if the Indians' supposed attack had really been averted, I would shake the dust of New Amsterdam forever from my feet and go back to Massachusetts, there to take up again my long interrupted farm life among my own father's own people.

I had once more scored a failure. This time a ludicrous one. The Indians' assault that I had so mock-heroically proclaimed, was doubtless a figment of the imagination; born in the brain of the messenger who had visited the Tappan Zee village.

For, Indians are ever wont to be egregious liars; and this one had heard of the proposed intertribal conclave and had distorted it into a New Amsterdam attack.

On the morrow I would bid Blanche farewell—and my heart throbbed heavily at the thought! I would see her safe on her way, to her father, in the Pomp-i-ton country, under escort. Then I would leave forever this scene of so many dead hopes.

I did not awake. At least, not consciously. Of a sudden I found myself on my feet in the middle of the room, my hand on the hilt of my hunting knife, my ears full of a wild confused clamor.

Shouts—screams—the report of a gun—a death yell! Then from the steeple of St. Nicholas's church rang the harsh clangor of an alarm bell. And the fort bugle caught up the din.

To the door I rushed. The little city was alive with commotion. Below me, toward the Bowling Green, stretched the white, dusty Broad Way.

And up the thoroughfare came tumbling, through the gloom, an awful avalanche of leaping, half-naked, shouting creatures. The Way was blocked from wall to wall with Indians!

Their weapons glittered under the starlight, their plumed headdresses tossed fantastically against the sky. From a thousand throats came the shrill war shout.

Waiting till midnight, the savages had crossed from Staaten Eiland, had landed under the very noses of the careless Battery guards, and were swarming up through the city.

And I—*I,* whose senses should have kept me apprised of peril—had slept like a log instead of being on hand to give the alarm.

The tavern, behind me, was full of swearing men and of weeping, hysterical women. The landlord, a bald, fat dwarf, with a fringe of red whiskers, bustled to the door beside me, in his night gear, a blunderbuss in his hands, a horse pistol caught between his teeth.

"At 'em!" he bellowed right valiantly. "At 'em, everybody!"

He waddled out into the street. I caught him by the arm and jerked him back. But I was too late. From the vanguard of the advancing Indian throng an arrow sang. The landlord, with a queer little choking sound in his throat, collapsed in a heap upon the ground.

I pulled him back into the doorway, where a woman and a young girl at once threw themselves on their knees beside him, their lamentations filling the house.

Scarce had I time to snatch up his pistol and blunderbuss when the red mob was abreast of us. A young brave raised a tomahawk to hurl it at the crouching, weeping women at my side. I discharged the blunderbuss full in his face.

Then, slipping the awkward weapon under my left arm, as he fell, I had barely scope to cock and fire the horse-pistol at a savage who was hacking at me with a hatchet.

Down he went. From the yell his comrades raised, he must have been a man of note. While the main body dashed on, a dozen or more Indians rushed the doorway where I stood.

Keeping well between the two protecting posts of the threshold, I clubbed the blunderbuss and laid about me with all the strength I had.

An arrow stuck in my shoulder. A knife thrust reached my forearm. But I fought on, wielding the heavy blunderbuss with a swiftness and force that for the moment held my foes at bay.

Then came another concerted rush. Down whirled my gun-butt on the shaven scalp of an Indian. And as he crashed earthward at the impact, the stout wood of the blunderbuss stock shivered to splinters.

A huge savage took advantage of my instant of helplessness to fling himself upon me, knife in hand. I was just able to flash out my own knife, to parry his wild slash and to stab furiously at his chest.

I felt my blade drive through bone and flesh. The dying man clasped me about the arms and body in a convulsive grip that I could not shake off.

As he did so a warrior behind him leveled a blow at me with a knobbed club. I saw it coming. But the weight and the death struggle of the man who grasped me impeded my motions as I sought to fling myself to one side.

For one instant I saw the whole scene—the choked street, the houses whence the flames were already beginning to burst, the wild, inhuman faces of my foes, the giant who was aiming the club-blow at my defenseless head.

Then, as the Indian who had seized my body fell limply to the ground, and I ducked sharply to avoid the other's club, I knew instinctively that I was too late in my movement of precaution.

For, all at once, the air burst into a million varicolored lights. There was a crash that blinded and stunned me. I felt my knees double under me through no volition of toy own.

Then I fell an interminable distance, felt my body thud noisily against the door lintel and—and—

That was all! Afterward I knew nothing except that, far—*very far*—away, women were screaming and that their shrieks caused my anguished head untold tortures.

Then I fell asleep.

CHAPTER XXV.
AT THE MERCY OF THE MERCILESS.

"YOUR EXCELLENCY," Van Cortlandt was saying, "I have had the honor to describe to you his services to our city. Had we heeded his advice more closely many a life and many a house would have been spared."

I listened dully to my advocate's pleas. For I knew well enough what judgment Petrus Stuyvesant would pass. I knew naught could ever turn him from a decision once formed. And, well nigh a year agone, he had formed the decision to execute my unworthy self.

Much time had passed since the night of the Indian raid upon New Amsterdam. The savages had looted the city, slaying and burning, and had fled back to their Palisade wilderness, burning Pavonia village as they went.

On the morning after the massacre, I had been found lying just outside the burned tavern, in the midst of a grim little ring of my slain.

It was Oloffe Van Cortlandt who (inspecting the dead and wounded as they were carried to an impromptu hospital in St. Nicholas's church) had recognized me. He had made sure there was still a flickering ember of life left within me, and had had me borne to his own house, that faced the street now bearing his name.

There for weeks I had lain 'twixt life and death; too drowsy, too stupid to heel aught that went on about me. My soul was held by very feeble bonds, just then, to my battered body. For I had no yearning to live on.

Then came a change. I opened my tired eyes one day to find Blanche Goffe leaning above my pillow. From that hour I improved. And from that hour she had never left me; nursing me tenderly as an angel of mercy.

And at the last I emerged weak and thin, but convalescent, from the Valley of the Shadow.

Stuyvesant, meanwhile, had returned from the Delaware. So busy was he in supervising the rebuilding of the half-destroyed city and in caring for those who had lost all by the raid, that I half hoped my own case might be forgotten by him.

I was strengthened in this by learning that Louis Van Hoeck had been slain during the massacre—fighting gallantly at the head of a detachment of soldiers.

I was daily growing stronger. Soon it would be safe to move me from my sickroom. Van Cortlandt and Blanche and I planned that I should be rowed by night across Hudson's River and should make my way, with Blanche, in easy stages, to the Arareek country.

On the morning before the night of the date set for my escape, the clank of spurs and scabbards sounded in the lane in front of the Van Cortlandt house. I went to my window, Blanche at my side, and looked down.

There, before the door, stood a squad of the city watch. Their officer was talking with Oloffe Van Cortlandt who, from his gestures, was apparently making vehement protest of some sort.

At last Van Cortlandt turned and re-entered the house. A moment later he had come into my room.

"Lad," said he, his lips twitching, "I've black news for you. We delayed your departure a day too long. I—"

"I understand," I answered, touched at his emotion, "I am to be sent to prison until the gallows can be prepared."

"No," he muttered, "not quite that—yet. You are summoned to appear forthwith, before his excellency, in the council chamber. I have sent for a litter to bear you thither. And I will go with you. Whatever poor eloquence or influence I may have shall be used for you."

He tramped hurriedly out of the room, growling something about going for his hat and staff. The watch captain and one of his men stood just outside the door, to prevent any possible chance of my escape. Though—faith—I could not have run a hundred yards on those tottering legs of mine.

Blanche brought me a cloak and a hat—part of the costume of civilization with which Van Cortlandt had provided me—and then proceeded to throw her own scarlet-lined mantle over her shoulders.

"*You* are going away, too?" I asked.

"I am going with you," she replied.

"But I—"

"I am going as far on your road as they will let me, Dirck."

"That road, Blanche, leads to the gallows foot. I pray you spare yourself the suffering. You cannot aid me. I shall be but the unhappier, knowing that you are distressed on my worthless account. And I must keep a calm mind now if ever."

"Then you do not want me to go with you as far as I may?" she asked, troubled.

"Want you? *Want* you?" I echoed, almost fiercely, "I want you always and everywhere! Each moment you are not with me is drear loneliness."

"My good, *good* comrade!" she whispered softly, her big eyes raised to mine.

"Comrade!" I repeated. "No! I stand in the shadow of death, sweetheart, and I dare not lie. I am *not* your comrade. I am your *lover!*"

"No, no!" she protested, shrinking back. "You told me once—and you meant it—that you loved me not. Let me remember you as the honest, dear comrade whom I have learned to look on as a beloved brother—"

"So be it!" I sighed, my sudden elation dying and leaving me strangely weak. "So be it. Forgive me that I annoyed with love words a girl who is too wise to care for me in that same mad way. But I *do* love you, Blanche. With all the heart and soul of me!

"Ah, do not grieve," I hurried on, as her brimming eyes took on a wondrous light. "You *could* not love such a man as I. And I am thrice happy, just to have been near you so long. I—"

Oloffe Van Cortlandt bustled into the room, making much pother and haste to mask his feelings.

"Come," he called, "the litter is ready. Captain, we are at your disposal. Lean on my arm, lad. So! Now, march!"

And we set forth thus for the council chamber.

With Van Cortlandt and Blanche on either side of me, I entered upon the council's session. Stuyvesant's ruddy face grew redder as he caught sight of me.

Blanche would have had me sit down, for I was still pitiably weak. But I preferred to meet my fate standing.

So there, leaning on a corner of the table for support, I stood. And if my body was feeble, there was at least no flinching in the gaze wherewith I met Petrus Stuyvesant's wrathful glance.

And we two remained for a space, wordless, eying each other— while the councilors looked on in uncomfortable silence.

News of my arrest had preceded our coming. My case had caused the wildest interest among the people. Nearly the whole population of New Amsterdam was gathered in the square before the White Hall, to hear the tidings of the verdict.

It was Stuyvesant who first spoke.

"Well, Mynheer Spy!" he observed.

"Well, Mynheer Silver Leg," I returned, with an air of grave courtesy.

He grew purple.

"You dare call me—*me*—by an odious nickname?" he howled.

"Even as your excellency has just dared call me by a far more odious one," I assented quietly.

"Pardon, your excellency," intervened Oloffe Van Cortlandt, rising at this juncture and clearing his throat, "I crave permission to address this council and your honorable self."

Without waiting for further leave, the gallant burgher plunged into a fervid defense of my unworthy self, and a still more fervid plea that my life be spared.

He pointed out that my supposed work as spy had evidently profited England nothing; since no British attack had been made upon New Netherlands. He cited, in glowing colors, my action in returning at life's risk to warn the city of the Indian raid.

He was pleased to say that the arming of the burghers as a result of my warning, had saved New Amsterdam from total annihilation on the night of the massacre.

He gave a right dramatic description of my fight with the savages at the tavern door; and pointed to my present weakened, emaciated state as the result of my so-called heroism.

Oh, it was a splendid plea! The burghers broke in more than once with scarce checked applause. Blanche's wan face was tinged with hope, and she covertly slipped her little hand in mine.

Even old Silver Leg forgot to scowl at me and listened; first reluctantly, then with very evident admiration.

With the words that open this chapter of my narrative, Van Cortlandt closed his speech and sat down. Instantly, five or six enthusiastic conclave were on their feet to indorse his appeal.

But Stuyvesant motioned them to their chairs again; angrily, contemptuously, as a fox-hunter might order a hound to its kennel. And—as ever when his fierce will clashed with theirs—the burghers obeyed.

"I have heard all that can be said in defense," snarled the governor. "And all the facts in the case were already before me. Dirck Dewitt, stand forward!"

I moved along the side of the table until I halted before him. He looked me full in the face again. And I met his gaze as fearlessly as before.

"Mynheer Dewitt," he began, his big voice as steady and emotionless as though he were reading from a scroll, "at your life's peril you returned to this city to warn its inhabitants. At your life's peril you fought, well-nigh to the death, that same night, in this city's quarrel."

He paused, while all wondered. Then he resumed:

"In recognition of those two services I herewith publicly thank you in the name of their High Mightinesses the States General of Holland. I thank you in my own name as Governor of the New Netherlands. I thank you from my heart in the name of the citizens whose lives and property you sought to save. And to prove a country's gratitude, I take pleasure in bestowing upon you the Order of Orange."

He took a blazing decoration from his breast as he spoke and pinned it to my coat.

The council chamber was in an uproar. The staid burghers cheered themselves hoarse. They slapped each other on the back, waved hats and wigs, crowded about me, then shaking my hand and congratulating me.

They even sent up three huzzas for the governor himself. Never before in all his eighteen-year administration had Stuyvesant come so near being popular as at that moment.

His excellency stood unmoved, and waited for the first noisy excitement to subside. Then, still facing me, he continued as though no interruption had occurred:

"Mynheer Dirck Dewitt, you have also been proven a spy of the English king. For that crime you have been condemned to death. The sentence will be carried into effect in half an hour."

CHAPTER XXVI.
THE GIRL.

A GASP from the incredulous burghers; a loud babble of protest— a stifled little cry from Blanche Goffe—and his excellency rapped angrily on the table for silence.

"The city hangman has been notified," said he, "to have the gallows in readiness. A file of soldiers, led by the provost marshal, will conduct you, forthwith, from this spot to the place of execution. And may Heaven, in its divine pity, have mercy upon your soul!"

I straightened my shoulders, saluted, and turned to face the provost marshal. The latter stepped forward, received the death-warrant scroll from Stuyvesant, and laid a hand on my shoulder.

The burghers, held in check thus far by Stuyvesant's glare, broke into a fresh clamor or expostulation.

"Silence!" roared the governor.

But, though the others halted irresolute one person in the great room knew no terror of the brutal man. Blanche Goffe darted forward and caught Stuyvesant's upraised hand.

"Your Excellency!" she panted, "you *cannot*—you *will* not—do this thing? Think what he did for you all! He—"

"Mistress Goffe," interrupted Stuyvesant, "you have deserved well of us. It was you who helped to bear the warning here, and who spread the alarm through Haarlem village. You have nursed the sick and wounded right zealously during the weeks that followed the disaster. I grieve that you should range yourself with such a man as this."

"It is an *honor!*" she declared. "And I would not part with it for all the wealth of this new land. Oh, Your Excellency, I entreat you, do not cast this blot on your fame! Do not condemn to death a brave, true man! In the name of all you deem holy—"

"You demean yourself," he broke in roughly, "to speak for so vile a creature as a condemned spy. What can such a man be to *you*, that—"

"What is he to *me?*" she cried, her face transfixed, her glorious eyes ablaze. "He is the man I love!"

"Blanche!" I cried, unbelieving.

"The man I *love!*" she repeated. "The man I have loved from the hour that first I saw him! And—and until this very day I knew not he returned my love! Now that I have learned it, will you take him from me? You praised my few poor services to your city. Repay those services ten thousandfold, and save yourself from ignominy, by setting him free! Oh—"

"You are beside yourself with hysterical fear!" he answered. "It is not meet that modest maid should speak as you have just done. Nor does it profit aught against justice. Provost marshal, take your prisoner!"

Again the provost marshal stepped forth. But ere he could lay hands on me, I had sprang forward to where Blanche still knelt before Stuyvesant.

Unmindful of the other's presence, unmindful of my fate, of everything save the blindingly beautiful light that had just burst upon my waning life—I raised her gently in my arms and held her against my heart.

She lifted her drenched eyes to mine, and our lips met in a long kiss. Then I released her, my whole body a-thrill with a heavenly joy.

"You have made it all worth while, dear heart!" said I. "Death—my wretched failure—and *all.* I can die right blithely now. For the longest, fullest life could hold no more divine moment than this!"

"Dirck!" she wept, clinging to me. *"Dirck!* I—"

The roar of a cannon shook the White Hall to its very foundation. From the street outside rose a babel of excited voices, and the running of countless feet.

Out of the window I glanced instinctively. There, just beyond, to the southward, stretched the sun-kissed waters of the upper bay. And at anchor, scarce a stone's throw from shore, a stately war-vessel rode. Behind her, with sailors busy at sails and anchors, were six other war-ships.

And—from their peaks, in the morning breeze, fluttered the flag of England!

"What does it mean? What does it mean?" raged Stuyvesant incoherently.

"It means, Your Excellency," I retorted, delirious in my unexpected triumph, "that seven line-of-battle ships of England's fleet lie off the Battery; ready, if need be, to blow your Dutch village to atoms. It means that my life has been *no* failure! It means," I blundered on, incoherent in my mad joy, "It means I shall—*live!*"

"Tell the fort soldiers to man the guns!" bellowed Stuyvesant to his orderly. "Ring the alarm bell to summon the whole city to arms! It is a trick! And—"

"Your Excellency," interrupted Van Cortlandt, stopping the orderly by main force, "you are condemning New Amsterdam to useless bloodshed. What chance have we, in our weakened, unprepared state, against the connonade of seven line-of-battle ships? It is madness! Do not take your people's lives in a futile defense."

"Am I master here or not?" screamed Stuyvesant. "This colony is still under Dutch rule. And, in the name of the States General, I—"

"No!" I interrupted. *"In the name of the king!"*

"Provost marshal," commanded Stuyvesant, stung to fresh fury by my words, "take this spy out and hang him! If it were the last order that ever I gave, I—"

"If the order were obeyed," put in Van Cortlandt, "the English would terribly avenge his death. Let him alone, provost marshal. By the council's authority, I order it!"

"The council?" stormed his excellency. "What is the council's word against mine? I order—"

"Petrus Stuyvesant," interposed Van Cortlandt, "for years you have ridden roughshod over the rights of this colony, and of this council. And we have endured it. But the hour for endurance is past. It is a question of our people's safety. *Mynheers,* what is your word? Shall we suffer this madman to bring ruin and slaughter on our city to gratify his stubborn pride? Shall we let the English lay our town in ashes; when by yielding, we may save all?"

"No!" came the unanimous answer.

For a moment, Petrus Stuyvesant glared about him like a baited lion. Then, as a welcoming cheer from the townsfolk at the water's edge greeted the arrival of the last English vessel, the old governor collapsed into his chair, buried his face in his great hairy hands, and groaned aloud.

The yoke of his despotism was forever broken. And he knew it. There was something almost tragic in his tense despair.

I felt a warm little hand grasp me fingers. All at once I forgot everything about me. I forgot that my golden plans had at last succeeded, that my country's future was assured—that New Amsterdam had just died, and that New York was newly born!

Yes, I forgot it *all.* I remembered naught; cared for naught, save that my wondrous dream maiden at last was mine!

All *mine!*

THE END.

Appendix I
Original source publication

This novel was serialized in six issues of *Argosy,* from April through September of 1911.

April 1911

Front text:
Author of "In Treason's Track," "The Spy of Valley Forge," "The Sword of the Emperor," etc.

Why Dirck Dewitt Was Sent by Charles the Second from Old England to New Amsterdam, and the Thrilling Adventures That Befell Him Under the Dutch and Among the Indians.

May 1911

Front text:
Author of "In Treason's Track," "The Spy of Valley Forge," "The Sword of the Emperor," etc.

Why Dirck Dewitt Was Sent by Charles the Second from Old England to New Amsterdam, and the Thrilling Adventures That Befell Him Under the Dutch and Among the Indians.

SYNOPSIS OF CHAPTERS PREVIOUSLY PUBLISHED.

THE story is told by Dirck Dewitt, born in New England, but sent to New Amsterdam as a spy by Charles II of England to ascertain the lay of the land with respect to the British attempting to wrest the New Netherlands from the Dutch. On board the ship Stadtholder, Dewitt loses his heart to Greta Van Hoeck, who seeks to make him reveal his purpose in sailing to the New World. He is about to comply when her brother Louis appears on the scene. There is no love lost between the two, and now they draw sword upon each other, and are hard at it when the combat is interrupted in startling fashion.

Began April ARGOSY. Single copies, 10 cents.

June 1911

Front text:

Author of "In Treason's Track," "The Spy of Valley Forge," "The Sword of the Emperor," etc.

Why Dirck Dewitt Was Sent by Charles the Second from Old England to New Amsterdam, and the Thrilling Adventures That Befell Him Under the Dutch and Among the Indians.

SYNOPSIS OF CHAPTERS PREVIOUSLY PUBLISHED.

THE story is told by Dirck Dewitt, born in New England, but sent to New Amsterdam as a spy by Charles II of England to ascertain the lay of the land with respect to the British attempting to wrest the New Netherlands from the Dutch. On board the ship Stadtholder, Dewitt loses his heart to Greta Van Hoeck, who seeks to make him reveal his purpose in sailing to the New World. He is about to comply when her brother Louis appears, between whom and Dirck there is no love lost. Later there is an explosion on board and Dirck is tossed into the sea, from which he is rescued in mysterious fashion while he is unconscious, to find a sprig of Mayflower in his hand and the memory of a sweet face bending over him. In New Amsterdam, he makes a favorable impression on Governor Peter Stuyvesant, who appoints him his secretary and later sends him on an errand among the Arareek Indians. He is saved from a rattlesnake by a maiden who turns out to be the same one who rescued him after his shipwreck. She tells him she is the daughter of the exiled regicide, William Goffe. She takes Dirck for Dutch, and when he must needs tell her he is English, she makes him prisoner with his own gun and takes him to her father among the Indians. When he tells her that his gun is unloaded and receives a warm greeting from a white-bearded man who meets them, the girl turns scarlet with mortification and blurts out: "I hate you! I hate you!"

*Began April ARGOSY. Single copies, 10 cents.

July 1911

Front text:
SYNOPSIS OF CHAPTERS PREVIOUSLY PUBLISHED.
THE story is told by Dirck Dewitt, born in New England, but sent to New Amsterdam as a spy by Charles II of England to ascertain the lay of the land with respect to the British attempting to wrest the New Netherlands from the Dutch. On board the ship Stadtholder, Dewitt loses his heart to Greta Van Hoeck, who seeks to make him reveal his purpose in sailing to the New World. He is about to comply when her brother Louis appears, between whom and Dirck there is no love lost. Later there is an explosion on board and Dirck is tossed into the sea, from which he is rescued in mysterious fashion while he is unconscious, to find a sprig of Mayflower in his hand and the memory of a sweet face bending over him. In New Amsterdam, he makes a favorable impression on Governor Peter Stuyvesant, who appoints him his secretary and later sends him on an errand among the Arareek Indians, where he falls in with William Goffe, the exiled English regicide; his daughter Blanche, and Macopin, an Indian chief. He makes confidants of these as to his real mission in New Amsterdam, and they return thither with him. There is a Meeting at the Governor's levee between Greta and Blanche, wherein the former is worsted in a wordy battle, and Dirck finds that she no longer exercises her former fascination over him. At the council Stuyvesant holds later, Louis Van Hoeck denounces Dirck as a spy, and puts in the Governor's hands the report he is supposed to have sent to the King of England. But this turns out to be a denunciation of Stuyvesant by Van Hoeck to the States General in Holland. The substitution has been made by Macopin, and it looks as if Dirck would be saved when Van Hoeck persists in claiming a hearing, declaring that witchcraft has been used. On the Governor's demanding proof of Dirck' s guilt, Van Hoeck asks that his sister be brought, whereupon Macopin whispers to Dirck that his fate hangs on a thread.

Began April ARGOSY. *Single copies, 10 cents.*

Editorial change:
"Dad," he went on, "I know men. Yes, and women, too.

was changed to

"Lad," he went on, "I know men. Yes, and women, too.

August 1911

Front text:
SYNOPSIS OF CHAPTERS PREVIOUSLY PUBLISHED.
THE story is told by Dirck Dewitt, born in New England, but sent to New Amsterdam as a spy by Charles II of England to ascertain the lay of the land with respect to the British attempting to wrest the New Netherlands from the Dutch. On board the ship Stadtholder, Dewitt loses his heart to Greta Van Hoeck, who seeks to make him reveal his purpose in sailing to the New World. He is about to comply when her brother Louis appears, between whom and Dirck there is no love lost. Later there is an explosion on board and Dirck is tossed into the sea, from which he is rescued in mysterious fashion while he is unconscious, to find a sprig of Mayflower in his hand and the memory of a sweet face bending over him. In New Amsterdam, he makes a favorable impression on Governor Peter Stuyvesant, who appoints him his secretary and later sends him on an errand among the Arareek Indians, where he falls in with William Goffe, the exiled English regicide, his daughter Blanche, and Macopin, an Indian chief. He makes confidants of these as to his real mission in New Amsterdam, and they return thither with him. There is a meeting at the Governor's levee between Greta and Blanche, wherein the former is worsted in a wordy battle, and Dirck finds that she no longer exercises her former fascination over him. At the council Van Hoeck denounces Dirck as a spy, and puts in the Governor's hands the report he is supposed to have sent to the King of England. But this turns out to be a denunciation of Stuyvesant by Van Hoeck to the States General in Holland. The substitution has been made by Macopin, but Van Hoeck persists in claiming a hearing, declaring that witchcraft has been used. On the Governor's demanding proof of Dirck's guilt, Van Hoeck asks that his sister be brought, and on her evidence Dirck is sentenced to be

hanged next morning. But through the connivance of Macopin and Blanche he escapes, and with Blanche as guide, takes a canoe for the other side of the Hudson. They are riding two horses that have been awaiting them when something strikes Dirck sharply across his throat and he is hurled from his horse to the ground.

Began April ARGOSY. *Single copies,* 10 *cents.*

September 1911

Front text:
Began April ARGOSY. *Single copies,* 10 *cents.*

Appendix II
Correspondence concerning movie rights
to ***In the Name of the King***

Publisher's Note: The following papers were purchased at auction at the 2021 Windy City Pulp and Paper Convention.

They are presented here in chronological order. The publisher knows no more than what the papers themselves tell. No evidence was found by the publisher that a movie based on this novel was ever made.

The images of these letters have been digitally enhanced for improved readability. Margins have been trimmed to reproduce letters (already smaller than original size, for this book) as large as possible.

Some of these are carbon copies on onionskin paper.

THE FRANK A. MUNSEY COMPANY

TWO-EIGHTY BROADWAY

NEW YORK

Munsey's Magazine
Argosy-All-Story Weekly

August 17, 1923.

Re. IN THE NAME OF THE KING
by Albert Payson Terhune

Dear Mr. Davis:-

I send you herewith a copy of a letter which came
in for you from Albert Payson Terhune, together with a copy
of a letter which he received from Grace H. Weir regarding
the motion picture rights to Terhune's story entitled
IN THE NAME OF THE KING.

This was a fifty-five thousand word story for
which we paid $475. in 1910. We own all rights to it.

Inasmuch as this may be a matter of some importance
to Mr. Terhune, will you kindly write him direct regarding
the matter and send us for our records here a copy of your
letter?

Mr. Dixon thought it best for us to handle it in
this way.

Very truly yours,

A.B.Gaunt

Robert H. DAVIS, Esq.,
P.O. Box 93,
Lachine, P.Q.,
Canada.

ABG:EH
(2 encs.)

April 10th, 1923.

Re: <u>IN THE NAME OF THE KING</u>
By Albert Payson Terhune

My dear Terhune:

In reply to yours of the 5th, the <u>book</u> <u>and</u> <u>dramatic</u> <u>rights</u> to this serial are herewith restored to you, free and un-encumbered without fee of any sort. These rights are yours to have and to hold and to do with as you see fit with the under-standing that we participate in no way, shape or manner. The <u>motion</u> <u>picture</u> <u>rights</u> and the <u>serial</u> <u>rights</u> we prefer to retain.

If you contemplate bringing out a book or turning the material into dramatic literature we will withold sale of the picture rights, as their value will be greatly increased by the appearance of the story in book or dramatic form. In that event we will be glad to divide with you on a basis of 50-50 whatever revenues may accrue from the picture rights.

I hope this is satisfactory. If it is to you, it is to us.

Here's hoping you have a violet-clad homecoming to Sunny-bank and that all the dogs paw you affectionately at the front gate.

Ever sincerely,

Albert Payson Terhune,
126 Riverside Drive,
New York City.

RHD:T

THE HIVE FARM
MONROE, NEW YORK

My Dear Mrs Terhune.

At your suggestion I am going to try to put on paper the purpose for which I wished to see Mr Terhune in the illness of my husband. I don't know how successful I will be, but I will do my best.

Mr. Weir has been grievously — part of the time desperately — ill for over four months. Beginning with intestinal complications, due to a long neglected hernia, he was seized with a series of hemorrhages, brought about by his weakened physical condition, and a serious heart and lung trouble was discovered. The operation that had been arranged for had to be called off suddenly, and, apart from his physical suffering all summer (we have just brought him back from the mountains of Sullivan County where the altitude was too much for him), you can understand that his work has had to be dropped completely.

One of the matters in which he was most enthusiastic was the project of dramatizing Mr. Terhune's argosy story "In the Name of the King", and he had already done considerable work on this when his illness interrupted, and he was compelled to lay it aside.

A short time ago one of his motion

Picture friends, who has produced a great many of his scenarios, came out to see him in an effort to get him to write an American historical picture play for his firm. Mr. Weir, of course, was unable physically to do this, but while the film man was here, Mr. Weir told him of the dramatic version he was doing of Mr. Terhune's historical story for a stage play. He was so interested that he insisted on being told about it in detail and reading parts of it, altho. to him as a film.

Lately, however, his concern has written to Mr. Weir, evidently very anxious to produce it, and offering $5000.00 for the rights and even agreeing if Mr. Weir is unable to do any more work on it, to have one of their men make a continuity based on his ideas and from his dictation, if necessary.

Mr. Weir knows of course that Mr. Terhune had explained when the matter first came up, that until the story was first produced as a play, or published as a book, he has no connection with the film rights, and even then would have to divide anything that would be received "50-50" with the Munsey people; otherwise that they would have all of the motion picture rights, as the publishers of the story and the owners of the original copyright.

Mr. Weir is most anxious that Mr. Terhune should be given a fair and square treatment in the matter, and in view of his own very serious illness is wondering if an arrangement could not be made whereby the film rights could be sold and Mr Terhune's interest protected. In other words he believes that the Munsey people would sell all picture rights to the story for any where from $1000.— to $2000.— judging from what he knows they have been willing to sell similar rights before. And of course without being adapted or built up for motion picture purposes, such a price from their view-point would be acceptable, probably.

Mr Weir is wondering if he would have Mr. Terhune's consent to take up the question of the motion picture sale with the Munsey people, and if desirable to Mr Terhune without mentioning his name in any way in the matter. Then if possible to buy the rights from the Munsey people. Mr Weir will divide the balance equally with Mr. Terhune, whatever this balance may be. And while Mr. Terhune's name would be kept out of the dealings with the Munsey people completely he would share equally in all profits remaining.

Will you please be good enough to give me an answer by return mail, as the picture people either cannot or will not wait, and have said they would have to make immediate arrangements for another production if there is any delay.

Mr Weir wants me to send his best wishes to Mr Terhune.

Cordially

Grace H. Weir.

Aug 11th 1923

Did you like this book?

Well, then...